# ON THE WAY DOWN

JENNIFER FARWELL

**On the Way Down**





Front cover design by Miblart
miblart.com

ISBN 979-8-9994018-2-3

*For those who've explored second chances, stood on business, sought redemption, or wondered "what if?" about a past love—this book is for you.*

# Chapter One

Like most of my questionable life choices, the overnight trip to Vegas masqueraded as a good idea at the time.

"What isn't fabulous about this plan?" Ava, my best friend, asked me two days ago after she suggested going. "We get out of LA for a night and finally catch Torin's band. You've wanted to see them play for ages, and you haven't left your condo in weeks."

She was right on all counts, and especially the part about me being a recluse. It's what I do when I'm neck-deep in research for a new novel. Ava knows this, and it drives her bananas when I decline her invitations for weeks on end, but she understands why I do it and loves me anyway.

I owed her a night out, though. Countless hours of holing up at home with only my laptop and news articles about a murder case for company also had me starting to climb the walls. So I said yes, and now here we are in Sin City, smack in the middle of casinos and chaos.

It still seemed like a good idea as recently as three minutes ago, when Ava and I abandoned our blackjack table in The Auriga and headed for Nebula, the casino's hidden speakeasy where our friend's band has a standing Saturday night gig. It hit me then, as we glided past the cacophony of clinking poker chips and whirling slot machine chimes, that I'm in this for the long haul tonight. Torin's band doesn't go on until eleven, and he already texted Ava about the after-party at his house when they're done. The bar better have energy drinks to keep me standing.

"Ava Sinclair plus one."

The doorman checks a list and unhooks a rope to let us inside a cozy café adorned with a starlit ceiling, flickering candles on each table, and twinkling fairy lights in every corner. I'm confused when we walk past people sitting at tables, since the café is small and there's no stage in sight, but Ava appears to know where we're going. We follow someone to a door marked as a supply closet. It turns out to be the entrance to a small enclosure outside of another metal door that's opened for us a moment later.

"Isn't this great?" Ava's hazel eyes sparkle as she nudges me forward.

I step inside a lounge decorated with dark wood, tufted velvet sofas, ornate chandeliers, and a starlit ceiling like the one in the café. A crowd is already gathered at the bar on one side of the room, and another one is forming in front of the empty stage.

"Hold us a spot near the front," Ava says. "I'll get our drinks."

"I don't drink when I'm writing a book," I remind her. "It

disrupts the flow."

"You aren't writing a book tonight. You're in Vegas, at a bar, enjoying life."

She winks at me and takes off before I can ask for something with caffeine in it. I resign myself to a single drink and make my way to an unoccupied spot close to the stage.

"Delaney Sharpe," a familiar voice booms from behind me. "How did Ava manage to drag you out of LA?"

Torin sweeps me into a hug the instant I turn around. "Didn't she tell you I was coming?" His shoulder muffles my words.

"She did, but I had to see you here with my own eyes first. It's been forever." He loosens his hold and takes a step back, his gaze sweeping over me. "You look amazing, by the way."

I'm not sure how my current vampire ways of staying indoors all day, tapping at my keyboard, and barely letting my skin see sunshine have led to a compliment about my appearance, but I'll take it. I did at least make an effort to add curling-iron beach waves to my normally straight blond hair, and I let Ava talk me into wearing a short silk skirt she just happened to bring with her. The black knee-high boots I'm wearing also snuck along for the ride to Vegas, since Ava grabbed them from my closet when she came to pick me up this morning and declared herself my stylist for the day.

"Kind words from the glamorous rock star." I pretend to look Torin up and down. He dyed his hair an indigo-tinged black at some point since I last saw him, and the color makes his blue eyes stand out even more than they already did. "You need to share your eyeliner tips with me."

"Everything I know, you and Ava taught me in the dorms. Where is she, by the way?"

"At the bar, hopefully not buying shots. She should be back soon."

"No shots?" Mischief lights up his face. "Come on. All your best dance moves come out with those."

I groan, recalling the last time the three of us did shots together at our college graduation party, eight years ago. Torin and Ava swear they deleted all incriminating photos and videos from that night, part of which involved me dancing on top of a bar with the most attractive guy I had ever laid eyes on, whom I'd spent the last semester of college crushing on from afar. His name was Phoenix Alden. He was a theater major with an agent and a couple of TV and film roles on his IMDb resume, and he'd had an entourage of women following him around campus every time I saw him.

I was too shy to approach him until the alcohol made my inhibitions disappear. Phoenix asked me out that night and I said yes, which was another decision that seemed fine at the time but led to disaster in the end. I don't do shots anymore.

"Mixed drinks are safer for all of us," I assure Torin. "You and the rest of the band don't want me turning into your tambourine girl."

"I doubt the guys would mind. And what happens in Vegas..."

"Oooh, are we discussing finding a hookup for Del tonight? Because there are some prospects I spotted at the bar."

Ava hands me a glass filled to the brim with God knows what. She sets her own glass on the stage, then flings her arms around Torin.

He laughs and hugs her back. "Nash is single, and he's sticking around for the after-party tonight. You never know what might happen."

"I'm not hooking up with your guitar player," I inform him. "That's trouble waiting to happen and about a million red flags."

"You say that now, but who knows where the night will lead?" He exchanges a conspiratorial glance with Ava. "Speaking of Nash, I need to find him before we go on. See you after the show?"

"We'll be there," Ava promises. "Tell Nash that Del is showing up just for him."

"You two are the worst." I look up at the ceiling and then take a sip from my glass, trying not to choke on the strong taste of vodka and sugar. "What is this?"

"A vodka ginger ale. Your first of many tonight, as we scope out your prospects. Now that I have you out of your condo, my mission is also to get you laid."

"What prospects?" I protest. "I'm here for one drink and to enjoy the music. That's all."

"That's too bad, since the guy who just walked over to the bar looks like your type."

I turn around so I can see the bar, but it's mostly to humor Ava. If I pretend to check out who she's talking about, then tell her I'm not interested, she might let this drop. "What guy?"

"Tall, dark hair, wearing a white shirt and black jeans."

I scan the patrons at the bar and spot who Ava means. I start to reply, but then stop, no longer able to form words when I catch sight of something that knocks the air out of my lungs.

No, not something. Someone. I'm struggling to breathe.

It can't be him. Torin would have warned me. Christ, Ava was just at the bar and she would have come running to let me know. But Phoenix's sun-streaked, shaggy hair is unmistakable, and so are the tattoos covering the bronzed skin of his arms.

He's here in Las Vegas. In this bar. The ex-boyfriend who waltzed out of my life without an explanation or a goodbye before he attained the status of a Hollywood god for a hot second and then lost it just as fast.

I am not prepared for this tonight. I would not be prepared for this on any night, in any lifetime.

Ava snaps her fingers in front of my face. "Wow, I must have been spot on about that guy being your type. You should see how hard you're staring."

I rip my eyes away from the horror film my night just became and take another gulp from my glass. The liquid burns my throat, but the sensation jars me back to reality enough that I remember how to speak.

"Tell me you didn't see him and didn't know he would be here."

"See who?" Ava's auburn waves bounce around her shoulders as she twists her body for another peek at the bar.

I shuffle to the side, trying to hide behind her as I risk another look. The spot where Phoenix stood less than a minute ago is vacant. My stomach drops. Where did he go?

Ava faces me again, wearing a puzzled expression. Then her eyes widen and her mouth forms a small O.

"Del." A hand lands on my shoulder. I would know Phoenix's voice and touch anywhere.

A night in Vegas might be the worst idea Ava and I have ever had.

# Chapter Two

THE APPROPRIATE SOUNDTRACK FOR this moment would be the abrupt scratch of a needle pulled off a vinyl record. Whoever controls the music at Nebula gives me a Journey song instead. So help me, I wish I could jump on a real-life version of its midnight train and go far away from here.

Phoenix's hand drifts away from my shoulder. He materializes in front of me, and now I have no other option but to acknowledge him.

"Hey." My tone is surprisingly indifferent, and even confident. I'm not an actor, but all the times I helped Phoenix run lines when we dated must have programmed my neural pathways with the ability to convincingly play pretend.

I force myself to meet his stare, then immediately regret it. His honey-brown eyes have always been expressive in ways where words fail. It's some sort of superpower that knocks all coherent thought into another galaxy.

"You look incredible. How are you?" He touches my shoulder again, as if the years of separation between us don't exist. As if he isn't the one to blame.

My brain fumbles to form a reply. What am I supposed to say to that? *I'm fine now, thanks. I gave myself my own closure after you walked out and left me on read for six years.*

The truth is, I don't know if I'm fine. I thought I was over this a long time ago. But now that I'm standing mere inches from him, inhaling the scent of his aftershave and hearing his voice, a part of me is transported to a time when we knew each other intimately. Phoenix and Delaney. Nix and Del. He always came first in those days, especially to me.

"Would you look at what the cat dragged in?" Ava's question is colder than the ice cubes that clink together in her glass as she sips her drink and gives my ex-boyfriend the once-over. "Shouldn't you be somewhere shooting your comeback blockbuster, or are you back to low-budget indie films these days?"

God, I love her. She always has my back, and she never minces words.

"Ava, it's always a pleasure to see you." Phoenix shifts his gaze to her. "And funny you should ask. I'm on location out here, but I have a few days off."

"I hope it goes better for you than *North Node* did."

I'm not sure whether to gasp or laugh at Ava's jab, so I bite my bottom lip and watch Phoenix for his reaction. I'll give him credit, because he doesn't even flinch. Lord knows he should. *North*

*Node* is the box-office flop that knocked him off of Hollywood's A-list and was the catalyst for a tabloid scandal that cost him his agent and the lead role in a production he had already signed on to. The ordeal allegedly drove him into hiding. Whether the rumor about him intentionally disappearing is true or not, he dropped off the celebrity radar almost entirely after everything went down and hasn't appeared in any films since. I haven't missed seeing his name on Hollywood billboards.

"It can't be worse, right?" He flashes a megawatt smile at Ava, like he's in on the joke, then locks eyes with me again. "What happened with *North Node* is just one more thing on my list of decisions I regret."

I should look away. I need to. And yet here I am, powerless in his presence. It's as though years haven't passed and I haven't climbed upwards in my life and career with book deals, film options, and fans, and he hasn't fallen from grace in every conceivable way.

*No.*

I can't go back to who I used to be around him. Not after I built my success brick by insufferably heavy brick, after he did all he could to destroy me right when my dreams started coming true. I'm stronger than this, and he doesn't get to act like everything is cool.

"Why are you here?" I purse my lips, hoping this comes across to him as icy and unimpressed.

"I'm friends with Nash. He told me about the show."

It doesn't answer why he's in front of me, acting as if he didn't once shatter my heart and not give a damn, but it tells me Torin had no part in him showing up tonight. Torin knows what happened between us, but Nash didn't enter the scene as his bandmate until long after my personal life imploded.

"Let me rephrase that. Why are you talking to me?"

He flinches, and his response takes longer this time. "Because we had a deep connection once, and you were a big part of my life. I still think about you."

"Bullshit. You made yourself dead to me for years." I down the rest of my drink. Liquid courage is definitely kicking in.

Ava's gaze darts from Phoenix to me like she's watching a tennis match. I'm about to excuse myself and bolt for the restroom before he can say something else, when the volume fades on the song in the room. A thumping drumbeat emerges in its place.

I look up to see Torin behind his drum kit. He twirls a drumstick and grins at me, but the joy on his face fades when he spots Phoenix.

"Are you okay?" he mouths. I bob my head, since I'm physically fine and don't want to distract him from playing. Emotionally, though? That's a different story.

Phoenix leans in closer. "I know I owe you an apology," he murmurs, his words tickling my ear. "I was an asshole. You didn't deserve what I did."

This must be what an out-of-body experience or falling into an alternate universe feels like. For all the times I imagined Phoenix apologizing to me, before I gave up on ever hearing from him again, nothing quite prepared me for it actually happening.

It also doesn't change a thing—or it shouldn't. But the stage lights blur for a moment, and I'm suddenly lightheaded, a jumbled mess of thoughts and feelings I didn't see coming. Self-preservation demands that I shut this whole thing down.

"Let me enjoy the music, okay? It's what I came to Vegas for."

I stare straight ahead at the stage, because there's a good chance I'll sway or tip over if I turn my head or body toward him. Falling into Phoenix's arms is the last thing I need to do tonight.

"Can I talk to you after the show?" he asks.

"I have plans after the show."

Any qualms I had about staying out all night have evaporated now that going to Torin's house gives me a reason to not continue our conversation. Torin and Ava's scheming to set me up with Nash is suddenly on the level of solving for world peace.

"If you mean the after-party, Nash invited me to that. Maybe we can talk then if you're going."

My heart sinks straight to my feet. I wouldn't be shocked if it fell out of my body and splattered blood across the concrete floor. Of course he'll be there. Why would Torin's house be my safe haven?

Ava taps my shoulder and wedges herself between us. "I'm going to the bar for a refill. Want another drink?"

"I'll come with you." As much as I would like to keep my front-row view of the band, I want the escape from my personal sideshow more.

Ava grabs my hand and leads me away from the stage and

Phoenix. I half-expect him to follow us, but he remains where he is. Perhaps he senses Ava is holding back on letting him have it. I do.

"What'll it be?" she asks. "I'm buying this round."

She also bought the last round, but we can settle the bill later. "Something strong that comes in a shot glass. You choose."

Forget everything I said to Torin about not doing shots. If the way tonight has played out so far is anything to go by, I'm going to need more than one.

# Chapter Three

Some force in the universe must take pity on me. Either that, or Phoenix takes the hint. He remains where he is for the first three songs, which is long enough for the lemon drop shot Ava bought me to kick in and ease the fight-or-flight feeling that's made it impossible to focus on the performance I actually came here for.

Ava offers me some of her drink during the band's fourth song. By their fifth, I'm swaying to the music's beat, and I even catch myself smiling and laughing. Then the next song begins. My smile dies with it.

The band's cover of "Total Eclipse of the Heart" isn't the problem. No, that would be the memory it triggers, and the images from years ago now flooding my brain.

An infomercial for an '80s music collection lights up the TV in my living room, but I don't watch it. Only the opening piano notes of "Total Eclipse of the Heart" filter into my awareness, since I have my eyes glued to the words on my laptop screen. Phoenix isn't watching it either. He's at the other end of the sofa, reading a script.

I almost always keep the television on when Phoenix is at my apartment these days, no matter what else we're doing. It's background noise to fill the silence between us when he's a walking storm cloud, which has been more often than not during the last two months. But he's been in a good mood since arriving at my door today, and his brightness is contagious. He hasn't been this happy and relaxed in weeks. Neither have I.

"Should we go out for dinner?" he asks, looking up from his script.

I could suggest our favorite restaurant and a night out together. We could text our friends and meet up at a club, or see what's happening on Sunset Boulevard. We have a lot to celebrate. His latest film just wrapped, and my agent recently sold my first book. From an outsider's point of view, we're the young Hollywood dream in the making. There's every reason to live it up.

Still, the peace inside my apartment is like breathing pure oxygen after nearly suffocating on fumes. Alone together here, and shielded from the outside world, most things are within our control. Leaving will expose us to people and places and situations I can't predict. Everything could change in an instant. It often does.

"Let's stay in," I suggest. "We could order takeout and watch a movie."

"Netflix and chill?"

His eyes sparkle, telling me he's kidding. Except this is the most attracted to him I've been in weeks. He's vibrant and alert, and his speech isn't slurred. He hasn't touched a drop of alcohol today that I'm aware of, but it's more than that. Phoenix is warm and upbeat and the guy I know again, after what's started to feel like dating a stranger. This is who I fell in love with.

"If you play your cards right," I kid back. But I move my laptop to the table, then scoot closer to him on the sofa.

Phoenix's script joins my laptop on the table. His arm loops around my shoulders, and he pulls me closer. I sink into him, tilting my head slightly so I can see his face.

"Challenge accepted. Always bet on the house."

His gravelly voice is already enough to make my stomach flutter. When his lips sweep gently along my neck, I close my eyes, blocking out visual distractions. All I want is to feel how I used to when his mouth explored any exposed skin on my body, but he pauses and moves his head away.

"What's wrong?" I ask after a moment, still keeping my eyes shut. There's been more wrong than right with us lately, which makes me nervous about Phoenix's answer.

"Not a thing." His voice carries a softness it hasn't had in ages.

I open my eyes and find myself peering straight into his. "Why did you stop?"

"To look at you." He traces my jaw with the tip of his finger, holding my gaze. "You really are everything to me. I wouldn't have made it through this film without you."

Words fail me in that moment, but I don't need to speak. His mouth brushes over mine with a kiss so tender, it breaks the iron grip I've had on my emotions for weeks. Tears spring to my eyes, and I can't hold them back. One teardrop rolls down my face, then another.

He stops kissing me again. "Is everything okay?"

How do I tell him it feels like he's lifted an anvil off my chest? Weeks of crushing anxiety have evaporated in seconds, and now I'm nearly overwhelmed by the relief pumping through my veins. I haven't lost him. We haven't lost us.

"I'm just happy right now," I whisper, wiping the tears from my cheek.

For a heartbeat, nothing moves but the air between us. Then Phoenix rests his forehead against mine, and I thread my fingers through his hair. We're still for another beat, eyes studying eyes, until his face lights up in a smile. He's still smiling when his head dips and his mouth returns to mine. I melt into the familiarity of him, the sweep of his tongue, and the gentle caresses that carry a tantalizing promise of so much more.

Bonnie Tyler's voice blares from the TV speakers while my

fingers work at the buttons on his shirt. She's still singing about forever starting tonight when he slips my shirt over my head and it falls to the floor. I don't hear what song comes next, or if the infomercial ends. I'm too lost in the moment with Phoenix, consumed by the growing passion and dizzying sweetness of every kiss and touch, and the heat of his skin as each layer of our clothing joins the pile next to the sofa. I've missed him, and I've missed this.

His mouth finds the curve where my shoulder meets my neck, and he lingers there. My palms skim over his chest, and then I slide my arms around him, urging him closer to me. It's more than just physical desire. It's an all-encompassing need to feel his body pressed against mine, as if this will prove we still fit together as perfectly as we once did.

Maybe he has the same need, and the same reason. His arms tighten around me, holding me like he's afraid I'll slip away. He buries his face in my hair, inhaling the scent. When I press my lips to his shoulder, he shifts one of his arms. Then he's tracing the contour of my body with his hand, each stroke of his fingers igniting sparks along my bare skin. And when he touches me where I ache for him, something in me wants to believe we've dodged what had us falling apart. That here, in this moment, we're back to being in love.

It was only a rough patch. The film shoot was stressful, and the hours were long, and he partied too much with some of the cast and crew so he could solidify connections for his career. It's over now, and the guy I was head over heels for has returned to me.

Phoenix eases me back into the cushions, and I curl into him as if there's nowhere else I belong. As the light from outside slips away with the evening sun, so do my worries about our recent past.

❧

"Another lemon drop?"

Ava's question breaches the gauzy curtain between the music-filled bar and my reverie. I blink hard, bringing the room into focus, even as I remain tangled in the memory of my final night with Phoenix and the last time we made love. He cooked us breakfast the next morning, smiling and whistling off-key while eggs sizzled on the stove. He kissed me goodbye and told me he loved me before I headed out the door to work. And when I came home that evening, he walked out and left our world in shambles. Seeing him now is like raising the dead after trying everything short of an exorcism to expel his ghost from my soul.

"Del?" she asks, nudging my arm this time.

I shake my head, both as an answer and as an attempt to clear the cobwebs from my brain. "Just water for me."

I don't meet her eyes, because one look at mine will tell her where my mind was. She always knows. Instead, I focus on the stage and Torin, and try to ward off any other image from the past that tries to surface now that the floodgates have opened. Having the back of Phoenix's head in my peripheral vision doesn't help.

Ava presses a bottle of water into my hand a few minutes later.

It's cold, and I hold it against my forehead, only now realizing how warm I've become.

"Ignore him," she says. "He isn't worth the energy."

I nod, but say nothing. If only it were that easy to do. Ava must read my mind, because she grabs hold of my elbow and drags me to the opposite end of the stage from where Phoenix is, so he's out of our line of sight. We stay there, with Ava dancing and singing along to the music.

*He ruined years of my life. Don't let him ruin this.*

I look at the band, and then at Ava again. I should be doing what she's doing. Phoenix doesn't deserve my energy or attention—Ava, Torin, and the band do. And I deserve to enjoy my night.

"I changed my mind," I tell her. "Can I steal a sip of your drink?"

She grins and passes me her glass. "Have as much as you'd like. I know where to get more."

By the time the band announces the last song of their set, I'm dancing and singing with her. She notices and grabs my arm to twirl me around once, then a second time. My joy comes to a screeching halt mid-turn, and so do I.

Not everyone in the bar is watching the band. Phoenix is watching us.

"What do you think about bailing on the after-party and finding something else to do tonight?" I suggest. "Maybe more dancing at Hakkasan?"

If there's one person I can't fool, it's her. She throws a dark look in Phoenix's direction, then turns her side-eye on me.

"Not a chance. We aren't letting that sparkle pony change our plans for the night." She tosses her hair over her shoulder, then reaches out her hand. "Can I have some of your water?"

I pass her the bottle and don't hear what she says next. Phoenix is headed our way.

"We should go." I turn on my heel and beeline for the exit. I'm already past the door and in the casino by the time she catches up to me.

"Whoa, slow it down. Where's the fire?"

"Hopefully not following us." I hurry past a few game tables, then turn into a row of slot machines. It's a good enough hiding spot for now.

"Sit," Ava commands. "Please remember who the hell you are, and I don't mean who you were six or eight years ago. There's no reason for you to run."

Uh-oh. She's wearing the "don't-even-consider-arguing-with-me" expression she has perfected throughout the course of her public relations career. I plop onto a seat in front of a slot machine.

"I can't help it. Seeing him brought me back there."

"Then I'm hauling you into the present, where you belong. Did you or did you not hit the *New York Times* bestseller list with your last novel?" She puts her hands on her hips and stares me down.

"Yes." I consider noting that it didn't crack the top five, but she fires another question at me before I can.

"How many of your novels are being adapted for film as we

speak?"

"Two."

"And what person in the bar tonight wrecked his career, nose-dived to the Z-list, and is completely irrelevant to anyone now?"

"Phoenix."

Ava arches an eyebrow. She appears to be satisfied with my answers. "Correct on all three. So ignore him and continue being the stunning and successful woman you are. We'll get an Uber, go to Torin's house, and have a better time than should be legal. Besides, I have a plan."

She whips out her phone, presumably to request a ride, and motions with her free hand for me to follow her. I can head back to our room and risk a several-hour lecture during our drive home tomorrow about hiding out, letting Phoenix win, and being the most boring almost-thirty-year-old to ever visit Las Vegas, or I can play along and find out what she's up to. I swallow a sigh and get to my feet.

"What are you thinking, and why am I worried?" The gleam in her eye makes me nervous.

"We let Nash in on the backstory, and you two flirt or make out in front of Phoenix for the rest of the night. You have some fun, and he chokes on karma. It's brilliant."

"I want peace tonight. I'm not out for revenge."

"But you should be." She gives me a wicked smile. "There's a reason for that saying about being nice to people on your way up, because you'll meet them again on the way down. It applies here."

I open my mouth to protest, then close it again. It's pointless to argue with Ava when she's decided the night needs a plot twist.

"Do you think Nash will agree to your plan?"

We reach a set of glass doors leading outside. Ava stops walking and gawks at me like I've grown a second head. "It's Nash."

"I don't know him that well," I remind her.

"He's the flirtiest guy I know, or he is with me. I'm sure he lives for this sort of thing." Her phone chimes, and she peers at the screen. "Our ride is two minutes away. Get ready, because the real show of the night is about to begin."

Something tells me I'm about as ready for this as I was to encounter Phoenix in the first place.

# Chapter Four

NO LIGHTS ARE ON in the two-story house our Uber pulls up to about twenty minutes later. But it must be where Torin lives, because Ava hops out of the car and strolls up the empty driveway, toward the front entrance. I thank our driver and also exit the car.

"Should we wait for Torin to get here?" I join her on the front stoop.

"Nope. It usually takes him a while to tear down and load out. He gave me the code so we can go inside and hang out until everyone gets here."

Ava taps a sequence of numbers on a keypad, which is followed by the click and whir of a lock unlatching. She turns the handle and pushes open the door, then flips a light switch on the interior wall.

I follow her inside and shut the door, leaving it unlocked. She kicks off her heels, so I follow her lead and remove my boots, then trail behind her through the foyer and to the kitchen.

"Torin sent a text that said to help ourselves to any food or drinks in the fridge." I expect Ava to pause in front of the aforementioned appliance, but she heads for a hallway, purse in hand.

"Where are you going?"

"Bathroom. Be right back."

I set my purse on the counter and walk over to the fridge. I'm debating between a hard seltzer and another water when I hear the front door open and footsteps enter the house. It must be Torin or one of his bandmates.

"The party is in here," I call out as I continue to scan the shelves inside the fridge. "It's a little quiet at the moment."

"I can fix that. Should we put music on?"

My head snaps up. Phoenix strides into the kitchen like he owns the place. His face lights up with a dazzling smile when he spots me. It's the kind of smile that also shines through in his eyes and puts the dimple in his left cheek on prominent display.

That dimple is one of my weaknesses.

*Used to be. Past tense.* Except it's difficult to look away from it now.

"Um," I stammer. "Music. Yeah."

Great start. Don't I write character dialogue for a living? There's no excuse for me to freeze up or be tongue-tied, especially not after the pep talk Ava gave me about remembering who I am. And yet, now that I'm cornered in the kitchen with no one else around to rescue me or back me up, I've lost my grasp on language.

"Any type of music in particular? I can put something on my phone to listen to until everyone else gets here."

"You choose."

I pluck a water from the shelf, even though the hard seltzer would help me more right now. Why isn't Ava back yet?

"I'm not going to bite you, Del."

His gaze flickers to my shoulder, and then to my neck. It's the wrong moment to recall that while no, Phoenix would never actually bite me, he used to gently nibble both of the places he glanced at. It always led up to him leaving a trail of kisses to other spots.

*Nope. Shut this down right now.*

My mind isn't going there again tonight, because it can't. The earlier memory at Nebula was more than enough.

"Excuse me?" I ask.

I must have imagined what he was looking at. Even if I didn't, he wouldn't dare try to flirt with me that way. The kind of audacity this would require is next level, but I feel as if we both had the same thought at the same time.

He interprets my question as an invitation to cross the kitchen and stand next to me. Every atom of my existence is on high alert.

"You looked like a deer in the headlights for a second. It was a joke. I'm not going to bite you." He pauses, then brushes a lock of my hair away from my face and tucks it behind my ear. "Unless you want me to, for old times' sake."

Holy hell.

Cool air hits my skin, reminding me I've left the refrigerator door open. The sudden chill smacks my brain awake and unravels the pretzel my tongue just became, thank God.

"Cute. Does that line work for you?"

I at least sound nonchalant over my heartbeat hammering in my ears. Phoenix's fingertips now rest against the side of my neck. Can he tell how fast my pulse is racing?

"You tell me. It's the first time I've used it."

Amusement sparkles in his eyes. His hand lingers where it is for another moment, his touch feather-light, then he draws it away. The idea that he finds this even remotely funny or entertaining is a match to dry tinder as far as my temper and irritation level go.

"Drinks are in the fridge if you want something. I saw one of those whiskey things you used to like so much."

My last sentence drips with sarcasm. I'm sure he knows why. He left a few empty cans of the same whiskey sour drink on my living room table when he walked out and didn't come back. His sobriety from the night before everything ended was exceptionally short-lived.

Phoenix leans in and takes a bottle from the shelf, brushing against me as he does. My instinct is to step back like I've gotten too close to an open flame.

"Water is fine. I don't drink anymore."

"That's probably good."

Ava would be proud of me for my passive-aggressive response if she were in the room to hear it. She was always the one to pull me together after Phoenix's benders tore me apart.

"It is." He twists the cap off the bottle, then pauses. "I'm completely sober now. Drugs, too. I've changed since those days."

I pinch the bridge of my nose. Does he expect me to say he's forgiven, and it's all water under the bridge? Or that I'm proud of him for whatever epiphany he finally had to change his life, after the damage to so very many things was done? Neither of these would be true.

"Glad to hear it. I should go find Ava."

"Wait. Please."

I bite back a retort about how I did wait once, and that his time ran out years ago. It won't help, and heaven knows he and I have argued enough to last several lifetimes. So I fold my arms across my chest instead, lean back against the counter, and stay silent.

He continues. "I was horrible to you when I drank, and I was probably worse when I was high. I put you through hell, and I'm sorry—more than you'll ever know. There might not be anything I can say or do now that will make up for the things I did, but I'd like to try."

Those damn expressive eyes of his. He always had a way of melting my heart with a certain kind of stolen glance when we were together. It's the one he gives me now.

*Don't fall for it. Remember how we got here.*

There's a saying about how the opposite of love is indifference. My insides are twisted in knots, but I'll be damned if I come across as anything but indifferent to his apology and intent to make amends.

"Why?" I uncross my arms. "Anything we had has been dead and buried for a long time, and you did that. It's what you wanted."

"I did awful things to people I love during that time of my life, but I still care about you. I never stopped."

Something is still off. I stare at a spot on the wall for several seconds so I can summon the courage to say what's on my mind.

"You didn't answer a single phone call or text from me after you left. It's been years since I've heard from you, so forgive me if I have a hard time believing you care about anyone but yourself."

His reply doesn't miss a beat. "Sometimes people keep their distance out of love, until they realize they can't."

My eyebrows ricochet somewhere into the stratosphere. "You waited until you ran into me at a bar by random chance to decide you can't stay away? That reeks of you trying for a one-night stand because I'm here and it's convenient."

"I don't believe in random chance, and you could never be a one-night stand to me. I'm not after that. I only want to talk."

"And hit on me," I point out.

His mouth turns up in a sheepish smile. "It's impossible not to."

If I could physically wipe the smile off his face right now, and then mop the floor with his over-the-top confidence, I'd do it in a second. He's infuriating.

"Spare me the flattery," I huff. "If you want to talk, start with what you're thinking, why you took off at all, and where you've been. You said you've changed, but have you changed enough to do that?"

A door opens and slams shut as I finish my sentence. Several raucous voices and sets of footsteps echo from the foyer. By the sounds of it, Torin, Nash, and a couple more people have arrived.

Phoenix lowers his voice. "Could we go out back by the pool to continue this? It isn't a conversation to have around other people."

Absolutely not. With Ava still missing in action, Torin is my safety net. I'm about to latch on to him for dear life until I figure out what's really happening and the motivation behind it.

"I came to Vegas to see Torin. I'm staying where he is."

Phoenix nods as if he understands, but his Adam's apple bobs and his entire demeanor shifts. For the first time since I spotted him at Nebula tonight, he seems nervous and uncertain.

He's never been uncertain around me. Ever.

"When do you go home?" he asks.

"I drive back with Ava in the afternoon." Our return to the hotel and our departure from Vegas both seem so far away, even though it's already past two in the morning. This isn't the night I bargained for at all.

"Can I convince you to continue this later?" He rakes a hand through his hair. The urgency on his face is unnerving. It's also baffling.

"Are you expecting to run into me again? I'm not coming back to Vegas anytime soon, and from what I can tell, you don't remember how to use a phone."

"I'll be in Laguna Beach next weekend. Can I see you then?"

I should tell him I'm busy until half past forever. Nothing but reopening stitched-up wounds can come of whatever he wants to hash out. I'm pondering the most direct way to phrase my answer when he takes my hand between both of his.

I didn't anticipate the shower of sparks that course through me when I feel his palm against mine and the warmth of his skin.

"Please? Just one weekend. That's all I'm asking for, even if I don't deserve it."

He's correct that he doesn't deserve it. I don't owe him a thing. Logic says I should tell him this, but my body is a live wire and my brain is still flailing to make sense of the last few minutes.

"Am I interrupting something?" Ava enters my field of vision. Seeing her grounds me again and throws me the lifeline I desperately need.

"You're fine. We're done talking, and I think Torin and Nash are here now." I pull my hand away from Phoenix's grasp.

"Did someone say my name?"

Torin walks into the kitchen. He stops in his tracks when he sees me standing beside Phoenix. Nash is right behind him, with two giggling women in tow. One of them tousles his dark curls and grabs the lapel of his leather jacket on their way in, which is followed by him wrapping his arm around her waist. Both are good signs Ava's plan for the night is already dead in the water.

"The party has arrived!" Nash declares. "Ladies, have you met my good friend Phoenix?"

"Wait, I recognize you!" one woman exclaims. "Aren't you that actor?"

Ava grabs my arm and marches me over to the hallway she left for earlier. Even though the women with Nash sidle up to Phoenix and pepper him with questions about a film he starred in before *North Node*, he watches me as I leave the room.

"What did I walk in on?" Ava demands, once we're no longer within earshot of the kitchen.

"It's nothing."

"It looked like something. He was holding your hand, and you looked stunned. You kind of still do."

Things could get ugly fast if I tell her Phoenix asked to spend the weekend together. It's better to wait until she isn't within striking distance of him before I divulge anything about what we discussed.

"I'll explain it later when we're alone. Where were you for so long?"

She rolls her eyes. "I had to do some quick damage control. One of my clients got wrecked in VIP at a club, started a fistfight on the sidewalk outside with a guy he saw filming him, and threw the guy's phone through a window of a store. Someone caught it on video and social media is all over it. I'm sorry I left you alone for so long, but don't worry. I promise to be your human shield for the rest of the night."

Her acting as a buffer between Phoenix and me is the most helpful role she can play while I decide what to do about his invitation for next weekend. My head screams at me to forget he asked, leave him without an answer, and go on with my life.

My heart is a different story. It doesn't know what to do at all.

Ava makes good on her promise. She's at my side for the rest of the night to make sure my focus is on hanging out with Torin, since the women who came in with Nash remain barnacles in his presence, wherever he goes. But when the party moves to the backyard, I catch Nash looking at Ava from time to time, as if he wants to sit next to her at the pool's edge where she's chatting with Torin and me. His stolen glances are frequent enough for me to wonder why he brought the two women to Torin's place. He could have hung out with Ava instead.

If Ava notices, she doesn't show it. Her attention stays on our conversation as we dangle our legs in the water and laugh with Torin about old memories of college pranks. Phoenix spends most of his time on the patio, talking to Nash and the two women. That's probably because of the death glare Ava beams in his direction any time his gaze shifts our way. It isn't until well after five in the morning, when we're back inside the house and saying our goodbyes, that he dares to approach me again.

"Can I text you about next weekend?"

He keeps his voice at a low volume, but he's still living dangerously by asking this when Ava is only a few feet away. She's busy joking with Torin and Nash about something, though, and her back is turned to us.

I pretend to rifle through my purse and avoid eye contact. "If you have my number and remember how to send texts, then I'd guess you're physically capable of it."

"Has your number changed?"

"Nope."

If he still has my number, then that's one up on me. Ava made me delete him from my contacts a few months after he walked out, when it became clear he wasn't going to answer my texts or calls. Letting go of the one tether I had to him at the time wasn't easy, but it prevented me from acting on later moments of weakness when I was tempted to try again. It would surprise me to hear from him after tonight, no matter how he's behaving at the moment. *Out of sight, out of mind* has been his modus operandi since the last time we laid eyes on one another.

"Can I hug you before you go?" Phoenix's words are even softer now.

I consider another non-answer that attacks his use of "can" and doesn't answer the question, but it isn't worth expending the energy. At least he's requesting permission to get into my personal space this time.

"Sure." My tone is flat. He doesn't notice my lack of enthusiasm, or he ignores it, because his arms sweep me into a hug the instant I agree.

The déjà vu almost knocks me over. I used to feel safe and shielded from the world when Phoenix put his arms around me, and like nothing could ever come between us. His embrace was my safe haven. I'm carried back to that place now, which might be why my arms return his hug.

"I'm so thankful I saw you tonight," he whispers. "You have no idea."

No, I don't. There are other things I also have no idea about, including why I inhale the scents of his soap and shampoo as an automatic reflex, and why my body relaxes, rather than tenses up, the longer I stay in his arms.

"Our ride is waiting for us," Ava chirps. She pats my arm. "Time to go."

Phoenix takes the hint and releases me. I didn't want to breathe the same air as him a few hours ago, so why am I reluctant to step away from him now?

*I'm tired, that's why.* It has to be. My brain will sort this out after some sleep.

"Good night." I study his face, and I don't know what for. It only reminds me of how attractive he is with a five o'clock shadow and surfaces the memory of when I used to run my fingers over his chin and along his jaw. He searches my face for something, too.

The spell breaks when Ava grabs my hand and pulls me away. She says nothing to me while we amble down the driveway and climb into the Uber's back seat. The quiet only lasts until we're buckled in.

"What was that about?" she asks.

I turn my head away from her to peer out the window. The sky is brightening with the first light of dawn. "We'll talk about it later. I'm too exhausted to explain it now."

I wouldn't be able to, anyway, until I've processed the events of the night. I'm having a difficult enough time explaining it to myself.

# Chapter Five

Ava knew what she was doing when she added a late checkout to our hotel stay. It's after 2 p.m. by the time we're out of our room, have hit a Starbucks for coffee and breakfast sandwiches, and are ready to leave Las Vegas. The city skyline fades into the distance after we merge onto Interstate 15.

Ava takes the first driving shift, which is an act of mercy. My few hours of sleep were broken at best, and flashbacks of last night filled my dreams. It's difficult not to ruminate about everything now, and exhaustion has a way of messing with my self-control. Ava may sense my struggle, since our conversation for the first hour of the drive tiptoes around what happened at the show and Torin's house. She hasn't mentioned the exchanges she witnessed between Phoenix and me since our early-morning ride to the hotel.

If anything, she seems determined to keep my mind on something else. Right now, this involves a singalong to a playlist of songs that are straight from our freshman year of college. With the volume cranked up and the two of us belting out tunes and not staying remotely on-key, I nearly miss the chime from my phone.

Nearly. Not entirely.

My phone is propped up in the center console, where it's connected to a charging cable. I glance at the screen and stop singing, mid-verse. The message label displays a phone number, rather than a name, since the sender isn't in my contacts. It doesn't matter. I know who it's from.

*I'm happy we got to talk last night, even if I wish it could have been for longer. I meant what I said about next weekend. Please think about it.*

I yank out the cable and grab my phone like I need it to put out a fire. Ava can't see this message, or the floodgate that's held her questions back will open and unleash a tidal wave.

"Is that a text from a certain ex who's attempting to rise from the ashes of what he burned down, or did you talk to someone else last night?"

Ava lowers the volume on the music, which means she expects me to answer and could be preparing for a longer conversation. I wonder how much of the message she saw.

"Before you start, I didn't give him my number. He must have had it saved."

"I'm sure he did. What about next weekend does he want you to think about?"

Dammit. She read the whole thing.

"It's nothing." This is the same lie I told her twelve hours ago.

"Is 'nothing' why you still haven't said a word about what I walked in on in Torin's kitchen last night, or what the deal with the extra-long hug was when we left? It sure looked like something was going on between you two."

She isn't letting me off the hook this time. We still have more than three hours together in the car to go, with nowhere for me to escape to. If there's one thing Ava excels at, it's interrogation. She'll get an answer from me one way or another, so we might as well discuss this now.

"He was hitting on me and making sure I knew it. That's all."

"Screw that guy." She sneaks a glance at me and then resumes watching the road. "I mean, not literally, unless you want to."

"Ava!"

My shock must come through in my voice, because she laughs out loud. "What? There's nothing wrong with a casual hookup with your ex. Lord knows I've done it. The best part is already knowing what to expect in bed."

I squeeze my eyes shut, trying to erase the memories of intimate moments with Phoenix from our two years together that now spring to mind, the same way one did last night. The physical side of our relationship was never an issue. Far from it. My problem is trying to forget that when it was good, it was so much more than that. I can't let my body crave him again.

"He asked me to spend next weekend with him," I admit. "That's what you walked in on, and what he wants me to think about."

I brace myself for Ava's reply, which is sure to include a few choice expletives about Phoenix and what he's up to.

"This will sound crazy, but hear me out. Maybe you should spend the weekend with him."

Wait, what? Is she kidding around, or using a reverse psychology strategy on me? Her poker face is more convincing than I realized if she is.

"Did we enter another reality when we crossed the state line?" I finally ask.

She smirks. "You know I can't stand what he did to you, and I'll be the first person to hunt him down and smack him into another solar system if he hurts you again. But if you're even the tiniest bit tempted to take him up on what he's asking, then I think you should."

I pinch the skin on my wrist as a test that I am, in fact, awake. Apparently I am.

"May I ask why?"

"So you won't spend months wondering 'what if' and questioning if you made the right choice, and so you won't waste another six years sabotaging your dating life because he left you with unfinished business."

"I've dated since then," I protest.

"You've also become the textbook definition of avoidant attachment."

"I've had a lot going on in my life since then. My career needed my focus."

Her mouth puckers. We've had this discussion before. It always ends with her accusing me of not opening up to new people because I'm terrified of vulnerability and rejection. I usually suggest we agree to disagree to keep the peace, instead of offering evidence in my favor. She would go round for round with me if I did. Not that she's wrong about this, but it wasn't like I could solve it by asking Phoenix for answers or one last conversation until now. I tried so many times in the months after he left. His silence and stonewalling only hurt me more.

"I want to see you happy in all parts of your life again," Ava says. "Spending a day or two with Phoenix might get you answers to the questions you've had for years, so you can truly move on. If you get some action along the way, so be it. There are worse things."

She makes it sound so easy, but I barely kept myself together during the brief interactions Phoenix and I had last night. What happens when it's just him and me alone? She has a point about getting answers, though, and about my tendency to second-guess things.

"Maybe." I slump down in my seat.

"You're conflicted about what to do," she observes.

"That's an understatement."

"Then do what I do when I'm stuck and overthinking things, and flip a coin. Heads, you get together with him next weekend, call him out on his bullshit, ask him everything you've ever wanted to know, and give yourself a fighting chance at finally getting over him. Tails, you ignore his message, forget you ran into him, and continue finding reasons to disqualify every guy you date. Let the universe decide."

"When did you become my therapist?" I grumble.

"When you stopped going to therapy, which was what? A year after Phoenix left?"

"A year and a half."

"And how many guys have made it past a handful of dates since then?" She waits for me to answer, then turns the music up and leaves me to stew in my thoughts when I don't.

Our stalemate lasts for two songs. Ava will keep this up for the entire rest of the drive if she has to, but I can't. "Fine. You win."

She takes one hand off the steering wheel and points at the console. "There's some loose change in there."

"I have to do it now?"

"You can always spend the rest of the drive agonizing over what to do, and then go home and lose sleep over it. It's up to you."

Why does she know me so well? It would be maddening if I didn't love her for it most of the time, but then there are times like this. I've already lost the battle, and she knows it.

"I'll get it over with, but then I don't want to hear another peep about it."

Agreeing with her doesn't stop me from sighing and noisily blowing a strand of hair away from my face while I open the console and rummage around. The first coin I spot is a quarter. It will do.

I grab the quarter and flip it into the air. It comes within a hair of the headliner, then makes its descent and lands on my seat. George Washington stares up at me. Heads it is.

"Make him wait a bit and sweat it out before you text him back," Ava advises. "You'd better believe I want a full report on what goes down when you see him."

---

Ava leaves me with strict instructions to forget about Phoenix's text until the morning when she drops me off at home. It's not as difficult as I expected it would be to do. I probably have my mental muscle memory to thank for that, after all the times I've blocked out thoughts of him before. Besides, my deadline to turn in a polished draft of my next book looms ahead of me. I need to write much more than I need to think about Phoenix, and when I write, I dial in. Focusing on my books is what got me through some of the worst times after he left.

After scrounging up something for dinner, I turn my laptop on and open my latest murder mystery manuscript and research notes on the Elenna Paseo case. The idea for my book was sparked by Elenna's disappearance from Aliso Viejo, the Orange County city she resided in, a little over two years ago. I first heard about her from a local news story on KTLA.

Her case has always been full of loose ends, because she vanished from her neighborhood without a trace or a reason. No one has seen or heard from her since. Her disappearance first caught my attention because Elenna and I are—or were—the same age. My connection became more personal a few days after the KTLA story aired, when another report was published online. In it, Elenna's uncle described how eerie it was to visit her house.

*"It looked like she had every intention of coming back. Dishes were left soaking in the kitchen sink, her fridge was stocked with food, and a book she'd been reading was on the counter."*

The book was my newest release at the time, according to her uncle. I probably wouldn't have seen the report or the part about my book if a few of my readers hadn't tagged me on social media. One of them mentioned that Elenna followed my accounts. I checked, and she did. She also had all of my novels in her Goodreads library. She'd rated every book except the one found on her counter. Learning all of this struck an emotional chord. I wanted to find out more about her and what happened.

But as her case went cold, I felt compelled to give it a conclusion. If she were a character in one of my books, what would the rest of her story be? Where did she go, and why? Was she alive or dead? I wanted to give her an ending, even if it was only a fictional world based around her, since the investigation hadn't. After the hours I've spent poring over news articles, online videos, and discussion forums, I understand why. She had no reason to vanish, no secrets anyone had uncovered, and no one with any known grudge against her. It could have been a random kidnapping or homicide. And that's where I've gone back and forth with my book, going so far as to outline and draft different versions of the plot. It's fiction, and

I can stray from the actual events and findings, but nothing I've come up with so far has fully satisfied me. Vegas should have been a quick writing break to reset my brain, so I could come home and brainstorm fresh ideas. It wasn't.

Now, skimming through the current chapter I'm at work on, I bite back a laugh. Like most of the book, it's set in Laguna Beach. I chose the oceanside town as the setting since it's close to Aliso Viejo without actually being the same city Elenna resided in. With its picture-perfect turquoise water and beaches, Laguna Beach seemed like an ideal location to juxtapose my character's sunny and idyllic California life with the dark nature of her disappearance. I could let it remind me of Phoenix and his message, and give in to the distraction, but I won't. He doesn't get to waste my writing time.

It isn't until hours later, when the words blur in front of me on the screen and exhaustion clouds every corner of my brain, that I close my laptop and grab my phone. I open Phoenix's message during the short walk from my office to my bedroom and read his words again.

"Why do you want to see me and talk?" I mumble. "Why now, after all this time?"

I'd be better off asking a Magic 8 Ball or a tarot reader for clarity than I am talking to my phone and expecting a revelation to fall from the sky. Only Phoenix knows why, and only he can tell me.

I flop onto my bed, phone still in hand, and bury my face in a pillow. As much as I hate to admit it, Ava was right about our unfinished business and how I've let it damage my life. Is she also right that one last weekend with him could be my chance to heal, or will it break me more?

Coin toss or not, I know I don't have to do anything. There's nothing I owe him, and I'm a grown adult who has free will. I can delete the text, block his number, and let him suffer with my silence this time. He deserves it after what I went through. But what if seeing him and clearing the air really is the way for me to finally sever this tie and open myself up to love again? Therapy didn't solve everything, and neither did time. Maybe this is it.

Ava wanted me to wait until the morning, but it's after midnight and technically morning now. I open his message again and type a reply.

*I can see you one day next weekend, not both. Saturday is better.*

He can take it or leave it. If he declines, I'm off the hook and can look forward to a peaceful weekend spent writing in solitude. If he tries to sell me on both days and a slumber party, then his true intentions will be clear.

My phone chimes a minute later. *I'm grateful you're even willing to give me five seconds. Thank you. I can come to you on Saturday if Laguna is too far.*

It's about an hour's drive from my place to Laguna Beach when traffic is light, but it's better to meet him there. My home is my sanctuary, and I'm not ready to see him at my door. Going to his place also means I can leave early if things get uncomfortable.

*Laguna works. Let me know where to go.* Let's hope everything I want for my life is on the other side of doing what I already dread.

And if the best-case scenario happens? If I actually enjoy Phoenix's company, hear him out on what he has to say, and decide to stay the entire time? I can't wrap my head around that idea and what it would mean just yet.

# Chapter Six

"NERVES ARE FOR PEOPLE who have something to lose," I mutter under my breath. "Calm down."

There's no reason for what feels like a frenzied flock of seagulls in my stomach as I approach the freeway exit that, according to my GPS, is only a few minutes away from the address Phoenix sent me. Being logical about it doesn't help. My palms are still clammy when I pull into the driveway of a sandstone-colored house with a tiled roof and park my car beside a maroon Mercedes SUV.

The street is a quiet crescent, and the houses here aren't ostentatious by any means, but it's Laguna Beach. Unless it's a rental, the modest-sized home in front of me came with a multi-million-dollar price tag. It's a far cry from the one-bedroom loft Phoenix leased when we started dating, and perhaps I shouldn't be surprised. His career may have tanked after *North Node*, but he was at the top of his earnings game before then.

Movement at a window confirms he knows I'm here, and that

it's too late to change my mind, reverse direction, and go home. This won't kill me, but it would be less brutal if I could skip to the part where sense and rationality take control again and my jitters go away. Damn coin toss, and damn nerves.

The front door of the house swings open as I step out of the car, and Phoenix emerges to greet me. I'd be lying if I claimed not to notice the way his sleeveless charcoal T-shirt hugs his chest and shows off the well-defined muscles in his arms, or if I denied how the fit of his jeans across his hips unleashes a torrent of memories that are in no way appropriate for the situation at hand. What is wrong with me? Taking inventory of his physical attributes isn't what I'm here for.

"Was the drive okay?" he asks.

"Mostly. I hit the usual traffic on the 5."

I'm a couple of feet from him now. He opens his arms for a hug, but stops short of putting them around me until I accept the invitation and close the gap between us.

"Thank you for driving all the way out here."

His breath tickles my ear and sends tingles up my spine. He's subtle about it, but I catch the dip of his head closer to my hair and the rise of his chest when he breathes in. Maybe he notices the scent of my hair, or the vanilla fragrance of my perfume. Maybe this isn't only me. Both of us hang on for longer than we should, like the moment we shared when we said goodbye at Torin's house.

I let go first. Our gazes meet when I step back, and I thank every higher power out there that I'm still wearing sunglasses. Phoenix isn't. If his eyes are truly a window to his soul, then today could be more than I bargained for.

"Would you like to go inside?"

"Sure." I'm not sure at all, though. Ava isn't here to play chaperone or interrupt if an exchange between us becomes intense, which means I'm the only one who can save me from myself.

Phoenix hangs back a few steps to let me enter the house ahead of him. Should I pause in the foyer and let him lead me somewhere? Or should I plunk myself down on the first chair or sofa I see? Will I recognize any of the artwork or framed photographs on his walls, or is everything in here from a part of his life I know nothing about? Nothing has ever made me feel like more of an awkward wallflower than stepping inside his house does now.

Phoenix must sense my hesitation. He touches my arm, which I take as a signal to stop and turn around.

"We could go to the beach for a while, if you're into that. If not, we can stay here."

I should be relieved. The beach means a wide-open public space. I'm less likely to do something I could regret later if we're in view of other people. But I recall Phoenix wanting to continue our conversation in private, which makes the beach an odd choice.

"I'm up for it if you think we can talk there. It's probably more crowded with people than Torin's house was."

This is my way of warning him he's still on the hook for finishing what he started in Las Vegas. I didn't come here for a beach date where we stroll along the sand, find seashells, buy ice cream, and watch the waves roll in.

"Not the spot we're going to," he replies. "Let me grab some things first, and then we can go."

I follow him into a gleaming white kitchen, where he opens the door of a stainless-steel fridge. He pulls out a plastic grocery bag, then puts it inside a larger canvas bag that's on a quartz countertop.

"Water and snacks in case we get hungry," he explains. "There's a beach blanket for the sand in my truck."

"Okay." The crazed seagulls have returned to my stomach. Food is the last thing on my mind.

"No." He looks at me in a way that makes me wonder if he's peering into my heart or reading my thoughts.

"No to what?"

"You said 'okay,' but I can tell it isn't and that you aren't. It's my fault."

"Pardon?" He's right, but the fact that he's caught on to my anxiety is unnerving.

"Want to sit down?"

It sounds like a request I can decline if I want to, but it's doubtful he'll let the subject drop for long if I say no and we continue on our way to the beach. The closest seats to us are stools at the counter, so I pull one out and sit on it. He takes a seat on the stool next to mine.

"You aren't comfortable around me," he continues. "I did that and I'll own it, but I want you to know I meant what I said last weekend."

He said a lot of things last weekend. "Remind me what that was?"

"That I don't know if I can ever make up for what I did to you, but I want to try if you'll let me. And that I won't bite you."

*Unless I want you to*, my mind finishes. Curse him, because now I'm remembering how he looked at me and played with a lock of my hair, and the images of us together that sprang to mind then and do the same now.

The corners of his mouth curve upward, as though he hears my thoughts. It was a decent ice-breaking attempt on his part, but he hasn't melted me yet.

"I'm still thrown by you wanting to talk and hang out all of a sudden," I admit. "I don't understand it, especially since I wouldn't be here right now if you hadn't run into me by accident."

"So, about that." He shifts in his seat to rest his elbow on the counter, then props his head up with his hand. "I need to confess something."

His expression reminds me of a puppy dog. I don't know what he's about to reveal, but I've experienced the same soulful, wide-eyed gaze of his before. It's nothing but trouble. My record for resisting him when he turns it on me and dials up the charm is abysmal. Despite this, my curiosity wins.

"Please do."

"I said I don't believe in random chance when we spoke at Torin's house. That's because I knew you would be at Nebula. Running into you wasn't an accident. I went there to see you."

Hold up. If he means what I think he does, then a certain drum-playing friend of mine will be getting an earful from me later. He'll be lucky if I don't sic Ava on him too. But something doesn't add up.

"Torin told you I would be at his show?" I stare at Phoenix, hoping I misunderstood. Torin is one of my most trusted friends. He wouldn't throw me under the bus that way and not tell me, and he was horrified when he saw Phoenix with me at the show and in his kitchen. Was it an act? And if so, why would he do that?

"Not exactly. Or at least not intentionally."

"Then how did you find out, 'exactly'?" I make air quotes when I say the last word. He's not about to speak in riddles on my watch.

"From Ava."

I pitch forward and nearly tumble off my stool. Phoenix's arm shoots out to steady me at the same time as I grab hold of the counter.

"What?" I sputter.

There's no chance. None. Then again, that's also what I would have said about spending today with Phoenix if someone had asked me before last weekend, so this could be the upside-down world.

"I was with Nash when he stopped in at Torin's house to drop off some gear. Torin was on a FaceTime with Ava when we got there and I heard her say you were coming to the show."

Thank God. I knew Ava wouldn't do me dirty like that and tip him off directly, but it's strange she didn't mention this. It's also strange that Torin hasn't said a word about being in contact with him, but then, he might have thought it would upset me. Phoenix has been a sensitive subject for years.

"One of them could have warned me."

"I was in another room. Torin didn't know I was there until after he hung up, or that I heard anything either of them said. I also didn't tell him I would be at the show."

"Nash must have known," I insist. "You said he invited you to the after-party." Mostly, I want to know how close Phoenix and Torin are these days that Nash would invite him to the house without saying something about it to the person who lives there.

"I sent Nash a text ten minutes before I got to Nebula. There was less risk of him telling Torin that way, since they would both be busy getting ready for their set. That also meant there was less risk you would find out."

I narrow my eyes. "You wanted to see me but didn't want me to find out you'd be there?"

Phoenix shifts in his seat. He's either uncomfortable about being called out for his covert actions, or with how I'm glowering at him.

"I was afraid you would change your mind about going, or that Torin might stop me from getting in," he admits. "He's protective of you."

His tone makes me suspect he's had a few exchanges with Torin that I'm not aware of. If I'm correct, then I'm beyond curious about what went down between the two of them.

"What makes you say that?" I ask.

"He only gives me one-word or two-word answers when I ask about you and then changes the subject. I thought he was going to punch me the first time I brought up your name to him after we stopped dating, but I understand why."

This sounds like he's asked Torin about me more than once. I had no idea. If he wanted insight into how I was doing, though, why didn't he reach out to me?

"You could have asked me what you wanted to know instead of trying to go through him," I point out. "You still had my number."

"It took a long time for me to get my act together after what I did. Too long." He rubs a hand over his chin. "I didn't think you would answer a call or text from me after all that time."

"That's fair, but there's still a lot it doesn't explain."

"I'll explain whatever you want to know. Should we head to the beach and continue this there?"

He gets to his feet and grabs the bag from the counter without waiting for a reply.

# Chapter Seven

It's hard to tell if Phoenix is stalling, or if he really will explain it all. I nod, slide off my stool, and leave the kitchen ahead of him. My questions will start the second we hit the sand.

A view of the sky through a window stops me mid-stride. It was overcast during most of the drive over, but the clouds in the distance now are an ominous shade of dark gray.

"Those clouds don't look good," I say. "We might want to stay here until they clear out."

"Was it supposed to rain? I didn't check after leaving Vegas yesterday." Phoenix sounds baffled. I understand why. Summer rain in Southern California is a rare event and it's hyped up by the news for a week before it happens.

"Maybe? I was wrapped up in writing this week and didn't pay attention to the forecast." I was preoccupied by thoughts of today, too, but I won't tell him this.

"Were you working on the novel that's based on a woman who

went missing from around here?"

It's an offhand question from him, but it sets off an alarm in my head. I haven't said anything publicly about what I'm currently working on, and neither has my agent. We always keep the details under wraps until the official book announcement comes out.

"How do you know that? This novel won't be announced for a while."

"Ava mentioned it to Torin when she told him you were coming to his show."

Ava is the closest thing I have to a sister, and I love her without question, but she and I should have a chat about how much she discloses to other people. She's also likely to lose her shit when she learns she was the reason for what happened in Vegas and where I am now, so that might be enough of a warning to filter what she says on its own.

"Are there any other details of my life she revealed that I should know about? Like where I'll be next Tuesday at two in the afternoon, or anything else I've said to her this year?"

He chuckles. "She's proud of you, that's all. We all are. You're such a talented writer."

Is he serious or trying to flatter me with an empty compliment he can't back up? I wrote when we were together, but I didn't let him read much of it back then, even when my first manuscript sold.

"You say that like you've read my books."

"I have. Come with me for a second."

He takes my hand and leads me to the living room. The hand-holding is unexpected, but I'll play along with it for now. We pass by an oversized ash-gray sofa and stop in front of a floor-to-ceiling bookcase. When he reaches for one of the shelves, I spy the familiar hardcover spines of the novels I've published.

He pulls out my first bestseller. "I was blown away when I read this. My agent sent me the script for the film adaptation the other day, and I was happy to see it does your book justice."

"So that's why I'm here. You want to ask me questions about the characters and get the inside track for your audition."

I'm teasing him, but his expression becomes more solemn than I've ever seen it. He returns the book to its spot on the shelf like it's a hot potato.

"I don't know if I'm going to audition, and I swear that thought didn't cross my mind. You're asking all the questions today."

It's the segue I've been waiting for. "Cool. Then I have one for you now."

My hand is still in his, which is why I'm able to detect the slightest tremor in his fingers. Is it because he's about to open up to me and doesn't know how I'll react? Does redeeming himself mean so much to him that he's nervous?

Raindrops patter against the roof and windows, which makes the final decision for us about staying here versus going to the beach. I guide him away from the bookcase to the sofa. When I sit, he does the same. I let go of his hand and settle against the cushions.

"If you really still cared about me for all this time like you claimed last weekend, why did you walk out and never come back?"

His head bobs, as though he's processing the question and agreeing it's a good place to start. There's silence for a moment, and then he speaks.

"Because I wasn't ready for anything that was happening in my life then. I panicked and I self-destructed. That's the short version."

"I would like to hear the longer one."

His lips form a grim line, and he closes his eyes. Is he acting, or should I brace myself for what the longer version is? When his eyelids open again a few seconds later, he trains his gaze on me.

"Do you remember when I started drinking? Like when it stopped being social and became excessive?"

"I remember the general time, but not a specific day or event." It hasn't occurred to me before now that his behavior could have been traced to a single inciting incident.

"It was the night of the *Summerlong* premiere. You were radiant on the red carpet, laughing and at ease with everyone you talked to. I acted the part, but I'd never felt more like an imposter, and my anxiety was through the roof. The entertainment media raved about the film and my acting, but I felt like a fraud. I thought someone would see it and expose me at any moment. It was fight or flight the entire night, so I had a few drinks at the after-party to try to relax. Then I had more when we got home. You helped me stumble to my bedroom at some point, and then I blacked out."

Memories of the night flash in front of my eyes. To me, he was celebrating the premiere and got carried away. He was hungover as hell the next morning, and his mood was off, but he didn't say a word about anxiety or inner turmoil.

"I remember that night. I didn't know you were going through that."

"I didn't tell you. It was stupid to hide it, but I was convinced you would see me differently if you knew how insecure I was about the accolades and attention, and how I felt like I couldn't live up to the hype. Toxic masculinity at its finest, right? That night was only the start of it."

"Because then the bigger scripts started rolling in, and all the interviews, and the spotlight got brighter," I recall. "Everything was so hectic all the time, but I was excited for you."

"You were incredible about all of it. You never complained about how long I was always on set, or how often I was away to film on location or to do late night talk shows, and I just got worse with returning texts and calling to see how you were. I hated myself for it when I was sober. You deserved better, and I wasn't giving it to you."

The disgust clouding Phoenix's eyes isn't something I believe he could fake, no matter how excellent of an actor he is.

"You were working. I expected you to be focused on what you needed to do, and I knew I would see you when you were home. I was working too, and then spending my evenings and weekends writing. It was fine until you were drunk or high on something more often than you weren't when we did have time together."

"That didn't take long to happen. The more attention and praise I got, and the more I neglected you, the more unworthy I felt of anything good. That led to drinking more. It was my messed-up way to calm down. Then one night after a press junket in New York, a castmate handed me a pill. He could tell I was on edge and said it would help. It did. I was on top of the world for a few hours and it silenced my self-doubt for a while. Coming down felt like death, but the escape it gave me made me want to do it again. And then again. You know how things went after that. Most people in my circle enabled me. You were the only one who cared enough to try to get me to stop."

I chew the inside of my lip, remembering. I did try, even though it ended in arguments and tears every time. He denied having a problem. I often wondered if I raised the issue one too many times, and if he left because he didn't want to hear about it anymore.

"Did you leave because I wanted you to stop?"

"No. I left because I was an out-of-control asshole who couldn't get a handle on anything."

"Is that the short version?"

A sad smile touches the corners of his mouth. "Yeah. There's a longer one."

"Could you tell it to me?"

Phoenix fiddles with his watchband. His chest heaves as he takes a long breath, then lets it out. The pause stretches on for so long, I wonder if he regrets promising to explain whatever I want to know, or if I'll regret wanting the details.

"The day I walked out was the same day my agent gave me the news I'd landed a huge part in a major film. You were at work when I got the call. I'd stayed at your place the night before and was still there, in your kitchen, at peace for once and having a sober day. I was going to go ring shopping for you that afternoon. But once I hung up with my agent, the panic started. I opened your fridge and grabbed the first thing I saw, which were those horrible whiskey drinks. They didn't help. You came home and I melted down."

What happened when I came home is burned in my memory forever, but it's not what I'm focused on now.

"Ring shopping?" I repeat. "You mean a surprise, just for fun, sparkly cocktail ring or something, right?"

He won't look at me. When he leans forward to rest his elbows on his knees, and then puts his head in his hands, my heart constricts and the air is sucked out of the room. No, he doesn't mean a cocktail ring.

"I wanted to ask you to marry me."

# Chapter Eight

GRAVITY MAY AS WELL be an illusion. Up feels like down, down feels like up, and the room swims in front of my eyes until I pull myself together enough to acknowledge what I heard.

"You wanted to ask me to marry you." Each syllable I speak sounds surreal. "But you left and didn't come back? I don't understand."

Adrenaline is kicking in now. Is it better or worse to know?

"The way we fought that day—" Phoenix stops, seeming to reconsider his words. "The way I lashed out that day, I mean. It was all me to blame and not you. It was never you. You were sobbing and heaving at one point because of me. Mostly, you were so sad, and everything you said to me that day was true. I loved you, but I did that to you and kept doing it, and it wasn't the first time. You deserved so much more than I could give you then. All you ever tried to do was save me from myself, and I was a selfish and insecure piece of crap who couldn't even make it out the door sober to buy a ring. When I left, I thought I would cool off and figure out how to pull myself out of the spiral I was in."

"But you didn't." It's a statement, not a question. Most of the Western world knows he didn't, thanks to the photos, videos, and stories splashed all over the tabloids. He was a train wreck.

"I got worse. I was toxic then, and I was aware of it. That's why I didn't answer your messages. I thought your life would be infinitely better without me dragging you down."

His lips move, and his words make it through to me, but it's like listening to him from somewhere underwater. I'm about to be caught in a riptide.

"I need a minute," I mumble, pushing myself up from the sofa. "Where's your bathroom?"

"Down the hallway, second door on the right."

I leave the room faster than I high-tailed it out of Nebula last weekend, before he can see the tears pooling in my eyes. Once I reach the hallway, I feverishly scan the open doors. The first one reveals a room that must be in the midst of a remodel, with half of a hardwood floor laid down and new, unpainted drywall lining the walls. The second one is the bathroom, just as Phoenix said. I slip inside and shut the door behind me.

*Focus on breathing. Don't cry.*

I asked for the truth and I got it, but I wasn't expecting that. The woman in the bathroom mirror looks shell-shocked. As I gaze at my glassy-eyed reflection, the *what-ifs* and *woulds* start to collide in my mind. What if he'd gone through with buying a ring and proposing? What if we'd made it down the aisle? What if we'd had kids? Would he have continued self-destructing? Would we still be together now? What would my life be like?

A bright flash at the window pulls me back to the present. It's followed by a loud crash of thunder and a howling gust of wind. The rain is more frantic now.

"Del? I'm going to put the cars in the garage. It's getting bad out there, and I just got a weather alert about hail and flash floods." Phoenix sounds like he's a few steps away from the other side of the door.

"Okay. My keys are in my purse, in the living room." I struggle to keep my voice from wavering.

Lightning flashes again, and then there's another loud rumble. If rain at this time of year is rare, a thunderstorm is an anomaly. The hail and flash flood warnings are alarming, and are also signs I can't just leave if I become overwhelmed. Driving in this from here to LA before it eases up would be a reckless thing to do, knowing how the freeways and drivers get during storms.

I also don't want to run away. There's more to uncover, including what made Phoenix clean up his act after my attempts failed, but I need some time between processing this and getting into that for my own sake. I take another minute or two to regain my composure and concentrate on breathing normally again. There isn't much I can do about the telltale red tinge of my eyeballs, which makes my irises almost comically luminous and green, but I can't hide out in here until that goes away.

The living room is empty when I return to it, and so I sit on the sofa and wait. My gaze flickers to the bookshelf, scanning the titles and colorful spines, and the framed photographs. I recognize a photo of Phoenix with his parents, and one of him with his older sister and nephew. Nothing I see offers clues into the years we were absent from each other's lives.

A door clicks shut somewhere in the house. Phoenix's footsteps approach the living room.

"Apparently it's an atmospheric river traveling through." He appears in the doorway. His hair is damp from the rain outside.

"Thanks for putting my car in the garage." My voice is steadier now, even if I don't feel that way as I watch him cross the room and take a seat beside me.

"Thanks for not climbing out the bathroom window and leaving."

"Thank the lightning for that." I try to smile so he knows I'm kidding. Wow, though. This is hard.

"What's going on out there is wilder than the monsoons in Vegas."

I can't let things regress to a weather chat again, even if I'm not ready to dive back into the deep end of what we just talked about. So I grasp on to the first non-breakup-related thought that flits through my brain, which might also give me a glimpse into the last few years of his life.

"Speaking of Vegas, how did you become friends with Nash?"

Phoenix blinks a few times. He probably expected another question to do with him and me. It's still coming, so I hope he doesn't think he's in the clear.

"We lost someone we were both close with," he says after a moment. "Our paths crossed before then, but losing Len brought us together."

So much for lighter topics. "I'm sorry. Did I know Len at all?" The name isn't familiar.

"No," he confirms. "We met on the set of a film we both worked on. It was after you and I were together."

"If Len knew Nash, then did he also know Torin?"

"She met him once, very briefly, but it was before Nash was in his band. They weren't friends."

She. This registers with me at the same time as Phoenix's description of being close with her and how they met does. Hollywood is rife with stories about on-set romances spawned from long hours together and weeks of close proximity. I pushed it to the back of my mind when we dated, and our problems had nothing to do with fidelity. But now something flags.

"Did you date her?"

I didn't mean to blurt that out. I don't even know why it matters, other than my mind's attempt to work through him being capable of a romantic relationship with someone else after his claim about spiraling too much to stay with me.

"Len became a good friend, but that's all. Losing her was the final wake-up call I needed to get my life together."

What does that mean? I want to ask him this, and why losing me wasn't enough, but I don't know how to do it without sounding jealous or petty about a friendship he had with someone who isn't alive now.

"She sounds like she was special to you," I say instead.

My heart aches at this thought. I wish I didn't understand why, but I do. Here I thought I was delaying the rest of a conversation that would trigger more of this feeling, but I've walked into a minefield full of it.

Phoenix has always been able to read me, and now is no exception. He touches my arm. "Len knew how special you are to me, if that helps to know."

He covers my hand with his. Embarrassment and confusion waltz together at my core. My soul is on display, and all I want to do is hide because it's clear he's dialed into my emotions and what I've refused to admit to myself until now. I still have love and a lot of other mixed-up feelings for him, and I'm not nearly as over him as I convinced myself I was.

"It does." I swipe at my cheek with my free hand, wiping away the moisture that's there. Of all the times for my tear ducts to spring a leak, it has to be now, when I'm already vulnerable and have shown every card I meant to keep close to my chest.

Phoenix brings his hand up to my face. He strokes another teardrop away with his thumb. "I'm sorry this made you cry. I'm sorry for everything I've ever said or done that made you cry."

I gulp a couple of times, desperate to regain control of myself. "Can we talk about something else for a while?"

His thumb lingers on my cheekbone, then retreats to my jawline, and lord, this isn't helping. "Of course."

The loudest cracking sound I've ever heard punctuates his reply, and then there's a bang. The wind howls outside, whistling through the trees and rattling the window next to us.

"What was that noise?" I ask.

Phoenix drops his hand and gets up from the sofa. He walks to the window, where he cranes his neck to look at something outside. "I'm hoping it wasn't what I think. Give me a second."

He leaves the living room. I follow him, watching as he opens the front door and holds it steady against the gusting wind as he peers down the driveway. He grimaces after a moment, then takes a step back and closes the door again.

"There's a tree down on the road and it's completely blocking my driveway," he reports. "I'm going to call it in and find out how long it will take to send someone out here to remove it. You won't be able to get your car out of the driveway while it's there."

"How big is the tree?" I open the door this time and look out. He wasn't kidding. The driveway is blocked in. The thick trunk and tangles of branches everywhere are quite a sight. I stare at the mess until an icy patter redirects my attention. The forecasted hail is here.

I shut the door and backtrack to the living room. Phoenix is on the phone, listening to something. He lowers it from his ear and taps the screen after about a minute, then places the phone on an end table.

"There's a recorded message about trees being down on major streets. The estimated time to get to side streets is twelve to fifteen hours, as long as the storm doesn't get worse than it is now."

"Twelve to fifteen hours?" I echo. "That's the middle of the night."

He nods. "You could be stuck here until the morning."

# Chapter Nine

THE TIMEFRAME FOR CLEARING a tree wasn't an exaggeration. It's still there when the clock strikes midnight. So is the storm. It has continued rolling through in waves all evening, leaving the two of us housebound with nothing to do but pass the time. We've played Scrabble. Phoenix gave me a house tour, and then he cooked dinner. We haven't said a word about what we talked about before the tree fell down, even though what came out hangs between us with a life force of its own.

I'm also now aware of something I wasn't before the house tour. There is only one bed in this house, and it's in Phoenix's bedroom. The half-finished room I passed by on my way to the bathroom earlier is the guest room, which Phoenix said he started renovating before he ended up on location in Las Vegas.

I still haven't asked what the sleeping arrangements are. There are other things puzzling me at the moment, as I sit beside him on the living room sofa, pretending to watch a movie. He's been a perfect gentleman ever since we realized I could be here overnight. It's gotten to where I'm convinced I only dreamed about him hitting on me last weekend, and that I hallucinated him holding my hand and brushing away my tears this afternoon.

My mind is in loops, mulling over what made him back off on the most innocent of gestures like touching my shoulder or arm, or saying anything I could interpret as flirting. We've been sitting together on the sofa for over an hour, a gaping space separating us, like two barely acquainted people who have seats next to one another at a theater. If it's a psychological tactic designed to heighten my awareness of him, it's working.

I sigh without intending to and slump further into the sofa cushions. He glances at me, which is the first acknowledgement I've had from him since a comment about the movie during its opening credits.

"Is everything okay?"

No, everything is not okay. I'm confused, annoyed with myself, and wondering if this storm will ever wrap it up so I can go home and overanalyze why the platonic treatment bothers me so much when it shouldn't.

"Mmm-hmm. All good."

A blinding streak of lightning flashes outside and illuminates the room, like it wants to call me out on my lie. The lamp on the table beside me flickers, and then it and the TV screen go dark.

Wonderful. Now the power is out.

"Maybe we should call it a night and go to bed," I suggest.

Sleeping will give us a reason for not speaking, anyway.

"You can have my room," Phoenix offers. "I think I have an extra toothbrush in the bathroom drawer. Let me find it."

He reaches for his phone and turns on its flashlight, then gets up from the sofa. I also get up and grab my phone from the table, then follow him down the hallway, up the stairs, and into his bedroom. He continues into the ensuite bathroom. I go as far as the doorway between the two rooms.

"Where are you going to sleep?" I ask.

"On the sofa." He rummages through a drawer and pulls out a new toothbrush in its package. "I'll leave this on the counter. Towels are on the shelf in here. If you want one of my T-shirts to sleep in, there are a bunch in the second drawer of the dresser. I just need to brush my teeth, and then I'll be out of here."

"Nix?" The nickname I used to call him tumbles from my mouth, surprising me.

He pauses in the middle of reaching for his toothbrush and meets my eyes in the mirror. I guess it surprised him, too. "Yeah?"

"You could just sleep in here, you know. It's not like we haven't slept in the same bed before."

He studies me in the mirror without saying anything. Thank God we only have the light from his phone's flashlight, because the longer he's quiet, the more my face feels like it's on fire.

"Are you sure you're okay with that?"

"It's totally fine. I'm sure it's a lot more comfortable than the sofa." I sound breezy, but now my brain is cluttered with questions about why he seems hesitant about it or if I'm imagining this, and about why I said what I did at all. Was it for validation?

"Okay. Thank you." He glances away from my reflection and plucks his toothbrush from its holder.

His stoic response is underwhelming, but it's in line with the last few hours. I turn away from the door and walk over to the dresser, where I open the drawer he mentioned. The only light in the room comes from a flash of lightning outside the window, but it's there and gone in an instant. I fumble in the dark to pull out the first T-shirt I find, and then perch on the edge of a chair in the corner to wait for Phoenix to finish brushing his teeth.

When he emerges from the bathroom, he's no longer wearing a shirt. This is normal, since he only wore his boxer briefs to bed when we were together, unless we fell asleep naked after making love. What I didn't expect is the magnetic pull his bare chest has on my attention. My gaze lands on his chest and six-pack abs, then roams to the V-line that is partly obscured by his pants. His body is still as incredible as it was when I used to spend hours exploring every inch of skin I see.

"Do you need anything?"

My head snaps up. He's looking straight at me, which means he knows I was checking him out. Let's hope he didn't also read my mind.

Years ago, if he'd caught me getting an eyeful, I would have replied to his question with something sexy or coy. Tonight, I shake my head and get up from the chair, because I don't trust myself to answer him. I'll return to my senses after I stop ogling him.

"Do you want my phone for the flashlight?" He holds it out to me.

"Thanks, I have mine." I continue past him into the bathroom.

Washing my face and brushing my teeth gives me the time I need to collect myself. When I change out of my clothes and pull Phoenix's T-shirt over my head, though, the nostalgia nearly knocks me back to where I was when I came in here. I used to wear his shirts all the time, especially in the mornings after I stayed over at his place.

The slate blue shirt is a mini-dress on me, hitting mid-thigh. It's modest enough thanks to its size and my small frame, so I don't know what about it prompts the flutter in my stomach when I pick up my phone from the counter and open the bathroom door.

Then it strikes me: It isn't the shirt at all. It's what wearing it makes me remember.

Phoenix is already in bed, propped up against the pillows and watching something on his phone. I turn my phone's flashlight off as I approach the other side of the bed, and then set the device on the bedside table. He glances at me when I lift the corner of the duvet, and I swear he tenses up. Whatever is going on with him, my nerves and patience are both too frayed to want to think about it.

He clears his throat. "Are you okay with that side? I just assumed—"

He cuts off his own sentence, perhaps because he was about

to make a reference to when we shared a bed more often than we didn't. This is the side I slept on, at least when we didn't end up spooned together in the middle of the bed. And now I have memories of spooning to deal with, thanks to my overactive brain. I should have let him sleep on the sofa.

"Yup. It's still the side I sleep on." I keep my tone light as I get into bed and pull the covers over me. "What are you watching?"

"A comedy thing I found on YouTube."

He sits up and reaches for one of the pillows behind him, then uses it to prop the phone up between us so I can see the screen. It gives me a reason to stare at something other than him and his chest and those damn abs. My overstimulated senses welcome the reprieve.

We've been watching what's on his phone for about ten minutes when I finally start to relax. I adjust my head on the pillow and close my eyes, listening to the monologue and intermittent laughter.

"I can turn this off if you want to sleep."

There will only be strained silence if he turns it off now. I can't deal with that. It will get me keyed up again.

"I'm awake and listening to it. I'm just resting my eyes."

"Famous last words."

I smile, but keep my eyes closed. He's teasing me, whether he meant to do that or let it slip out by accident. It's the most normal exchange we've had in hours.

"I only used to fall asleep watching something when we were

snuggled together," I remind him. "That was on you, because you were like a cozy space heater and it made me relaxed and sleepy. I miss that sometimes."

I didn't mean to say the last part out loud. If it makes him clam up and become overly polite again, I might scream.

"Me too."

My eyelids fly open at the softness in his voice. He meets my gaze, and I'm reminded of what I glimpsed in his eyes when I got here today.

"Do you want to..." He doesn't finish what he says, but he moves his arm that's closest to me away from his side and raises it so it's up near the pillows, creating an open space for me to lie next to him. Then he looks at me again. "Please don't kick me out if I misread that."

Phoenix is asking to hold me. Less than half an hour ago, he was uncertain about us sleeping in the same bed. I'm so perplexed right now, but I move his phone and the pillow away from the center of the bed and slide closer to him, until I'm settled in the crook of his arm with my head against his chest and my hand resting on his stomach. Now if my heartbeat would only settle down, and if I could stop noticing how good he smells, I might not give away how being in his arms makes me feel.

"You aren't getting kicked out for cuddling." I sound infinitely calmer than I am. "You've made it clear you aren't trying to put the moves on me. You haven't even tried to flirt with me all day. I got the message."

What I technically got was an indecipherable mishmash of hot and cold signals that are doing my head in. It's a message, all the same.

"Do you know why I haven't tried to flirt with you?" he asks after a minute.

What a question. It feels like I'm one precarious step away from falling through a trapdoor, whether I answer him or not. I could stay quiet and ignore the bait. It might be safer to. Asking him why will only tell him I care, but I'm certain he already knows. I tipped my hand hours ago.

"Not a clue, since you were last weekend."

"You thought I was after a one-night stand last weekend. I didn't want you to think the same thing today, especially when you didn't have a choice about staying the night. You gave me another chance to spend time with you. I'm trying not to come on too strong, or scare you, or screw it up, even though I was sure I did this afternoon."

"When you told me about the day you left, you mean?" *When you told me you once wanted to marry me.*

"Yes, and after that. I felt like I hit a boundary when you left the room, and then when you were in tears and asked to talk about something else. I wanted to respect you and how you felt. It doesn't mean I don't want to flirt with you. I just want to do this right."

His words about wanting to do this right jog my memory back to the first weeks we dated, and I don't know how I didn't remember until now. Phoenix was so careful with me in the beginning, as though I were a diamond he wouldn't risk dropping. On our first date, he held my hand and put his arm around me, and that's as far as anything physical went. Our second date ended with a lingering hug and him pressing his lips against my forehead, before we parted ways at my door. He didn't ask to kiss me until our third date. It worked, because I fell for him hard.

This is eight-years-ago Phoenix behavior, even with the history we have. It's the guy who didn't want to move too fast, too soon, or it is if he's telling the truth. As much as I want to protect my heart at all costs, the ice shelf around it is cracking.

"You aren't trying to friend-zone me, then?"

"For the record, I am far too attracted to you to do that. I'm sorry if the message got mixed up."

"Oh yeah?" I arch an eyebrow, even though I'm kidding.

"Fair warning that if your hand goes any lower than where it is, you'll discover that for yourself and probably without meaning to."

It takes a few seconds for me to realize that I'm tracing circles down his abdomen with my fingertip, and I'm about to reach the waistband of his underwear. *Oh*. I don't know whether to be amused by the moderately embarrassed tone in his voice, or to be mortified that my hand is doing things to his body outside of my conscious awareness. Old habits are hard to break.

"Sorry about that." I bring my hand back up to where it was before.

"You have nothing to be sorry for. I'm the only one in this room who needs to apologize for anything."

"Or we could both stop apologizing for a while," I suggest. "It's kind of been a day."

He chuckles at this. "It has, but I'm grateful you're here. I hope I'm still a decent space heater."

"So far, so good."

He holds me closer and I snuggle into him more. I don't know what the morning will or won't bring, but I'm okay with this for now, and maybe that's all that matters.

I watch the subtle rise and fall of his chest until my eyelids feel heavy. The last things I'm aware of before I fall asleep are him stroking my hair, and the hypnotic sound of the rain.

# Chapter Ten

THE BEDROOM IS STILL dark when I next open my eyes. I must have rolled over at some point, because my head is against a pillow now, and I'm facing the bedside table I left my phone on. There's also a buzzing sound I can't place. Is my phone making the noise? Or is it Phoenix's phone, wherever that ended up after I moved it?

It takes a few seconds of scanning the darkness for the source before my sleep-addled brain recognizes it as the buzz of a chainsaw. The sound is from outside somewhere, and not from something in the room, but it's loud. No wonder I woke up.

I turn over to see if Phoenix is awake and discover his side of the bed is empty. Did he end up on the sofa? Things between us were peaceful when I drifted off last night, so I know I didn't kick him out. Maybe he couldn't sleep. I reach over to touch the indentation on his pillow. It's still warm, which means he couldn't have left very long ago.

The sound of running water interrupts my thoughts. I listen more closely, and I barely make it out over the revving from the chainsaw, but now I realize Phoenix is brushing his teeth in the bathroom. What time is it that he's already up?

I'm debating between reaching for my phone to check the time and pulling the duvet over my ears to muffle the chainsaw noise, when light spills into the room. It only lasts for a split second—long enough for me to also realize the power is back on—and then Phoenix emerges from the bathroom, wearing a bathrobe. He glances at the bed as he heads toward the bedroom door, then stops when he sees me watching him.

"Hey." My voice is raspy from sleep.

"Hey. Did I wake you up?" He changes direction and walks over to the bed. The mattress dips slightly when he sits next to me.

"No, I think it was the chainsaw."

"I was just going to check on that and see if someone is removing the tree. Go back to sleep if you can. It's early." He brushes a strand of my hair away from my eyes, then rests his hand against my cheek.

I turn my head and touch my lips to his palm. It happens like a reflex, and before I'm aware I'm doing it, much like my wandering hand last night. Again with the old habits. It feels like we've rewound time.

I move my head again, so my mouth isn't against his hand. "Are you coming back to bed?"

"I'll be back in a minute." He leans over and drops an air-light kiss on my forehead.

Maybe it's the feeling of waking up in his bed after falling asleep in his arms. Maybe it's how gentle he's being with me, or that I'm coming down from the emotional rollercoaster of yesterday and recalling what he said last night. Whatever the reason, it makes me want to nudge his head down so his mouth covers mine.

He stands up before I decide if I should act on the impulse or not. Then I remember I've been asleep for several hours. If this is a sign of how the morning might go, I should also brush my teeth to be prepared.

I wait for Phoenix to leave the room, and then I slip out from under the duvet and head for the bathroom. He's already back when I return, his bathrobe strewn over the chair in the corner. He tries to keep a straight face while I climb into bed, but it's obvious he heard what I was doing and likely suspects why.

"Don't act like you didn't brush your teeth five minutes ago," I tell him.

He laughs softly at this. "I didn't say anything."

"Your face gave you away. I could ask why you did it first at whatever ungodly hour of still-dark-outside it is, you know."

"You could. And it's four-thirty."

As much as I want to know what he would say if I asked him why, I settle for curling up next to him and resting my head on his shoulder. The past is still far from being water under the bridge, but something has changed since yesterday. The energy between us is more comfortable now, even if the touch of his fingertips running up and down my arm sends my mind places it definitely shouldn't be at this stage of things.

"When do you go back to Vegas?" I ask instead.

"This afternoon or tonight, if the roads are clear. The storm looks like it's over."

"Didn't you get here on Friday?"

"I did. Friday night."

I do the mental math. He's been here for less than thirty-six hours, and he's already leaving later today. A lot of the time he's been here has been with me, and that raises a new question.

"Were you already planning to be here last weekend when you asked to see me?" I glance up at him. His sheepish expression is my answer.

"Does the second or two before I said I would be here and asked to see you count as planning?" He gives me a hopeful smile.

Unless I'm missing something, Phoenix came to Laguna Beach to see me and that's all, even though he didn't know how long I would stay when I pulled into his driveway yesterday.

"Did you only drive here this weekend to see me?" I'm ninety-nine percent certain of this, but I have to ask anyway.

"Guilty. And I'd like to do it again soon, if you'll let me." He says it casually, but there's a hitch in his breath, like he's holding it while he waits for my reply.

Is he nervous about me saying no, even after our conversation last night, and even though I was the one who just initiated snuggling with him? Does he have any idea that the smallest touches from him are lighting my body on fire this morning, or that I was two seconds away from trying to kiss him earlier, morning breath or not?

"Oh yeah?" I do my best to sound equally as casual. "When were you thinking?"

"I was wondering if I could take you out for your birthday, or on a day that's close to it if you already have plans."

My birthday is next Saturday. I'm always pretty low-key about it, and I was planning to ignore turning thirty. It helps that Ava has to be in New York for a client event all of next weekend, but she's still insisting we have a postponed celebration with a few of our friends the following week. Despite my mixed feelings about my twenties being over, it hits me that I really do want to spend time with him that day.

"I would like that."

"I'll plan something in LA and drive to you this time. No more of this getting stuck in a house in a storm stuff." He presses his mouth against the crown of my hair, and then he loops his arm around me. "The storm looked like it was over when I checked, by the way. They should be finished clearing the tree by the time we get up."

Right. Time still exists, and so does life outside of this cocoon of him and me. We're going to get out of bed at some point in the next few hours, and I'll go home after that. Phoenix will drive back to Las Vegas later. This moment will end, but I'm not ready for it to yet. Not without finding out one more thing.

"There's something we should talk about before I go home today." I place my hand on his chest. This time when I trace patterns along his skin, I'm fully aware of what I'm doing.

"Of course. Anything."

"What you said last night, about trying not to come on too strong. Does that mean you aren't planning to kiss me until after you take me out?"

There's a pause, like he's thinking about how to respond. "It doesn't have to be when we go out for your birthday," he finally says. "I won't try to do that until you want to, if you do."

If I do? I guess I need to make something clear.

"I'm glad it doesn't have to be then." I tilt my head up to look at him. "Because I want to, and I don't really want to wait until my birthday. It's already been a minute or six years of minutes, wouldn't you say?"

I watch him take this in. He's silent, and now I'm afraid he'll ask me if I'm sure, like he did when I suggested he sleep in here last night. Then his face brightens like someone turned up the sun.

"So you're saying now is okay?" Phoenix shifts his position on the bed so he's facing me, and then reaches out to stroke his thumb along my jawline. He traces it over my lips next, and that alone sets my nerve endings ablaze.

It still isn't what I want.

"If I have to spell it out for—" The rest of my sentence disappears when he presses his mouth against mine.

I close my eyes and sink into the feeling of kissing him again after so many years. And God, does he remember what to do. The way he cradles my face in his hand and focuses on my bottom lip first, soft and sweet and slow, makes me think I might combust from the anticipation of more. There's a gentle nibble, and then his tongue sweeps over my lip, teasing me. I nudge him upward and feel him smile before my mouth parts under his and I let instinct take over as our kiss deepens. My hand snakes up his back and I pull him closer, like we can't be close enough, and like the growing heat of our lips crushed together can't be intense enough.

We're both breathing in shallow bursts when Phoenix slows our kiss down. It's probably the right decision, since there are other places this could easily lead to if he feels even a fraction of what I do. I give us credit, because we haven't yet let our hands or lips wander to places I'm sure we're both tempted to go. Even so, the desire pooling in me from our kiss already has me questioning my self-control, and there's still so much I need to figure out when it comes to him.

When we finally break apart and I open my eyes, the first things I notice are Phoenix's flushed cheeks and dilated pupils, and the absolute tenderness he radiates. Lord, the chemistry we still have between us. My brain is a mush of nonsensical thoughts, and his might be the same, because he wraps his arms around me and simply holds me without saying a word.

I've never been more thankful for atmospheric rivers and fallen trees than I am right now.

I'm still thinking about the morning and our kiss after I get home that afternoon. I go through the motions of showering, changing into different clothes, and pulling out my laptop to write, but my mind is still sixty miles away in Laguna Beach and reliving those predawn hours.

There are things I need to do, though. Answering Ava's many texts before she sends out a search party for me is one of them. When I finally looked at my phone today, I had a slew of messages from her that started last night and resumed this morning. The last message from her was a question about whether I'd spent the night with Phoenix, only she phrased it in a much more R-rated way.

*I'll call you tomorrow, okay? Everything is good.*

I send the cryptic text to Ava and put my phone down. There are thoughts and feelings I want to process before I talk to her about the last twenty-four hours, and I don't know if I want to tell her everything. Not yet, when all of this is still so new.

It's funny. Yesterday, around this time, I was in tears and irrationally envious of someone I've never met, and who isn't even alive, for being the force that made Phoenix get his life together again when I couldn't. Now I'm grateful to Len for her part in bringing him back to me.

I didn't ask him anything more about her before I left today. My questions about her didn't even cross my mind while we lay together in bed, or while he made us pancakes for breakfast. But now, alone in my condo, I'm curious about who she was.

I pick up my phone again and open Instagram. It's a long shot, but maybe I can find an old picture of her in Phoenix's posts somewhere. I blocked him on social media after we broke up—it was something else Ava had me do, right after I deleted him from my contacts—so I haven't kept up with what he's posted over the years.

There are surprisingly few photos on his profile. Most of what's there is film-related, and from the days when he had the lead role in a few major movies. The most recent post on his page is from several years ago, but it makes sense. He all but vanished after *North Node*, and that's when the posts stopped.

I'm about to close the app when I remember he said Nash also knew Len. I can't remember Nash's last name, so I go to Torin's profile and look through some of his band posts. When I find one Nash is tagged in, I tap his name.

Most of Nash's recent posts are band photos, but I keep scrolling to the older ones. A familiar image brings my scrolling to a stop. It's a missing person poster for Elenna Paseo—the same one I saw on billboards and utility poles around LA and Orange County after she vanished. Did Nash know Elenna, or was he just one of the countless people who shared the poster back then?

I tap on the post. There's a caption under it. *Please be safe, Len. Please come home. I miss you.*

I read the caption again. *Len.* Is Nash's nickname for Elenna a coincidence, or is she the same person Phoenix knew?

My mind skips back to yesterday, when Phoenix asked about the novel I'm writing. He was aware of the high-level details. Presuming Elenna is Len, did he put the pieces together and realize the missing woman it's based on is her? If he did, why didn't he mention it when his friendship with Len came up?

This could be a coincidence, but there's also a chance it isn't. And now there are a few things I'm curious about, starting with exactly what Ava told Torin about my book during the call Phoenix overheard.

# Chapter Eleven

"You honestly expect me to believe you spent the night at his place and didn't sleep with him?" Ava side-eyes me hard from her spot on the sofa in my living room, like I've breached the ex-boyfriend code somehow and she can't accept that this possibility exists.

"Correct," I confirm. "Do you want something to drink?"

"I only want tea, and you'd better spill all of it to make up for the cagey texts and dodging my calls."

"There is no tea, literally or figuratively. I have coffee, sparkling water, regular water, vitamin water, and some of those fruit soda things."

"Like hell there isn't figurative tea," she scoffs. "You're all glowy and shit."

"I'm not glowy," I protest. "I wrote by the pool today. It's a rare sighting of what I look like when my skin sees sunlight."

"I love you, but remember who you're talking to." She steeples her fingers in front of her and peers at me over the top of them. "If I can pull the truth out of my celebrity clients who live in delusional alternate realities where they think they can do no wrong, you don't stand a chance. What happened?"

I pinch the bridge of my nose. Ava's dog-with-a-bone mode is relentless, and I'm well aware of this fact. I truly don't stand a chance.

"Fine, you win. We kissed on Sunday morning, nothing scandalous. Are you satisfied now?"

She blinks a couple of times, then drops her hands to her lap and groans. "It's worse than I thought."

"How is it worse? You walked in here assuming we'd done much more than that."

"I didn't expect him to dust off the gentleman act again, or that you'd be floating on air from it."

"I'm not—"

She holds up her hand and cuts me off. "Don't say you aren't, because I know you. This is how you were after your first couple of dates with him, when you were falling head over heels. That's how it's worse."

Sometimes it's comforting that Ava knows me so well. Other times, like now, it's more of a curse than a blessing, because she won't let anything slide. My ability to deflect is no match for her interrogation skills.

I try anyway. "Didn't you encourage me to see him when we drove back from Vegas?"

"I did. I also had a karma-fueled daydream you would get answers to everything you've ever wondered about, have hot sex, decide there's nothing left between you but physical attraction, and never talk to him again."

"Then you'll probably hate that he's taking me out on my birthday." I get up from the sofa, hoping her best friend telepathy is tuned into me enough to recognize I'd like to change the subject. I don't want to argue with her about Phoenix, or what I may or may not feel. "I need water. Do you want something to drink for real this time?"

She doesn't answer right away, so I turn on my heel and head for the kitchen. I'm already at the fridge when she calls out to me.

"I'm sorry. That sounded awful. I'm not trying to be a lousy friend, just the voice of sober second thought. But you seem like you're happy, so I'll shut up."

I grab two cans of lime-flavored sparkling water from the fridge and return to the living room. "You're never a lousy friend. I get it. I'm sure I'd also have mixed feelings if a guy who broke your heart sashayed back into your life out of nowhere."

She takes the water I hand to her and watches me sit down. "You must have talked about a lot and gotten the answers you wanted if you're seeing him again."

"Yes and no. It got a little heavy for me after I learned things I didn't expect to, so we stopped talking about some topics at my request. To be continued, I guess."

Ava is quiet for a moment. She keeps her gaze focused on the top of the coffee table, and this, along with the crease between her eyebrows and the set of her jaw, tells me she has something on her mind.

"It's none of my business, but I'm going to ask anyway," she finally says. "Did any of what you found out involve a ring?"

Phoenix mentioning a ring stunned me. Ava knowing about it has me dumbstruck. How was I the last one to find out?

"You knew."

"Yeah. I knew."

She picks at the aluminum tab on her water can. The clinking becomes a metronome of sorts. I focus on the rhythm while I digest this news, until Ava stops and sets the can on the table.

"You never told me," I say.

She folds her arms across her chest and rests the back of her head against the sofa cushions. The angle lets her look up at the ceiling, rather than at me.

"I was convinced it was just another fight at first, and he would come back and ask you to marry him after things settled down. I couldn't see him spending all that time planning how he was going to propose, to then throw your entire relationship away like that. After it was clear you two were done, I thought telling you would hurt you more."

She's probably right about the last part, but my mind zeroes in on what she said before it. Phoenix only told me about his intent to go ring shopping, and not that he'd already planned how he would propose.

"How do you know how much time he spent planning it?"

"Because he asked for my help." She continues to study the ceiling, but uncrosses her arms. "He wanted it to be perfect for you, so he asked if you'd ever mentioned how you wanted to be proposed to in all the years we've been friends. And he wanted my opinion on a few different styles of rings. I thought he'd realized how much of an asshole he'd been with the drinking and everything else, and that he was trying to get it together for your sake."

"Did he tell you how he was going to propose?"

Ava presses her lips together, then shakes her head. "That's something you should hear from him if you really want to go there. It isn't my place. Shocking I think something isn't, I know." She offers me a weak smile. "Want to talk about something else now, like how your book is going?"

I'm still grappling with how she kept this a secret for six years, and what else she may be aware of that I'm not, but I bob my head in silent agreement.

"I'm working out some gaps in the plot, but I'll get there. There's actually something related to it I meant to ask you."

She shoots me a bewildered glance. "You're asking me about your book? My writing skills are limited to press releases, texts, and emails."

"It's not a writing question. I need to know how much you told Torin about it."

"I told Torin about your book?" Her forehead crinkles, and then her eyes widen. "Oh! I guess I did in passing when I talked to him about us going to his show. It was mostly in the context of being glad to tear you away from it for a night, because I missed you."

"Did you tell him what it's based on?"

She scrunches up her nose, as if she's trying to recall. "I don't remember everything I said, other than joking about how you've been obsessed with a local woman's disappearance and what happened as part of your research for it. I told him you're like Keith Morrison investigating a case for your own episode of *Dateline*."

"Did you mention Elenna Paseo's name at all?"

"I'm not sure. Maybe?" She looks and sounds more serious now. "Wait, did Torin say something? I was kidding about you being obsessed, and I thought he knew that, but there I go sounding horrible again. I was just ecstatic you'd agreed to go to Vegas."

"He didn't say anything. Phoenix brought up my book this weekend, and what he knew about it caught me off guard since nothing has been announced yet. He said he was at the house with Nash and heard your call with Torin."

"Oh no." Ava's hand flies up to her mouth. "I'm sorry. I had no idea anyone but Torin and Nash were there and could hear us talking, and Nash was in and out of the room, carrying mic stands and amplifiers somewhere. He didn't seem like he was listening."

"Torin didn't know Phoenix was there."

"Hang on. If Phoenix heard what I said, then he knew you'd be at the show." She snorts, and something resembling mirth lights up her eyes. "It would be sort of hilarious if what I said about getting you and Nash together is what made him show up and talk to you.

Typical territorial ex-boyfriend bullshit he has no claim to."

"Back up. You were already trying to make something happen with Nash and me then?"

"Nash walked by while Torin and I were talking, so I said hi and told him I was bringing you to the show for him. I have a running joke about setting him up, but as you saw, he can pull perfectly fine on his own. So can you, by the way, so keep that in mind. You can drop Phoenix in a second if he mishandles you again."

"Do you expect him to mishandle me?"

She doesn't have to answer. Her doubt about Phoenix is written all over her face.

"I have a healthy dose of suspicion when it comes to exes who spin the block." She shrugs, as though this should be obvious. "He has to prove he's worth another chance, and don't go by one night. Grill him about anything you didn't get answers for yet, and make sure nothing is off with what he says. If things check out, and if he genuinely makes you happy, then I promise I'll be happy for you. I'll even try to like him again, although I may need a hypnotist to make that happen."

"Listen to you, the dating guru." My voice has a teasing lilt to it, but I'm starting to feel like the human version of a flat tire. So much for the glow Ava insisted I had when she got here.

"Hardly. I've just learned to look for the dealbreakers and be picky about who I date. My cut-off game is strong." She raises her water to me, then takes a sip.

"You seem to think Nash is fun, and you get along with him. I'd love to hear why you're his wingwoman and haven't gone for him yet."

She nearly chokes as she swallows. "Nash is the male version of me," she replies, once she recovers. "The world isn't ready for that kind of chaos."

"Maybe I'll suggest it to Torin. Stranger things have happened."

Ava tosses a throw pillow at my head. I duck and lean to the side, laughing as it narrowly misses me. She's only known Nash for about a year, since he first joined Torin's band, but the way she talks about him makes it seem like they've been friends forever.

"You'll do no such thing," she informs me. "Torin is enough mischief on his own without you giving him ideas. Besides, Nash moved to Vegas when Torin did, and I live here. End of discussion."

"We'll see." I toss the pillow back at her. "You're protesting too much, which makes me think I'm on to something. We could go on another Vegas trip and double date."

"Not a chance, and you're brave for thinking I wouldn't spend the entire time cross-examining Phoenix about his intentions and sudden change of heart."

I was kidding, but Ava isn't. While I didn't expect her to be this skeptical about my decision to see Phoenix again after our time together on the weekend, I understand why she is. Ava was there for me when Phoenix wasn't. She's my best friend in the world, and even more protective of me than Torin is.

I also agree with her on one important thing: There's more I need to uncover and ask Phoenix about. Finding out if Len is Elenna and why he'd hold that information back from me if he made the connection between her case and my book only scratches the surface. Even if Len was a different person, I want to know why losing her was Phoenix's big wake-up call, and what else has happened over the last few years of his life.

# Chapter Twelve

My thirtieth birthday finds me awake at the first light of dawn, as the sun's morning rays paint the sky outside my bedroom window in gradient pastels. I could blame the usual city noises for rousing me from my dreams, but I doubt the sirens or car alarms are at fault. Anticipation is, and so are my nerves.

Last Saturday began as an up-in-the-air, informal reunion with Phoenix to hear what he had to say and figure out how I felt. Today is an actual date. When he asked if he could pick me up at my place, I had no reservations about texting him my address. The concerns I had at this time last week about my home being my sanctuary and inviting him in have vanished into the ether, so I can't explain my racing heartbeat as I lie in bed, thinking about our plans.

Not that I have insight into what those plans are. He hasn't told me where we're going. I tried to pry it out of him a couple of times this week, in text conversations and when he called me. He would only say dinner is involved and we'll be near the coast, so to bring a sweater or jacket. Outfit planning with these vague details has been a challenge. His answer when I asked if dinner is at a casual place or somewhere dressier didn't clear things up.

*You'll be perfect no matter what you wear*, he replied. *You always are.*

I wish I could say the compliment didn't make me smile at my phone. I wish I could say I haven't thought about our kiss and how I want to kiss him again about eighty-four million times since leaving his house on Sunday. That's also why I'm nervous. It's a little terrifying to feel this way so soon, especially about the person who shut me down to love in the first place. What am I opening myself up to?

I bury my head in my pillow, blocking out the sunlight from outside and trying to muffle my thoughts. More rest is what I need, and not this. There are hours to go until Phoenix gets here, and I don't want to be exhausted tonight.

*Focus on breathing. Focus on right now.*

I try this for a while, and then I close my eyes and resort to mentally repeating a mantra I learned a few years ago in a meditation class I took to tackle the anxiety I had then. It must work, because it's after nine o'clock when I next open my eyes, and I'm calmer than I was in the early hours. Now I just have to stay that way.

Once I'm out of bed, I make my way to the kitchen to brew a cup of coffee. My doorbell rings as I'm pouring water into the coffee maker. I freeze, mid-pour. It can't be Ava, because she's in

New York. My family lives on the other side of the country and wouldn't show up unannounced. That leaves Phoenix, but he isn't supposed to come by until late this afternoon. I haven't showered yet, and I'm still bleary-eyed and in my pajamas. Did I somehow get the time wrong?

I abandon the coffee maker and hurry to the door, combing my fingers through my hair as I do. When I get there and glance through the peephole, I'm relieved to see a woman I don't know holding a floral arrangement.

"Hi," I greet her, opening the door.

"Delaney?" she asks. I nod, and she hands over the largest and most fragrant arrangement of long-stemmed roses I've ever had in my possession.

"Thank you," I call out as she leaves.

After nudging the door shut with my foot, I carry the flowers to the kitchen and set them on the counter. There are definitely more than a dozen flame-red roses in the glass vase, mixed with greens and sprigs of baby's breath. There might be more than two dozen, actually. Curious, I count them. There are thirty roses in total.

Thirty roses for thirty years old. Someone put thought into this. I reach for the card nestled among the flowers.

*Del,*

*You are brighter than the sunrise, more stunning than the sunset, more exquisite than the constellations, and the most loving and talented soul I have ever known.*

*Wishing you a birthday as wondrous and beautiful as you are. Thank you for letting me be part of your day. -Phoenix*

I expected today to involve romantic moments with Phoenix, picking up where we left off on Sunday and building on some of the cute and slightly flirty texts we've exchanged since. I didn't expect the roses or his message on the card.

"This is real, right?" I ask out loud, reading the words for a second time. It feels more like I've landed in the middle of a dream.

There was a time when I would have immediately sent Ava a photo of the roses and the card. She used to gush with me about Phoenix's romantic gestures and sweet words when I was first getting to know him and starting to fall. But our conversation from earlier in the week weighs on my mind. It's tough to predict what her response would be if I told her about this, or if she'd remind me to be wary of love bombing and to not fall too fast.

Texting her might be out, but I should send a note to Phoenix to thank him for the flowers. I finish setting up the coffee maker and leave it to brew, then head for my bedroom where I left my phone plugged into its charger on the bedside table.

A birthday greeting from Ava is the first thing that greets my eyes when I tap the screen. *Happy birthday! I love you to the moon and back. I hope you have the most incredible day and that you get nothing less than the princess treatment. Have a great time on your date tonight, wherever the night takes you. Talk soon. xoxo*

Something in me softens. No matter what her reservations about Phoenix are, and no matter how cautious she thinks I should be, Ava is still my best friend. It's clear she's in my corner and is trying to be supportive, even if she's concerned and wants me to be careful. I may tell her about the roses and the card, but it can wait until after my night out.

*Thank you! Miss your face and I'm a little jealous NYC gets you this weekend. See you in a few days!*

I send the text, then open my conversation with Phoenix. The last message I have from him was from one minute after midnight, when he texted to say happy birthday and to let me know he had just gotten to his house in Laguna Beach after a few hours on the road.

*Thank you for the roses, they're gorgeous! And that card... wow. I'm speechless.*

It doesn't take him long to answer. *Was the card too much?*

*Don't tell the guy who sent it, but the card is perfect.*

*Not a word. My lips are sealed.*

A flirty reply takes form, and I put it in a message before I have a chance to filter myself.

*Not completely sealed, I hope, or at least not when it comes to other things you'd use them for...*

*Hmmm. What other things are you thinking of?*

*You'll have to use your imagination, then show me what you come up with later. See you soon!*

I laugh at the eyeball emoji and ellipses he sends in response, but there's a butterfly on the loose inside of me when I put my phone down and return to the kitchen. Autopilot takes over while I spoon sugar into my coffee, with thoughts of roses and everything I'm already aware Phoenix's lips are capable of now occupying my mind.

When my doorbell rings again at three-thirty, I'm showered, dressed, and ready for the person on the other side. Or I think I am until I open the door and lock eyes with Phoenix for the first time since I left his house last weekend. His warmth and unbridled happiness render me senseless for a good five seconds while I take in the curve of his mouth and the sparkle in his eyes.

I don't even realize he has something in his hands until he holds out a small cube to me. "Happy birthday."

"Thank you." I take it from him, our fingers brushing together as I do. A single red rose is inside of the cube, and the color of it is the same as the ones that arrived this morning. It's just the flower, with no stems or leaves, encased in a clear acrylic box.

"It's an infinity rose," he explains. "The other ones will last for a week or so, but I wanted you to have one that would last for this whole year of your life."

"I didn't know these existed. It's beautiful."

"So are you." He touches my arm, which has the effect of sending tingles up and down it and all over my body.

"Come in for a second," I say, realizing he's still in the hallway. He steps inside and I close the door behind him, then set the rose on a nearby table. "You're spoiling me with all the roses."

"Nope. It doesn't even compare to what you've given me by saying yes to today."

He kisses the top of my head and puts his arms around me. I lean into him, resting my head against his shoulder. This feels so natural today, and like I could just angle my chin up, meet his lips, and lose myself in kissing him the way we kissed last weekend. There's also a part of me that wants him to take the lead this time and make the first move that goes beyond fleeting touches and lingering hugs, even though he might be waiting for a signal from me.

Maybe he reads something in my hug, or maybe it was our text exchange earlier that does it. Wherever the motivation comes from, he releases his arms so he can brush the hair away from one side of my neck, then dips his head lower. I hold my breath in anticipation.

He doesn't disappoint me. His mouth is soft as he trails gentle kisses along the sensitive skin from my collarbone up to just below my ear. My head tilts seemingly on its own, on instinct, giving him greater access to my neck. His lips feel like heaven and the devil's work at the same time.

"Is this what you meant earlier about using my imagination and showing you what I came up with?"

His teeth graze my earlobe, and my self-restraint comes precariously close to flying out the window as I clutch his arms in an attempt to remain steady on my feet.

"Gold star," I manage to tell him.

"Glad you rate it so highly." He continues to my jawline.

I no longer have words to reply with, but it doesn't matter. A second later, his lips find mine, and our kiss does the talking for both of us. I thought last weekend was something, but this is a brand-new level of fireworks that leaves me breathless and dizzy when we finally come up for air.

"That was quite the hello, Mr. Alden." I'm still holding onto him, trying to regain my balance as I gulp in a couple of breaths.

"Was it too much?" Genuine concern flickers across his face, like he fears he took it too far and needs to dial it back to the innocence level of last weekend, before we kissed. We aren't going back there if I have anything to say about it.

"Did I seem like I wanted you to stop?" In case the answer isn't clear, I press my mouth to the hollow of his throat, and then take my time working my way up his neck. "Let me know if it's too much for you."

The flash of desire in his eyes is reply enough on its own. He bends his head over mine and kisses me again, but it's slower and more controlled this time. I feel him smile, which causes laughter to bubble up inside of me. This reminds me of how we used to be, and I missed it more than I knew.

"I'm trying to remember that we have to be in Marina del Rey by four-thirty." Phoenix leans his forehead against mine.

"Finally, a detail," I tease. "What's in Marina del Rey?"

"It's a surprise."

He's full of surprises today, between the long-stemmed roses and the card, and the infinity rose, and a greeting better than what I imagined. I know there are important things we need to continue talking about. I also know I should listen to Ava's advice from the other day and not get in too deep before I find out everything I have questions about. It's my birthday, though, and so far it's playing out like a fairy tale. All I want to do for the next few hours is see where the evening takes us and stay floating among the stars, come whatever may.

# Chapter Thirteen

I GIVE THIS MAN credit. He spent four hours driving from Vegas last night, and then another hour driving from Laguna Beach to my place to pick me up this afternoon. Now he's willing to brave Saturday stop-and-go traffic on LA's west side to get to Marina del Rey.

I would make a joke to him about how that's love, like I used to do when he surprised me with an impromptu weekend road trip somewhere that involved a freeway traffic jam on our way out of the city, but the words become stuck in my throat. Thank God they do. As familiar as Phoenix is, and even with the moments last weekend and already today that have transported me back to old times, now is now.

There will be no uttering of the L-word during this date, not even in the lighthearted, kidding around sense. Not with him. We have a history filled with it, and I took the word and the concept it symbolizes for granted too many times. I won't sprinkle it into casual conversation with him.

"I haven't heard this song in years," I say instead, opting for a safer comment on the music. It sparks memories of a playlist he made me when we started dating, and of the shiny, dreamlike bubble my life was to me then. This was the first song on it.

Phoenix smiles and keeps his eyes on the road. Neither action tells me if he recalls the significance of the music filling our ears, so I let it go for now.

We're four songs deep into our drive when I can't ignore it anymore. The music isn't a coincidence. This is the same playlist. If he's using it to evoke warm feelings and breathless memories of the days I listened to these songs on repeat, smiling and humming along while I lost myself in the honeymoon stage of our relationship, it's working.

*What are you doing to me, Nix?*

I decide to call him on it. "This is our playlist."

"You recognize it." He sounds happy about this, and his eyes tell the same story when they light up. Did he think I would forget?

"Of course I do."

The sequence of these songs is ingrained in my mind for eternity. "Thinking Out Loud," the Ed Sheeran single that became our song, should be five tracks from now. We'd best be in Marina del Rey before it comes on, since I can't be sure how I'll handle hearing the melody and lyrics while I sit next to Phoenix. I've avoided listening to it since we crumbled, and I always lunge to change the station any time I hear a note or two on the radio. I used to assume it would be our wedding song if we got married, and that was before I found out he'd planned to propose.

The traffic gods grant me mercy, because Phoenix signals to turn into a parking lot at Fisherman's Village before we reach that part of the playlist. Once we're parked, he exits the vehicle and is at the passenger side in a flash. He takes my hand as he helps me out, my palm easily finding its place against his as though we've still been doing this every day for the last six years in another timeline.

I keep hold of his hand while he leads me from the parking lot to the boardwalk that runs along the harbor. As we stroll past the brightly colored shops and restaurants, I scan the signs for anything that could be our destination.

"Are we going to a restaurant here?" I ask. It seems like the answer to this would be yes, but it's also an early hour to be eating.

"Not quite, but there will be dinner later. I think we should check out the yacht over there."

"Yacht?" I scan the harbor. My eyes land on the first yacht I see.

I'm too intrigued by the sight of the boat and that we're heading in its direction to ask more questions. Once we're closer, a man who's standing on the dock and holding a tablet in his hands comes into view. He glances up at us when we approach.

"Ms. Sharpe and Mr. Alden?" he inquires.

"That's us," Phoenix confirms. He shakes the man's hand.

"It's a pleasure to meet you both. I'm Daniel, one of the crew here and your host for tonight." Daniel extends his hand to me. "Happy birthday, and welcome aboard. Go ahead and follow me this way."

This isn't the appropriate time for the "I'm on a boat" song from an old *Saturday Night Live* sketch to pop into my mind, but I can't help it. The song is forever linked with my memory of the last time Phoenix and I were in Marina del Rey together, leaving the restaurant where we'd celebrated Torin's birthday.

It was a couple of weeks before the *Summerlong* premiere. Phoenix didn't drink anything at dinner because he was driving, but I was cheerfully buzzed from a few cocktails. Being stone sober didn't keep him from agreeing when I insisted we would own one of the boats docked in the harbor one day, or from chuckling and singing the silly song we'd learned from late-night *SNL* reruns with me after I declared, "I'm on a boat, everybody look at me!" When we walked past a lounge and I heard "Thinking Out Loud" playing inside of it, I asked him if he wanted to dance. There on the boardwalk, under the night sky and shimmering moon, he took me in his arms and danced with me until the song was over. We seemed invincible then.

The images in my mind's eye make it impossible to suppress a grin as we trail behind Daniel. I lean in to whisper to Phoenix. "How long until one of us has our arms spread wide on the starboard bow?"

The corners of his mouth twitch when he recognizes the song reference. "It's that or flying this boat to the moon somehow," he whispers back, amusement sparkling in his eyes.

He puts his arm around my shoulder and we continue following

Daniel, who has been narrating something about different parts of the boat while we weren't paying attention. Daniel stops walking when we arrive at a deck with cushioned seats and a dining table that's under the shade of a canopy. Phoenix leads me to a seat on the side of the deck, which overlooks the water. We sit down with his arm still around me.

"May I start you off with some champagne or sparkling cider?" Daniel asks.

"I'll have the sparkling cider," I reply.

"Same for me, thank you," Phoenix says.

"Coming right up."

Once Daniel leaves us and disappears into the ship's interior, Phoenix moves his arm from my shoulder and turns to look at me. "Are you sure you don't want champagne for your birthday? There are a few more verses of that song to go."

He's making light of the subject, but the silent form of communication we used to have kicks in for me now.

"It's not because I'm worried about having champagne when you don't drink anymore. I don't drink much in general these days, and I try not to when I'm writing a book. The Vegas drinks were an Ava thing." The first one was, anyway, but I'll leave it at this.

"You've always been so disciplined with your writing, and I've always admired you for it. I wish I could have been the same way a lot sooner in my life. I'm sorry I wasn't."

He gazes into my eyes as he says this. I'm startled by the regret and tenderness I hear and see, and it's only the approaching footsteps that keep me from falling headfirst into a wave pool of my feelings.

"Your sparkling ciders, and a little something to start you off before we head out on the water in a minute or two," Daniel announces. He places a tray on the small table next to our seat, then hands us our drinks and moves a charcuterie platter from the tray to the table. "Enjoy. I'll be back in a little while to see if there's anything you need."

He leaves us again. It dawns on me that the only other people I saw on board while following Daniel through the ship were crew members. No one else has joined us on the deck. If we're leaving shore in a minute, then Phoenix and I are the only passengers. I'm aware of the public dinner cruises that depart from the marina, but this doesn't appear to be one of them.

"Is this a private charter?" I ask.

Phoenix's face takes on an expression so angelic, I half-expect a halo to appear above his head. "The crew is here. That's probably good, because we'd be stuck at the dock if I had to steer this thing."

Along with a few over-the-top romantic gestures today, he's also trotting out his inner comedian. I shake my head and try again.

"We aren't waiting for other passengers?"

"Not unless a sea lion hops on board. It's disappointing when you consider it means you're stuck talking to only me until sunset and won't meet your dream guy on the boat, unless that's Daniel, but—"

"Oh my God, stop." I place my hand over his mouth before he

can get another word out, even though I'm on the verge of either dissolving into giggles or kissing him.

A laugh escapes me first. He gently turns my hand and presses his mouth against my knuckles, and my world cartwheels somewhere into euphoria. It's like being tipsy in the best possible way, minus the actual alcohol.

"Here I thought taking me out for my birthday meant you made dinner plans."

"I did. They'll serve dinner around six, over at the table." He points at the dining table a few feet away, as if I missed the setup when we walked past it.

"That's not what I meant, and you know it." I reach for Phoenix's hand, then lace my fingers with his. "Thank you for all of this. I can't believe you chartered a yacht."

"It isn't quite a gondola ride down the canals in Venice, but I thought asking about your passport and if you were up for some really long flights this weekend might be pushing my luck. Plus, who wants to hang out at LAX in the Tom Bradley terminal on their birthday?"

At first I think it's another of his jokes, but then I realize how serious his voice sounds in comparison to a minute ago. "Nice try. You weren't actually considering a trip to Italy, I hope."

"You used to talk about wanting to go. I wish I'd taken you."

He doesn't seem like he's kidding. Never mind that I'm about to hyperventilate at the idea of him dropping thousands of dollars on plane tickets and hotels to take me to Venice for my birthday and what is technically our second first date. Or maybe it's our second second date, if last weekend counts as our second first date. I don't even know anymore. Where are the brakes for my brain?

"I'll visit Venice one day." I keep my tone light and say "I'll" instead of "we'll," because now I'm scared he'll drop everything and book us a European vacation at the first sign of encouragement from me. Considering he paid for a private chartered dinner cruise of the coastline on this yacht tonight, it's a reasonable concern.

"I'd like to go back and actually appreciate it this time."

"Did you make it to the canals any of the times you were there for work?"

I can't remember what films he was in Venice for now, because I didn't watch the ones that came out after we broke up. But I recall something about him and a movie and Venice, or maybe I saw a trailer from something shot on location there.

"No," he admits. "I wasted the experience. I was too messed up back then to do anything but go to clubs at night and pass out in my hotel room. The last time I was there was for a film festival, but I don't remember much of it other than the film I was there for getting panned."

A memory of Ava's glee about Phoenix's downfall in Venice suddenly floods my mind. She said the critics who attended his film's showing ripped it to shreds, and she insisted it was karma coming for him. *North Node* was screened at the film festival there. The fallout related to it that ripped through the tabloids happened a week later, after Phoenix was back in California.

I actively avoided entertainment news then, but some things made it onto my radar. Most of what I caught by accident had to do with physical blows Phoenix instigated and exchanged with *North Node*'s director, Chaz Beckenbauer, outside of a bar in Newport Beach. There was also a video of a producer and cast-mate pulling him away from Chaz, blood smeared on his hands, while he screamed and swore at different people and made a few heavily bleeped-out threats. Grainy photos of him passed out in a hospital emergency room were published later, along with a flurry of accounts about his drinking and drug use, and his belligerent behavior while shooting *North Node* and while in Venice. Then he dropped out of sight.

"What happened after *North Node*? You were never violent with anyone when I knew you, but there was everything that was all over the tabloids, and then you disappeared."

The question is out of my mouth before I consider how much it could change the tone of our evening, and that there's no way off this boat for a couple of hours.

# Chapter Fourteen

TODAY HAS ALREADY BEEN a more perfect birthday than any scenario I could have dreamed up on my own, so why am I sabotaging things? Any other time and place would be better for talking about this.

I backtrack before Phoenix can reply. "Wait, no, don't answer. It's the wrong time for me to ask. What were we talking about before Venice?"

His thumb strokes the back of my hand. "It isn't the wrong time. You deserve to know what happened more than anyone, and I want to be an open book with you."

If I expected the topic of *North Node* and its aftermath to change his demeanor, it hasn't. His voice is calm, and he seems as relaxed as ever, just like the night in Vegas when Ava brought it up.

"I'm guessing you saw the Newport Beach video?" he asks. I nod, and he continues. "That night was bottom. I'd been home from Venice for a few days, and obviously I was drinking. I'd decided the reviews of *North Node* were completely my fault. My performance was bad, and I knew they should have fired me the first week of production. There was talk about it, because I was a mess on set. Chaz stood up for me, though, and said he would walk away from the film if I was axed."

"Because you had worked together before?"

Chaz isn't a stranger to me. He directed a film Phoenix had a supporting role in when his career was on the rise and we were still together, and I talked to him a few times at different events back then.

"Filming started right after I'd had back-to-back number one films. I think he was convinced my name would make *North Node* hit the top of the box office, and that he could get the performance he wanted out of me if he tried hard enough. He was my biggest cheerleader for a while and probably the only one who believed I could pull it off."

"So why did you punch and threaten him in Newport?"

I know what Phoenix was like in those days when he went on a bender, but I was never afraid of him getting into a physical fight with me or anyone else. Even wasted, it wasn't in his nature.

"We'd been on shaky ground since Venice and the screening. I couldn't make it to anything on time or sober, and then there were all the reviews about my performance. I don't think he expected me to show up at the cast and crew event in Newport Beach, and he was beyond pissed off when I stumbled in, already three sheets to the wind. We were at each other's throats from the time I got there.

I deserved every dig he made at me, but then he said something about you and it went too far. I lost control."

"He said something about me?" Phoenix and I had been broken up for several years at that point. I can't fathom what Chaz might have said or why.

"Yeah." A muscle works in his jaw. I get the feeling he doesn't want to elaborate, in spite of his claim about wanting to be an open book, but he continues. "I don't know if you remember, but it was around the time you hit some of the bestseller lists with one of your books and were doing daytime talk shows. There had just been an announcement about the film rights, which Chaz read about. He had the announcement open on his phone and showed it to me, then made a few derogatory comments, and I—"

I interrupt him. "What were the comments? I'd like to know."

"Mostly things I don't like repeating." Phoenix rubs the side of his face with the hand that isn't holding mine. He keeps his jaw clenched and his lips pressed together for so long, I start to wonder if this is all I'll get from him. Then he speaks again.

"The gist of it went something like, 'Look at your pretty little ex-girlfriend, using the connections she made with you to get ahead after she left you to destroy yourself. I don't know what she did to make you end up like this, but get it together. She isn't worth it.' And then he said some other trash about who you must have slept with to get the publicity and deals you did." He pauses there. His chest rises as he takes a deep breath, then falls when he lets it out. "I'm sorry. You said you wanted to know, but you shouldn't have to hear this."

I can't say he didn't warn me. "It's fine. I don't care what Chaz thinks of me." And I don't, even if finding out what he said just set my blood burning. The man had a lot of nerve to invoke my name in something he knew nothing about.

"I did. I cared a lot. He was blaming you for everything I did to myself and to our relationship, and he was attacking your talent and talking absolute garbage. It went too far, and I snapped. That's when I punched him. He defended himself and fought back, of course, and it escalated from there."

I let this sink in, trying to process the story the tabloids didn't tell about what happened. Phoenix's brawl with Chaz has always been cited as the tipping point that cost him his career and ran him out of Hollywood.

"That entire thing was because of me?" Dazed doesn't even start to describe how I feel about this.

"No." He takes my other hand now, so he's holding both of them. "None of it was because of you. It happened because I was a few drinks past wrecked already and Chaz ran his mouth. He'd also had a couple of drinks, and he was still angry with me about my public behavior in Venice. Neither of us were being reasonable. I wouldn't have punched him if I'd been less intoxicated than I was. I wouldn't have let it go, but I would have handled it differently."

I take a moment to mull this over, glancing out at the water as I do. We're miles down the coast from where we started. What began as a light breeze a few minutes ago picks up now with a stronger, chillier burst of air that raises goosebumps along my bare arms. I release Phoenix's hands so I can reach for my sweater, but he must see the goosebumps because he's on it before I make a move. He drapes the sweater over my shoulders and runs his hands up and down my arms a few times, restoring warmth to my skin.

"Thank you." I pull the sweater tight across my chest, even though the wind has subsided again.

"For what it's worth, Chaz apologized for what he said later. He admitted he was trying to get under my skin because he was angry and didn't understand why I was throwing my career away."

I squint at him against the blinding rays of the evening sun. "You talked to him after that? The tabloids made it sound like there was a war between you two, and that he got you kicked out of your next film and shunned by all the studios and execs."

"He called me a couple of days later, after we'd both cooled off and I'd had time to recover from my trip to the emergency room that same night to have my stomach pumped."

"Why didn't one of you say something to set the record straight?"

I'm at a loss to understand this. Either one of them could have stopped the barrage of headlines and rumors that grew like a tumbleweed with each passing day, instead of letting the tabloids torpedo Phoenix's reputation and career.

"I didn't care what they said about me, and I didn't want your name brought into it. The paps would have hounded you, especially since your career was taking off and people knew who you were. Chaz agreed not to talk about what happened on the condition I entered rehab. He helped me get out of the contract I'd signed for his next film so I could."

There's defending someone's honor, and then there's this. I stare down at my palms, quiet while my mind strings together the scenes of a story I couldn't have predicted. I don't know what to make of it yet, but one thing has become clear. Phoenix wasn't kidding when he said he never stopped caring about me.

"Is rehab where you went when the tabloids claimed you were in hiding?"

"Yes. Chaz had connections that got me into a facility in Antigua, which kept my location under wraps and kept me from leaving when it got rough. I wasn't convinced rehab would work for me, since I'd tried it once before then and checked myself out after five days, but I went. The only people who knew were Chaz, my family, and Len."

His mention of Len pulls the question that's been at the back of my mind since last weekend straight to center stage. After the roses and text messages this morning, I'd almost talked myself out of bringing her up today.

"Can I ask you something else?"

"Ask me anything you want to know. Nothing is off limits." Phoenix raises my chin up so I have to meet his eyes. His gaze is as gentle and open as it was when I asked about *North Node*.

"What happened to Len? You told me you lost her, but you didn't say how."

If the subject change catches him off guard, nothing in his face or posture shows it. He answers without faltering. "No one knows. She went missing one day and didn't come back. The last sighting of her was on someone's home security camera, when she was walking down the street she lived on."

My pulse speeds up with each word. By the time Phoenix finishes his last sentence, I'm certain of what I suspected when I saw Elenna's missing person poster on Nash's Instagram page and read the caption where he called her Len.

"That sounds a lot like the last sighting of Elenna Paseo, the woman who went missing from Aliso Viejo." I watch him as I speak. Nothing in his expression changes.

"That's because Elenna was Len. Or is, if she's still out there somewhere."

He sounds laid-back about it, and unfazed that I've made the connection. Now I wonder if I had it wrong, and if he didn't know Elenna's unsolved case inspired my novel.

"When you overheard Ava telling Torin about my book, did she say it was based on Elenna's disappearance?"

"She didn't mention her name, but what she described was too similar for it not to be. I assumed it was."

"You didn't say anything when you mentioned my book, or when you told me about Len."

"I didn't," he agrees. "You seemed spooked I even knew the basis of the story and I didn't want to make it worse or come across like a stalker. Then when Len came up, I was more concerned about you and how you felt at that moment. It didn't seem like the right time to bring it up."

He says it so matter-of-factly, I almost feel foolish for letting this fester in my mind all week. Of course it didn't seem like the right time. I was in tears for the second time in twenty minutes and asked him to talk about something else.

"Do you think she's alive?"

The shake of his head is so slight, it's almost imperceptible. "I wish I could say yes. I've accepted she might not be."

Anyone who doesn't know Phoenix the way I do would take one look at his face and think he was unaffected by what he just told me. They would assume he's past the grief that came with losing Len and not knowing what happened, or if she's dead or alive. But I notice when the corners of his mouth droop and his body stiffens, and how his hand trembles when he raises his glass of sparkling cider to his lips to take a drink.

It hits me then, what he's struggled through and overcome since our world together fell apart. I've had tunnel vision the last two weeks, focusing on how I felt, the questions I had, and what I went through after we weren't in each other's lives. I may have tiptoed through purgatory after we broke up, spending weeks bawling my eyes out and months going through the motions of my life while I oscillated between sad and angry, but he has also been to hell and back. He lost his career, got and stayed sober, and dealt with the disappearance and presumed death of a close friend. And yet, all he's done is focus on me since he said hello at Nebula. Phoenix has done everything but move heaven and earth to make me feel like the sun orbits around me, and like my emotional needs and comfort come first and are all that's important.

I place my hand against his back and move it in a slow, circular motion. I continue until the muscles there relax under my touch and he sets his glass on the table.

"I think I see sea lions near the shore," I murmur, easing us out of the silence we've fallen into.

He circles his arm around my shoulder, the same as he did when we boarded the boat, only this time he pulls me in closer. I turn my body so I lean against him, and he puts his other arm around me.

"Are you warm enough?" he asks. Sitting together the way we are, with his arms around me, I didn't notice the wind pick up again. His body shields me from it.

"You're a good space heater like this, too," I joke. "I'm perfect right now."

"You really are, you know."

My heart nearly bursts inside of me when I catch what he says. He rests his head on top of mine. We stay that way, watching the sea lions and the passing scenery until Daniel emerges from the ship's interior with another crew member to set the table for dinner.

The menu at dinner was Michelin-star-worthy as far as I'm concerned, but the true surprise and crowning glory was Daniel showing up at our table with my favorite Milk Bar birthday cake for dessert. Phoenix feigned innocence when I asked him if the cake was a coincidence, or if he was behind it. I may never know for sure.

The sun is already below the horizon when we dock at shore and say our thanks and goodbyes to the crew. I think we're headed back to the parking lot after we step off the boat, but Phoenix has other plans.

"There's one more place I'd like to take you tonight." He touches my elbow, then guides me in the opposite direction of the parking lot. "It's just down here."

"There's more?"

His eyes twinkle under the boardwalk lights. "You gave me the whole night. I wasn't going to lose out on hours of your company by taking you home this early."

He reaches for my hand. We stroll along the harbor until we're in front of a nondescript building that's sandwiched between a seafood restaurant and a souvenir shop. I glance around for a sign, but I still can't tell what the building contains. Then I listen. There's music coming from inside.

Phoenix opens the door for me. I nearly gasp when we walk into a space lit up by hundreds of flickering LED candles. A string quartet is set up at one end of the room, already playing a song I recognize the melody of, even if I can't place the artist and song title.

"I saw something about candlelight concerts here on weekends," he explains. "I thought we could check it out."

I take in the glow of the darkened room, and how the candlelight gives way to private spaces in the shadows where seats are set up. Phoenix pulls his phone out of his pocket and opens a screen with a barcode, then holds it out to a woman with a handheld scanner. She points at a corner of the room and says something I don't hear, then hands him two leaflets. He passes one to me as we wander further inside, but I'm too mesmerized by the sights and sounds to read it.

We head for the area the woman pointed at. There's no one else occupying any of the seats there, and so we have the corner to ourselves for the moment. It isn't until we sit that the name of the song being played by the string quartet pops into my mind. It's John Legend's "All of Me," another song from our playlist.

I open the leaflet Phoenix gave me and discover two things at once. Each concert listed in the calendar is a themed performance, and tonight's is a modern soft rock hits tribute. The last notes of "All of Me" fade as I read this, and a new song begins. It takes approximately an eighth of a second for me to recognize it, and a lump forms in my throat when I do. My eyes land on Phoenix. He knows what song this is, too.

He holds out his hand. "Will you dance with me?"

I don't trust my voice to answer, so I take his hand without saying a word. We both get to our feet as the quartet continues to play "Thinking Out Loud." It's only when I'm in Phoenix's arms, my head against his shoulder and our bodies swaying in complete synchronicity, that I let myself listen and feel. The lines between the past and now blur when I close my eyes. In an instant, I'm twenty-three, dancing with the man I love under the moonlight on a boardwalk, in possession of a heart that hasn't yet been broken. When I open my eyes, I'm thirty again. Now I'm dancing in a candlelit room with the same man, remembering how perfectly our bodies fit together, and aching to forget every scar the years between then and now left us with. There's no way to predict if our story has a happy ending this time, but the one thing I'm certain of is my yearning to find out.

Ava will have opinions, Torin might think I've lost my mind, and don't get me started on what my family will say. None of it matters. For the first time in six years, I'm letting my heart lead and trusting what it tells me. In its steady beat, I hear it whisper what it hinted at last weekend.

I am falling in love with Phoenix all over again.

# Chapter Fifteen

If I could stop the world from turning and the hours from passing, and if I could keep dusk from becoming daylight again, I would do it and stay in this night forever.

My emotions are still bigger than I am after the concert ends and the quartet leaves the stage. They threaten to carry me away like a hot air balloon the entire time Phoenix and I stroll along the boardwalk and through the parking lot. His hold on my hand is all that tethers me to the ground. The present drifts and fades and returns during the ride home, especially when "Thinking Out Loud" has its turn on the playlist.

When we park outside of my building and Phoenix helps me out of the vehicle, and when he walks me inside and to my door with his hand against the small of my back, all sense of time seems to collapse. Twenty-three-year-old me takes over before thirty-year-old me can second-guess myself or consider how the question might sound.

"Do you want to come in?"

His eyes search mine, as if looking for clues about what my words mean. Seven years ago, a night like this would have ended with us together at my place or his, a trail of discarded clothing leading to the bedroom. A kiss here, a caress there, tongue against tongue leading to skin against skin, leading to his hands and mouth exploring my most sensitive spots. My growing need for him, the fumbling for a condom, and the sweet ecstasy of what came next. Time slipping away and somehow ceasing to exist at all.

But before then, before our relationship became intimate in that way, our date would have ended outside of my door with a kiss and a promise of him calling me tomorrow, which he always did. Or, at the point just past that, him coming inside and making out with me for a while, as we progressed to the more serious relationship we later had. I don't know which version of us I'm asking for now, or what my words mean. I'm just not ready to say goodnight.

"If you aren't tired of me yet," Phoenix answers, his gaze still locked with mine. His mouth quirks up in a smile that shines through in his eyes and lets me know his reply is more teasing than it is self-deprecating.

"Yeah, good point." I scrunch up my nose as I open the door, but then grin at him to let him know I'm kidding. "I'm not, for the record."

He follows me inside. The door clicks shut, and the sound sends a flutter of anticipation coursing through me. There's something about being behind a closed door and alone with him that heightens the energy of the room. It could be the sweet perfume of the roses he sent me lingering in the air, or my larger-than-life feelings clamoring for release. Whatever it is makes me want to crash my lips against his and see where it takes us.

Phoenix opts for a more chaste approach, touching my shoulder first, then brushing his fingers along my cheek. "Kick me out when you are." He kisses the tip of my nose.

"And if I don't kick you out?" I wind my arms around his neck and peer into his eyes again.

"Then you might be stuck with me." His lips graze over mine, but he doesn't kiss me. No, this is a slow dance of close-but-not-quite, as his hands find the curve of my waist and he pulls me closer to him.

"Only until you go back to Vegas tomorrow." I run my fingers up the nape of his neck and through his hair.

"Shhh. Don't remind me."

He places his index finger against my mouth, as if he really doesn't want the reminder of his upcoming departure and drive. It's instinct for me to kiss his finger, but what seems innocent enough in my mind causes him to suck in his breath and hold it for a moment. For once, his expressive eyes work in my favor, because they reveal what his self-restraint doesn't. I'm not the only one with colossal emotions going on.

I tilt my head up. His finger slips away, allowing me to bring my mouth to his. This time, his lips do what I want them to, pliant against mine, parting, inviting me in. A switch flips in me somewhere, because now there's nothing else in the world outside of him and me, and all I want to do is taste him.

We end up on the sofa somehow, shuffling there in step with one another without losing rhythm or knocking something over along the way. He pulls me onto his lap, and then I'm straddling him, my hands working to unbutton his shirt while his head dips to my neck. The soft kisses that remind me of this afternoon turn into gentle nibbles, until he reaches my shoulder and retraces the path his lips left, trailing kisses up to my mouth again. I reach the bottom button of his shirt, and it isn't an accident when my hands roam over the bulge in his pants on their way to his bare chest, or when I adjust my body so I'm rubbing up against his pelvis.

"Del..." he murmurs. For a moment, his pause makes me wonder if he's going to stop, but then he kisses me with more urgency than before.

His hands find the zipper on the back of my dress and I feel it slide open, exposing the skin on my back to the air in the room. I help him move the straps off my shoulders and down my arms, until the top part of my dress falls away to my waist. I expect my bra to be next, but he doesn't reach for its hooks. Instead, his hands glide over my uncovered skin, while his tongue continues exploring my mouth. It only makes me crave his touch more, everywhere he isn't touching me. So when his hands settle on my waist and he starts to dial down the intensity of our kiss, I can't stop my whimper of protest. His quiet laugh when he hears me doesn't help.

"I know," he whispers. "I'm trying to remember this is technically a first date and that I leave tomorrow."

The still-aroused part of my brain doesn't see why this is a problem. "It's a second first date, and we're only making out. Things were still pretty PG."

Except a part of me knows. We both do. If he rains kisses over my body, if my bra comes off and his hands and mouth find my breasts, and if they wander from there to below my waist, between my legs, and discover the dampness that's already there, we will go far past making out. I doubt either of us would have the willpower to hold back, considering where we've been before and the blissful heights we're both aware we can take each other to.

It doesn't stop me from leaning forward and closing the space between us, or from pressing closer to him when our mouths meet again. It doesn't keep him from shifting us so I'm lying back against the sofa cushions, under him now, or from bringing the whisper-light touch of his lips to my neck and my shoulders, and then along my midriff and back up. But when his hands reach for my discarded dress straps and he pulls them over my arms again, and when he sits up, it's a signal he won't let himself do more than this with me tonight.

"At least one of us has self-control." It's supposed to be a joke, but my heart is racing and I'm breathing in bursts, and my voice sounds too gravelly for it to land that way.

I pull myself up so I'm sitting, too. A wayward lock of hair falls across my forehead while I'm in motion, and Phoenix brushes it away from my eyes before I can.

"I don't want to be leaving the next day and be four hours away from you for most of the week if it goes further." He twirls a different strand of my hair around his finger as he speaks, then tucks it behind my ear.

"If?" I raise my eyebrows. "And it's only an hour by plane."

He smiles at this, and cups my chin in his palm. "I'm trying not to make assumptions about how you'll feel tomorrow or two weeks from now, and I meant what I said last weekend. I don't want to mess this up with you."

If he had any notion of what last weekend and tonight stirred up in my heart, he wouldn't hesitate about making assumptions. I can appreciate how careful he's being with me, though, even if his unbuttoned shirt and the view I have of his chest and abs right now aren't helping me settle down.

My eyes scan the room for a distraction from the jumble of lust and longing still surging through me. They land on the TV remote, so I grab it from the table and hit the power button. The diversion works, because calm returns to my body after I've spent a minute focused on flipping through the channels, and my head wins back control.

"When do things wrap up in Vegas?" I return the remote to the table.

"Soon, I hope. I've been there longer than I expected to be."

"Things are that off-schedule?"

The vague timeframe isn't what I hoped to hear. Phoenix drapes his arm around me and hugs me close.

"I wish everything was done there. It isn't far off, and I'm going to keep driving here to see you as much as I can, when you aren't writing and don't have other plans."

"I could visit you there, you know. I don't need to be in LA to write."

"Mmm." He nuzzles my hair. "I would love having you there, but I don't feel right asking you to travel to see me. It's a lot of driving time."

"That you've done twice in just over a week," I remind him. "Besides, you didn't ask me to travel. I told you I could."

"Does chivalry really need to be dead?"

He turns his puppy-dog gaze on me—the same one he used at his place when he confessed that running into me wasn't by chance—but I'm not falling into his trap. I glance up at the ceiling instead, pretending to be exasperated.

"Fine. You've left me no choice but to plan a trip with Ava to see another one of Torin's shows, and to accidentally hang out with you while I'm there."

Phoenix doesn't respond. After a few seconds of silence, I glance over at him and witness something that looks a lot like panic in his eyes and on his face.

"Why do you seem worried?"

"I had a vision of what my next encounter with Ava might look like if she thinks I'm putting the moves on you."

It's hard to keep a straight face while I consider telling him Ava was certain we'd slept together last weekend until I said otherwise, and that she's already given me her unsolicited opinion about the birthday sex she thinks I should have tonight. That isn't what she would rake him over the coals for.

"Are you scared of Ava?" I'm barely able to keep my amusement out of my voice.

"That's a question?"

"Good point," I admit. "We'd need to find her a distraction. Maybe Nash could help?"

"Nash?" A crease appears in his brow.

"I think there could be something there." Ava would be mortified if she could hear me trying to play matchmaker right now by planting the idea with another one of Nash's friends. No matter what she said earlier in the week, I'm still convinced they would make a cute couple.

"I agree about distracting Ava if I want to make it through the experience in one piece, but not with Nash. Trust me on this."

"Then we'll think of something else. Or I could leave her at home, skip Torin's show, and spend time in Vegas alone with you. It's a genius idea, right?"

I lean my cheek against his shoulder and turn my own version of a puppy-dog gaze on him. I know I've won when he bites his bottom lip and closes his eyes.

"I still don't think you should have to travel to see me, but I'll say yes if you fly there and let me pay for your flights."

I consider disagreeing with the paying for my flights part, but discard the idea when he opens his eyes and looks at me. It's clear he means it, and it isn't out of character for him when I think about all the things he insisted on paying for the last time we dated. It's who he is.

"I'd like that. Are you busy next weekend?"

"Very busy." Phoenix places his hand over mine and bends his head down to whisper into my ear. "I'm spending every second of it with you."

# Chapter Sixteen

Landing in Vegas is always an experience, between the desert winds that bounce the plane around during the final approach and descent, and the view of the Strip from overhead and then from the taxiway. My flight there on Friday evening is no different, but I hardly notice the turbulence since my head is still somewhere in the clouds. It's difficult to believe it's only been three weeks since I was last here, with all that's changed since then.

*Just landed. I'll let you know when I have my suitcase and am outside.*

I send the text to Phoenix. A heart bubble reaction from him appears beside it almost instantly.

Once I'm off the plane and weaving past people and the airport slot machines, I expect to head for the baggage carousel to wait for my suitcase, and then to the passenger pickup spot outside. But when I exit the gate area into arrivals, Phoenix is at the carousel for my flight, waiting for me with a heart-stopping smile.

"Hi, you." His arms are around me before he finishes the second syllable. I melt into his hug on the spot, like the days between my birthday and now were hallucinations and we're picking up where we left off when we finally said goodnight.

"I thought you were meeting me outside the terminal?" I tilt my chin up to look at him. Our lips meet, and our kiss is soft and sweet. It's the family-friendly airport version of what I'd really like to do right now, and it's over far too fast.

He keeps an arm around my waist and peers into my eyes. "I couldn't wait that long to see you."

"The whole extra few minutes?" I tease.

"Too much to handle when I know you're here. Besides, you shouldn't have to lug a suitcase through here and across the bridge."

My suitcase is small, and although it's crammed with multiple outfits and pairs of shoes to be prepared for anywhere we might go during the three nights I'm here, it rolls and isn't heavy. I easily moved it from my condo to my car, then from my car and onto the shuttle from the parking lot to the terminal at the airport in Burbank, and then to the curbside bag check, but I'm not about to point this out or do anything but appreciate his thoughtfulness.

It doesn't take long for my suitcase to show up on the carousel. Phoenix pulls it off and takes hold of its handle, then threads the fingers of his free hand with mine. We make our way to the doors. A wall of desert heat hits me when we step outside.

"I thought we could stop by my place first and go out for dinner in a bit," he says, once we've crossed the street outside the terminal and are on the pedestrian bridge to the parking garage. "I made a reservation at Salt & Pepper, but if there's somewhere else you'd like to go instead, I'll change it."

"Don't change a thing. That sounds amazing."

I'm not exaggerating, because anything involving him and me and the lights and glitz of Las Vegas truly does sound amazing. Other than mentioning Salt & Pepper just now, Phoenix has been mysterious about what our plans are while I'm here, and has only said there are some places he would like to take me. The more he resists spilling his secret itinerary for us, the more intrigued I am.

My first hint at how carefully he's planned our time together happens soon after we reach his SUV in the parking garage. Once I'm settled into the passenger seat, Phoenix shuts my door for me and puts my suitcase in the back. After he slides into the driver's seat and turns the engine on, the stereo speakers come to life, revealing the opening notes of "All of Me," the song the string quartet played when we arrived at the candlelight concert last weekend. I steal a glance at him while he backs out of our parking spot.

"Is this a coincidence, or did you choose this song for our drive?" I'm pretty sure I know the answer, which makes it impossible for me to hide my smile.

If his face brightens any more than the megawatt level it just lit up to, he'll give the Luxor's sky beam a run for its money. "I'm putting a new playlist together. It's a work in progress."

That's fitting, because we're also a work in progress right now, in a sense. I'm already smitten with the idea of new songs to reflect our new memories and next chapter.

The drive from the airport to where Phoenix is staying takes about twenty minutes. I've seen some of the rooms at his place when we've FaceTimed, and so I'm aware we're going to a house and not a hotel. Even with this knowledge, and even though he's been out here for an extended amount of time, I didn't expect him to be staying at a two-story house with an attached garage and succulent garden out front. It isn't what I pictured temporary, on-location housing to be.

Once we're inside, with the front door closed and my suitcase in the foyer, Phoenix wraps his arms around me from behind and kisses the back of my head. I place my hands over his, enjoying the comfort and ease of this.

"What time is dinner?" My voice is soft, matching the mood of the moment.

"Seven forty-five." His mouth skims the edge of my ear, sending a delicious shiver through me.

"When do we need to leave?"

"In about an hour, but I can bump our reservation if you'd like more time to get ready."

If we move our reservation later, I doubt I'll want to use the time for choosing an outfit or touching up my makeup or hair. "Getting ready won't take me long. I was wondering how long we have to keep doing this."

"This?" He holds me tighter and kisses my head again, but then releases his arms from around me. "Or this?" His lips brush against my shoulder, and then the side of my neck.

I close my eyes and focus on the sensations coursing through my body and how the touch of his mouth feels against my skin. When I turn to face him, and when our lips meet this time, it's the opposite end of the spectrum from our brief airport kiss. Here, finally alone again, the passion of last weekend crashes through. His fingers tangle in my hair and caress the back of my neck, and then his hands roam to my waist. He pulls me closer to him until my body is pressed tightly against his, as though we could and should meld together right here. It's tempting to suggest skipping dinner and staying in tonight in favor of continuing this.

Even so, I'm the one to slow things down and come up for air first. The way Phoenix gazes at me when we break apart, with adoration in his eyes and his dimple on full display, just about knocks any remaining air out of my lungs.

"I'm so happy you're here." He tousles my hair, then lowers his hand to my shoulder. A million tiny sparks dance everywhere over my skin when he runs his fingertips along my arm.

"Me too."

If how my visit has started is any sign of what's to come, then my hope for this weekend is that what happens in Vegas doesn't stay in Vegas at all, and that my birthday and the next couple of days are only the beginning for us.

❧

The last time I walked past the game tables and slot machines at The Auriga casino, I was in a very different frame of mind. Then, Ava and I strode past everything to exit out the doors Phoenix and I just entered, when we were en route to meet up with our Uber and I was anxious and preoccupied. Now, I'm happy to be back, and to view The Auriga through a rosier lens.

We head in the same direction as Nebula, which is close to the escalator we'll ride upstairs to Salt & Pepper. The escalator and the curtain of sparkling star lights that surround it soon come into view, catching and holding my attention as we get closer. I'm so transfixed by the shimmering lights, I miss Phoenix slowing down until he touches my arm.

"Hey, man," a familiar voice calls out. I shift my gaze to where the voice came from and spot Nash approaching us. "Del, it's wonderful to see you again. You just missed Torin."

His gaze flickers from Phoenix to me, and then back to Phoenix, a question in his eyes. I'm not certain how close their friendship is, but I suspect Nash wasn't aware until now that I'm in town or that Phoenix and I are back together. He may not even be aware that we used to date, unless Torin, Phoenix, or Ava has mentioned it to him.

"Torin is here?" I inquire.

"Sound check," Nash explains. "Are you coming to the show

tonight with Ava?"

"I didn't know Ava was here," I admit. "I also didn't realize you guys have a show. Don't you play on Saturdays?"

"We switched nights with the band that's usually on Fridays for the next two weeks, since they have a couple of private gigs. Ava didn't tell you?" My face must reflect how baffled I am about the repeated mentions of Ava and her being in Vegas, because Nash continues. "She has a work thing here this weekend and came a night early for the show."

"Ah, no. She didn't mention that." This seems odd, since I saw Ava earlier this week for my postponed birthday dinner with her and a few other friends, and I told her I was flying to Vegas this weekend to visit Phoenix.

"You two should drop by if you don't have other plans. I'll add you to the list." He claps Phoenix on the back. "Gotta jet. Catch you both later, I hope."

I wait until Nash is far enough away to be out of earshot, then lean in closer to Phoenix. "We don't need to go."

He places his hand against my back and guides me to the escalator. "We might have to."

"Ava didn't tell me she'd be here, so I doubt she's expecting to see us."

"Maybe not, but Torin will want to see you when Nash tells him you're here."

He may be right about this, but it's not as though I see Torin every time he's in LA, so he shouldn't be upset if I don't see him tonight.

"It's fine," I insist. "I'll smooth it over with him later."

Phoenix's face is practically a flashing billboard that broadcasts his concern. In his expression, I read what he hasn't said, which is something that's also crossed my mind. Torin is bound to have questions if Nash mentions he saw me with Phoenix, and I'm sure he'll have a few choice words for Phoenix, too. He was there for me every bit as much as Ava was six years ago when my heart was destroyed, and it's why he's so protective of me now. I can't imagine what dealing with him and Ava as a tag team will be like if we go to the show. It's better if I handle Torin on my own, after I'm safely back in LA.

We get to the top of the escalator without saying anything more about Torin or the show, and I consider the matter settled for now. I step off, ahead of Phoenix, and am about to get on the next escalator to the third floor when a young woman in a sequined mini-dress approaches us.

"I'm sorry to bother you, but would you mind taking a photo of my friends and me?" She holds out her phone.

"Of course," I agree.

I take the phone from her and wait until she's standing beside two other girls in front of the sparkling curtain of lights. As I snap a few photos of them, it occurs to me what a gorgeous backdrop it is. Phoenix must have the same thought, because as I pass the phone back to the girl, he takes his phone from his pocket and asks if she would mind taking a photo of us.

Standing next to him, with his arm around my shoulder and our heads close together, reminds me of when we used to pose like this in front of step-and-repeats for event photographers. We became pros at it then, because of how often we did it. Positioning ourselves this way seems natural, like two puzzle pieces locking into place.

The girl raises the phone to take our picture, but then does a slight double take. She stares at Phoenix for a moment, recognition flashing across her face. Her eyes flicker to me next. While I'm not nearly as easy to identify as he is, if she was a fan of Phoenix during his early films, then there's a chance she also recognizes me. I don't get to find out if she does, because she passes the phone back after taking our picture and thanks us again, but says nothing else. She's still studying us with a thoughtful look when her friend grabs her arm to pull her away.

"Should we take one more?" Phoenix asks me.

His question pulls my attention off the girl and back to him. He extends his arm out to take a selfie of us and turns his head to kiss my cheek right before he takes the photo, which catches me by surprise and brings a smile to my face. The phone chimes while he takes a second selfie, and a message pops up on the screen. My gaze lands on Torin's name on the sender line, then moves to the message below it.

*What the hell are you doing with Del?*

My phone chimes next. It doesn't take psychic abilities to guess who texted me and why.

# Chapter Seventeen

NEBULA IS NOT WHERE I wanted or expected to be tonight. We didn't discuss Torin's texts to us over dinner, and neither of us sent replies. But as we finished dessert, Phoenix suggested dropping by the show for a few songs to keep things on the level with Torin, and then slipping out at the first opportunity to enjoy the rest of our night.

Torin's message to me was much friendlier than what he sent to Phoenix. *Nash told me he just saw you. Are you going to swing by the show tonight with Ava? I'd love to see you.*

It's possible I read too much into his emphasis on going to the show with Ava, with no mention of Phoenix, but the three lines gave off a particular vibe. Even if he tolerated Phoenix's presence at the after-party the last time we were all together, Torin was clearly wary of him being anywhere near me that night, and he probably still is. Did he intentionally exclude Phoenix from the invitation with the hope or expectation I would ditch him, or is he counting on him making an appearance so he can give him a piece of his mind?

"It's not too late to do literally anything else," I say as we approach the velvet ropes outside of Nebula. The glittering casino lights and lively music from the slot machines only reinforce my opinion of how much happier we'd be by choosing to stay out here, or by spending the night somewhere else in the city.

"It has to happen sometime," Phoenix reminds me. "It may be better to do this in a public place Torin invited you to, especially since he'll be on stage soon. I also don't want you to feel like you have to avoid your friends because I'm with you."

He has valid arguments, but none of them ease the dread gnawing at my insides. Visions of worst-case scenarios flit through my mind like a mental kaleidoscope of doom while he speaks with the doorman. If Torin once wanted to punch Phoenix for bringing up my name, what will he do now that we're romantically involved again? I hadn't planned on keeping him out of the loop forever, but I would have appreciated having more time to figure out the best way to approach the subject with him. I'd also have preferred it to happen after Phoenix wraps up what he's working on and is no longer in Las Vegas, where Torin can hunt him down.

Then there's Ava to deal with. She's chilled out a bit since the day at my condo when she raised flags and concerns all over the place, but she's also impulsive, and she doesn't trust Phoenix yet. It's a given that she'll be drinking tonight, and buzzed Ava has less of a filter than her sober self does. With alcohol in the mix, and

Torin's backing, this is a recipe for disaster.

The doorman unhooks one of the ropes. I clutch Phoenix's hand as we make our way to the hidden entrance. The tension in my shoulders must be visible to him when the metal door swings open and we enter the bar, because he places a hand on one of them and gently kneads it.

"Want something to drink?" he asks.

"Just water."

"Are you sure that's all?" His hand slides over to massage my other shoulder.

Perhaps I should break my own rule again. I could use some help mellowing out, and I doubt I'll be writing anything until I'm back in LA. Phoenix also doesn't seem concerned about having alcohol around him, or at least that's the impression I had on my birthday and the last time I was here.

I close my eyes for a few seconds, feeling my muscles relax under his touch. "Can I claim dire circumstances and ask for a vodka ginger ale?"

"One vodka ginger ale coming up, no dire circumstances or explanations needed. Want to find us a spot to watch the show from?"

I open my eyes again to scan our surroundings for the most inconspicuous place we can stand that will also permit an easy getaway later. The ideal place seems to be on the other side of the room, so I point it out and begin making my way over there to claim it for us.

I'm halfway across the room when someone taps me from behind. "Blink twice if you need my help."

I stop and whirl around. Torin leans forward to hug me, but his embrace feels tentative.

"You're funny," I reply.

He releases me from his arms and steps back. The way he studies my face, I get the feeling he's searching for the answer to something.

"I wasn't trying to be. What's going on?"

"What's going on?" I repeat, doing my best to sound cheerful and clueless about what he's asking. "Isn't it obvious? I'm at your show."

"With him." He jerks his head toward the bar.

"Correct."

"In Las Vegas."

"That appears to be where I am, yes." I give him my most dazzling smile, hoping it sends the message that I'd rather keep the mood light.

If he gets the hint, he doesn't play along. "Why didn't you tell me you're in town?"

The devil and angel within me have it out in record time, and we all agree a tiny lie is justified to keep the peace. I don't need Torin blaming Phoenix for me ghosting my friends.

"Because Nash did it for me. I'd just gotten here when we bumped into him."

"Where are you staying?"

"Have you become my mother?"

It's meant to be a joke, but it doesn't land that way. Torin's lips pucker as if he's tasted something sour, and he examines me for a long moment.

"You're staying with Phoenix," he concludes.

"Also correct."

"I might actually kill him. How does he think he has the right to weasel his way back into your life, just to get you into bed—"

I cut him off with a stern look. "Enough. Last I checked, I'm capable of thinking for myself and making my own decisions, and visiting him here was my idea."

Torin blinks a few times, surprise registering on his face. I'm tempted to ask if he's considered that I haven't been brainwashed and have willingly welcomed Phoenix into my life again, but decide to hold my tongue. Riling him up won't make this easier on me.

"Fill in some blanks for me, please. The last time I saw either of you, he had you cornered in my kitchen, and then you avoided him for the rest of the night until you and Ava went back to your hotel. What changed?"

I get why he's baffled, and I understand his concern, but I didn't travel here this weekend to explain or defend my romantic choices. "People get back together sometimes. It happens."

"After the ending you two had?" He shakes his head, clearly unsatisfied with my answer. "He must have said something out of this world to reel you in again, because the Del I know would have sent him packing before he finished saying hello."

The universe or some other force out there needs to grant me patience and strength. I'll require both if Torin is trying to shame me into feeling like I made the wrong choice during a moment of weakness.

"I know you're watching out for me, but this isn't up to you. I know what I'm getting into and I'm happy. That's all that should matter."

"I'm glad you're happy, because if he makes you unhappy again, you won't be able to stop me from putting him through a wall."

Torin's jaw tenses, and his hand balls into a fist at his side. He isn't kidding. If we weren't where we are and if he wasn't about to get on stage, he'd probably be over at the bar and in Phoenix's face right now, telling him the same thing.

"Violence won't be necessary."

"I'm sure it wasn't necessary when he and Chaz had it out, either, but look at who you're dealing with. You should think about that if you're against violent behavior."

"There are things you don't know." I rub a hand over my face, not caring what happens to my makeup. "I realize you'll never be besties, but can you try to be civil tonight?"

"Has he done something to deserve that?"

"Do it for me."

"Fine." He folds his arms across his chest. "If you think I'm bad, though, wait until Ava gets here and sees you with him."

"She's aware of my weekend plans." I sound unconcerned, but it's a front. While Ava has had several weeks to get used to the idea of Phoenix and me being together, it only means she's had more time than Torin has to devise a plan for exactly how she'll get under his skin.

"She knows about this and didn't tell me?"

"Relax, Torin." Ava's voice breaks into our conversation. "Focus on your show and we can talk about it later."

Ava throws her arms around me, then steps over to Torin and hugs him. She's smiling, and there's a lighthearted bounce in her movements. Either she hasn't spotted Phoenix yet, or she got in early enough today to have pregamed the show with a drink or two. Except she doesn't seem like she's been drinking, and now she peeks at the bar, so she has to see him. Something else is afoot.

I inspect her more closely. Ava is always careful with her appearance, especially when we go out, but tonight she's dressed to kill and looks like a goddess. She's also giving off *here-for-the-best-night-of-her-life* energy.

"Where's Nash?" she asks.

Torin's eyes sweep over Ava, also taking in her appearance, and then he and I exchange a glance. As upset as he might be about why I'm in town, the upward curve of his mouth and amused twinkle in his eyes tells me we're on the same wavelength and have guessed the same thing.

"I'll find him for you," he replies. "Excuse me for a minute."

Ava and I watch him weave through a group of people blocking the aisle. Once he's a few feet away, I nudge her.

"You're all decked out to see Nash, aren't you? And here you denied being interested in him."

She maintains a decent poker face, but she can't hide the flush of color that creeps into her neck and cheeks. "Never mind what's going on with me. You're the one living dangerously by telling Torin what you're up to."

"I didn't have a choice. Nash ran into us on our way to have dinner and told him I was here with Phoenix. Text messages happened. I assured Phoenix I could talk to Torin later, but he decided it was better to clear the air and face both of you now."

"You don't need to worry about me tonight. I'll behave."

"What have you done with Ava?"

She laughs at this. "Why do you think I didn't tell you I'd be here?"

"Other than your plans to hook up with Nash and keep me in the dark?" I tease. "What happened to the world not being ready for that kind of chaos?"

She ignores me and continues. "I wasn't about to interfere in your weekend of getting all loved up. I still can't stand what he did to you, and I don't like him, but I'm sure there will be other opportunities to question his ass without mercy."

A low whistle from nearby stops me from replying. Nash walks up to us with Torin right behind him.

"You look incredible." Nash kisses Ava's cheek. It's a friendly peck, but there's something in the way he looks her up and down and then pulls her into a hug that confirms my suspicions of something more brewing between them.

Torin catches my eye, and we exchange another knowing look while I struggle to contain a laugh. He appears every bit as entertained as I am, but then his entire demeanor changes, like sunshine giving way to storm clouds. His gaze shifts away from me.

Phoenix is at my side seconds later. He passes me my drink, then glances at Ava and Nash. "Did I miss something with those two?" he whispers into my ear.

"Your guess is as good as mine," I whisper back.

Torin couldn't watch us any more intently if he was an actual hawk, waiting to pounce on his prey. I pretend not to notice his dark glare.

Phoenix must see it, but he smiles and extends his hand out to him. "It's good to see you."

"I can't say the same about you. I thought we had an agreement." Torin's mouth pinches together, and he keeps his arms at his sides.

"I heard you out, but I didn't agree to anything."

"What agreement?" I ask.

Phoenix twists the cap off of his water and takes a drink, and then he and Torin lock eyes. Neither of them answers me.

# Chapter Eighteen

"A word in private?" Torin asks Phoenix. His request sounds more like a command.

"Torin." My voice carries a warning I doubt anyone misses.

"It's okay. I'll be back soon." Phoenix drops a kiss on my forehead and strokes my hair. Torin's mouth twists into a scowl before he stalks away.

"We're on in ten minutes," Nash calls after him.

He flashes the peace sign in response as he continues walking. Phoenix follows a few paces behind him to a dark corner of the bar.

Nash glances at Ava and me. "What was that about?"

"Phoenix is about to have his ass handed to him," Ava explains, as if this isn't obvious to all three of us. She looks and sounds much too gleeful for someone who claimed she didn't want to spoil my weekend by doing the same thing. "He and Del dated once before and—"

"It's a long story if you don't already know it," I say, interrupting Ava before she gets too animated with her account of things. "Practically a novel."

"I'll fill you in later," she assures him.

"Can't wait." He sounds amused, but the way his mouth quirks before he presses his lips together makes it seem like he's suppressing a grin for my sake. "Speaking of novels, Del, I overheard Ava say something about your latest book a few weeks ago. It sounded interesting."

"Shhh." Ava elbows him. "She just forgave me for vaguely spilling the beans. I wasn't supposed to talk about her book until it's announced."

"It's fine," I reply. If it gets us off the topic of Torin's beef with Phoenix and what I have to do with it, I might even be willing to get behind one of the microphones on stage and announce my new novel to the entire bar.

"Maybe I shouldn't ask, but did Elenna Paseo's disappearance inspire any of it? The premise sounded like it might have to do with her."

Thanks to Phoenix also connecting the dots, this time the question isn't out of left field. "It's loosely based on her case. You knew her, right?"

He doesn't seem taken aback by my knowledge of this. "Incredibly well. We grew up next door to each other. Phoenix knew her, too."

"He told me, and I'm so sorry. I can't imagine the pain you've been through, especially with her case still unsolved."

His head bobs, acknowledging what I said. Ava's gaze darts from him to me. This is new information for her, since we haven't discussed the connection between Len, Phoenix, and Nash. She was already so suspicious of Phoenix, his intentions, and what kept him away and silent all this time. Once I settled into gratitude for Len's role in his return to my life as the guy I used to know, I didn't want to risk Ava reflecting my initial insecurities back to me about how or why his friendship with Len was enough for him to work on himself and get sober when his relationship with me wasn't.

"What do you think happened?"

Nash's question catches me off guard. "To Len?"

"Yes. It might be a weird question, but I feel like the police fumbled everything from the start and gave up trying to find out. I've been over it a million times in my head, but I sometimes wonder if there are things I'm blind to because we were so close, that maybe you have theories about or pieced together while plotting your book." He shrugs, as if it's no big deal, but he absently twists the beaded bracelets on his left wrist, and speaks again. "I think I'm still just desperate for answers, you know?"

"I can't blame you. I've been working through a few plot points I'm stuck on and—"

"Are we playing a show tonight, or what? Where's Torin?" Jacob, the singer in Torin and Nash's band, cuts into our conversation. He taps his watch and scans the growing crowd, presumably looking for his missing drummer.

"I'll get him." Nash winks at me. "Let me go rescue your boy. If you don't stick around until after the show, get my number from Ava or Phoenix if you want to bounce theories or ideas off of me, or if you have questions about Len. I'd love to help if I can, as a tribute to her."

He gives Ava's elbow a squeeze and then heads off to the corner where Phoenix and Torin are. Torin still looks heated as he says something it's impossible to make out from over here. Phoenix appears calm while he listens, even though a couple of people standing nearby openly stare, slack-jawed, at whatever comes out of Torin's mouth. He stops speaking when Nash joins them, but irritation remains written all over his face when he turns and walks toward the stage.

Why can't he follow Ava's example and chill out for a couple of hours? There's no chance I'll be talked into staying here for a possible second round of this after the show is over, but I will reach out to him after I'm back in LA to discuss why he's so upset and to make a few things clear about boundaries and what he doesn't have a say in.

"I'm going to the bar," Ava announces. "Want me to get you a shot of something strong? You look like you need it."

"I'm good, thanks." The tightness in my jaw and shoulders probably tells Ava otherwise, but she only gives me a quick side hug and doesn't say anything else before she saunters off.

As tense and annoyed as I am, the feelings begin to fall away as Phoenix makes his way through the throng of people crowding the space between where he just stood and where I am. Whatever went down, he doesn't seem fazed by it. His gaze softens when our eyes meet, and his lips curve up into a smile the moment he's next to me again.

"I'm glad you made it back in one piece," I tell him, only half-kidding. "Is everything all right?"

"Everything is fine. Torin wanted to remind me how amazing you are, and how lucky I am to be in your life."

"Why do I feel like that's a creative spin on things?" I straighten the collar of his shirt, then rest my hand over his heart, feeling its steady beat below my palm. "He was fuming at you. What did he really say?"

"That he cares about you and has concerns about me. I can't blame him for that. I didn't come here expecting him to be thrilled."

"And the agreement he mentioned?"

"It wasn't an agreement. He was concerned about me approaching you the last time you were here and had a few things to say about it after you left his house that night. That's all."

His heartbeat remains the same steady rate, which is a good indication he's telling the truth. Even so, this sounds like one of the short versions of the story he's so good at, and I want the longer one.

"What things?" I remove my hand from his chest.

He chooses that moment to take a long sip of water. For someone who used to be a top-rated actor, he's not doing a great job of hiding the fact that he's stalling.

"I can badger him about it later and get his version of events, or you can tell me now. It's your choice."

My tone should tell him I'm not here to play, and that he doesn't need to sugarcoat whatever Torin said. He puts the cap back on his water and meets my eyes.

"It was mostly that his drumsticks would stay away from my kneecaps as long as I kept my distance and left you alone. We're working that out."

I love Torin like he's my flesh-and-blood sibling and this doesn't change that, but he's taking his protective big brother role a bit too far. Making physical threats isn't okay, whether they're explicit or implied, and whether it was three weeks ago or tonight.

"Torin has watched too many reruns of *The Sopranos* and needs to remember he's a musician, not a mobster," I mutter.

Music blares from the speakers on each side of the stage as I finish my sentence, signaling the start of the set and the end of our conversation for now. This isn't a topic I want to yell back and forth about over drums, bass lines, and guitar riffs. Ava appears again, a drink in one hand and a shot glass in the other. She ducks past a few people and positions herself in the first row, in front of Nash.

Phoenix's eyebrows knit together when he spots where Ava is, and a frown crosses his lips when she hands Nash the shot glass. The frown deepens after Nash takes it from her, knocks it back, and then peers into her eyes while he begins playing his guitar.

What Phoenix said on my birthday about not wanting to distract Ava with Nash springs to mind. I understood it then, after what I witnessed at Torin's house with the women he had in tow, but something about this is different. Ava and Nash share an energy that's undeniable. He has to see it too.

I nudge him. "Don't be like Torin with this. They'd be good together."

He crinkles his nose at the comparison. "I don't want to see her get hurt. She may not like me, but she's your best friend, and we used to be friends. I care about what happens to her."

He's barely audible over the music, so I take his hand and lead him to the back of the bar and past a door to an enclosed hallway outside of the restrooms. It's quieter here, and we can speak at a normal volume.

"I thought Nash was your friend?"

"He is. As a friend, he's fine. It's his track record with the women he gets involved with that isn't."

If anyone knows how to play the player, it's Ava. She isn't easy to fool, and she doesn't walk into anything blindly or heart first. She's also Nash's friend and was previously his wingwoman, which means she's fully aware of what he's like. Either she only wants a fling or a one-night stand, or something else happened between them that has her overlooking it. I suspect the latter. As much as I appreciate Phoenix looking out for her, he doesn't need to worry.

"I promise you Ava can take care of herself, and we both know Torin will be all over it after the show if he thinks there's a reason she shouldn't get involved with him. Maybe this is the distraction he needs to get his focus off of you and me. It might be the perfect time for us to leave, so he only has them in his view."

Some extra enticement to persuade him can't hurt. I set my drink down on a ledge, then wind my arms around his neck and rise up on my feet, so we're at eye level. My mouth glides over his. The second this registers with him, his lips follow my lead and he pulls me closer. I'm aware of the door opening and someone walking past us to one of the restrooms, but the audience doesn't matter to me. For the first time since we bumped into Nash on our way to dinner tonight, the uneasy feeling in the pit of my stomach disappears. Maybe it's selfish, but spending time alone with Phoenix, like this, is why I'm here. I don't owe anyone an explanation, and hearing more of Torin's concerns and opinions can wait.

"Let's get out of here," I murmur to him, in case he hasn't yet gotten the point.

It takes no more convincing to get Phoenix to walk to a door marked with an exit sign that's a few feet away. He holds it open for me, and then we're outside of Nebula, in the casino, and free to go wherever the night wants to take us.

"There's one more thing I thought we could do tonight," he says, guiding me past the slot machines. We seem to be heading for the doors where we entered the casino earlier this evening.

"If it means going somewhere far away from here, then I'm listening." I stretch my mouth into a dazzling and slightly sarcastic smile, hoping he senses how much I'd rather be anywhere else but The Auriga when the show is over and the band loads out.

He catches it, because a chuckle slips out and he puts his arm around me. "If being in the sky is far enough for you, then I think I have it covered. How do you feel about helicopters?"

# Chapter Nineteen

I'VE BEEN IN PLENTY of airplanes in my life, but I hadn't set foot in a helicopter before tonight and didn't expect to. Helicopters in my Los Angeles life are associated with the LAPD airship buzzing my neighborhood, and with news choppers circling when there's a major event somewhere in the vicinity. It wouldn't have occurred to me to book a city tour in one, nor was I aware nighttime views of Las Vegas from one were a thing until Phoenix filled me in on the reservation he made and drove us the short distance up the Strip to where the helicopter and its pilot awaited us.

While I'm a pro at airplane takeoffs, the straight vertical climb of the helicopter is a new experience. The feeling of being pushed down in my seat makes my stomach twirl, and I have to close my eyes until the feeling subsides. When I open them again, my breath catches at the sparkling sea of lights below me that stretch on for miles. The view of Las Vegas from a helicopter is infinitely more dazzling and panoramic than it is from a tiny airplane window. Now it makes sense how the city's lights are visible from space.

"That's the Sphere," I say, when I spy the enormous orb that's currently projecting images of glowing flames. Close by, color-shifting lights illuminate the High Roller Ferris wheel. "Everything is so beautiful."

I turn my head to glance at Phoenix. He must have heard me through his headset, because he shifts his gaze from the scene outside of the helicopter to me.

"Everything really is," he agrees. *Especially you*, he mouths, silent this time so only I catch the words. The same adoring look I saw in his eyes earlier this evening makes another appearance now.

Pure happiness melts away any remaining thoughts I had about what happened at Nebula tonight. Forget about Torin's irritation, and forget about whatever is going on between Ava and Nash. The mesmerizing city panoramas, the almost weightless sensation I have as we soar over the Strip, my joy at being able to do this, and Phoenix are all that exist for me now.

"Look at the Strat tower from here," I marvel. It's the tallest observation tower in the United States, and the top of it is right outside the window. The much shorter Eiffel Tower replica at Paris Hotel is also visible from here, and I point at it. "Look how it almost seems to shimmer. Can you imagine what the real one must look like from a helicopter?"

"We'll find out one day," Phoenix vows. "We'll go there and to the canals in Venice."

Our pilot probably thinks we're bantering about future plans, but the reminder of the canals brings me back to our conversation about Venice last weekend, and what Phoenix said about wishing he'd taken me. He sounds equally serious about a trip for him and me that also includes Paris. It isn't his vision of us traveling together in Europe on a romantic getaway that has me suddenly fumbling for words. It's the repeated promise within it that he's here for the long term this time and sees this as possible for us.

Life has sparkle again by the time the helicopter tour ends and we're back on the ground. Phoenix controls the playlist for our drive home, and it starts with an ethereal, beat-driven dreamscape of a song I haven't heard before. I sink into the passenger seat and let the music wash over me in relaxing waves. But when the melody fades and a familiar song begins, my stomach flip-flops. The distinct notes of "Lovesong" by the Cure always awaken my memory of a cozy weekend morning, years ago, cooking breakfast with Phoenix in the kitchen of my old apartment. The same song came on the radio then as I set up the coffee maker. He put his arms around me and murmured the lyrics in my ear. Neither of us heard the toaster pop or ate the slices of bread that stayed there long after the song was over, and the coffee maker remained off for another couple of hours as we lost ourselves in one another.

Does he remember that? God, we were so in love then. I swallow hard, attempting to clear the thickness in my throat.

"Nix?"

He eases the vehicle to a stop at a red light and then looks at me.

"Yeah?"

The tenderness in his voice and in his eyes tells me he has the same memory, and that his song choice isn't a coincidence. I'm interpreting it the way he meant for me to.

"Same." *I will always love you.*

Neither of us has uttered the words we used to speak all the time, but I don't think I could feel more open-hearted and vulnerable even if that's what I had said. The light turns green, but the road is empty and Phoenix doesn't move his foot from the brake to the gas pedal until after he's reached for my hand and held it in his for a few seconds.

There are no guardrails left standing around my heart. I'm in this with all of me, a trust fall that will either end in happily ever after or another devastation, with no option in between. I want to believe he feels this at the same depth I do. The lengths he's gone to with traveling to see me, paying for my flight here, the flowers, the birthday dinner cruise, the candlelight concert, the helicopter ride, the new playlist, his attentive and sweet phone calls and texts, and putting things out in the open with Torin, give me every reason to think he's also all in. It's only a matter of us definitively saying it, but a conversation about our relationship status isn't something I'm going to start while we're driving. We'll be home soon. Then it will just be him and me, with no focus on navigating a vehicle or on anything else but each other.

I don't mention what's on my mind when we park in his driveway about ten minutes later. The words are still stuck inside of me when we're in the house and he asks me if I'm tired at all, or if I'm hungry, or if there's anything I need. But everything I want to say still lingers at the forefront of my mind after we've gone upstairs and I've exchanged my night-out-in-Vegas clothes for a silky sleep camisole and shorts, and as I sit upright in bed, fidgeting with my rings, and waiting for Phoenix to join me. I'm keyed up about something that's nothing more than a formality—it's only words and a relationship label, really—but try telling that to a heart that's partly terrified about being wide open again after hiding behind fortress walls for so many years.

*Relax.*

I roll my shoulders backward a couple of times, and then I tilt my head forward and slowly move it from side to side in a semicircle, trying to stretch out some of the taut muscles in my shoulders. I stop when the mattress shifts and Phoenix's fingertips graze my neck. It's a familiar action, one that he used to do to silently ask if I wanted a neck or shoulder rub after I spent long hours hunched over a keyboard at the content design job I had in those days, and during the evening and weekend hours when I worked on a manuscript. My way of answering was always to straighten my head up and lean into his hand, like I do now.

"Neck and shoulders only, or your back, too?" he asks.

"All of those, if you're willing. Thank you."

The choreography of how we do this is still nearly perfect. I change my position to sit cross-legged and turn so my back faces him, and he positions himself so he's behind me and able to use both of his hands to work on the knots in my muscles.

"Let me know if there are places you don't want to be touched."

He might mean this in the context of the back rub, but I hear it as a request for consent. Perhaps that's because this often used to lead to something more, or because we're about to spend the first of three nights together, and this time is an entirely different situation than when I stayed over in Laguna Beach.

"You're good. I'm trusting you with all of me." My heart pounds as I say this, and it continues when the kneading motion of fingers pauses for a moment. Does he understand just how much I mean what I said? Part of me wants to spill my guts now and put everything out there, but I again hold back, focusing instead on the brush of his hands over my skin.

His fingers find the spot on my shoulder that always gives me the most trouble, as if he's magnetized to it or somehow remembers. I don't know how he could after all this time, but he also seems to recall exactly what to do to get it to uncoil and release.

"Remind me why you didn't go pro with this?" I keep my tone light and joking. The question is as much to pull myself out of my head as it is to break the silence that's settled over us.

"It was some pipe dream I had about an acting career. That, and you're the only one I ever want to do this with." His tone matches mine.

"Sounds like a pretty exclusive client list."

"It is." His breath tickles the back of my neck, and then his lips are light as air against my skin. At the same time, his hands slide forward over the top of my ribcage, and his fingers brush ever so softly along the underside of my breasts.

It's innocent, but it's also sensual enough for my pulse to pick up the tempo. Awareness stirs in places deep inside of me when his thumbs trace the outer curves of my chest, and when his mouth works its way up the side of my neck, and then to my earlobe. He knows exactly what he's doing, but I don't mind.

No matter what he alleged last weekend about not wanting to have the geographic distance between us if or when touches and making out go past that to steamier foreplay, and then to us making love, we've been here before. It's his enticing game of catch and release; an intentional slow burn where he brings me to the edges of arousal and then retreats. It's a caress here, but not there, as his mouth lingers on my skin. It starts with my neck, just as it has now. In a different phase of our lives, after the declarations of commitment and the boyfriend-and-girlfriend labels on what we were, it continued south of there, with him purposely skirting around the sensitive places until the ache of anticipation threatened to overpower us both.

Will it go that far tonight? If I know him, and I think I do, he won't make a move on me beyond the fleeting touches and more surface levels of making out until we've defined our relationship, even though I'm staying here with him all weekend and sleeping in his bed. He didn't the last time around.

Almost as soon as I have this thought, his hands return to my shoulders and there's space between us again, as if the interlude was only a figment of my imagination. On impulse, I reach for his hands, covering them with mine.

"Is it too soon to talk about what we are?" For the nerves I battled ahead of voicing this question, I sound astonishingly calm asking it.

"It's not too soon if you're ready to. I didn't want to rush you." He doesn't seem caught off guard. If anything, he sounds like he's thought about this, knows what he wants to say, and has been holding back until the time is right.

I nod, then let go of his hands so I can reposition myself. Once I'm facing him, I speak again. "I don't want to assume anything, but I get the sense you aren't seeing anyone else right now?"

"I'm not." His hand settles on my knee, and he gazes into my eyes. "And so there aren't any questions about how I feel, I don't want to see anybody else but you."

"I don't want to either, and I haven't been. It's only you." I touch the side of his face, then run my fingers along his jaw. He takes a page from my book, turning his head to kiss my palm.

"It's always been you," he says, looking directly into my eyes again. "Maybe I don't have the right to say that given what I did, but it's true. It will always be you."

As I lean forward into his waiting arms, and as he holds me close to him, I no longer care about what was. Tonight is about what is and what will be.

"I believe you," I whisper to him. And I do.

# Chapter Twenty

It's a night that doesn't end until long after the sun comes up.

After being in Phoenix's arms turns into the brush of his lips on my forehead and over each of my closed eyelids, and after that leads to a soft kiss that deepens into more, and after that turns into making out and exploring one another in ways I once thought we never would again, the passion between us combusts. Any hesitation or caution we had last weekend about our temporary geographic distance is abandoned in the moment, no looking back.

There's something about the way our bodies fit together, like two perfectly interlocking puzzle pieces. The weight of him, the heat of his skin, and the warmth in his touch. How the rhythm of us takes over, as if the years between the last time we made love and now evaporate into nothing and linear time becomes a fable. It's the feeling of falling headfirst into an endless ocean of him and me when I look into his eyes and he gazes into mine, and the pleasure that ripples through me and grows until I'm moaning and clutching onto him, fingernails against skin, surrendering to sweet release.

It was always good with us, but somehow never quite as good as it is now in this current incarnation of who and what we are. Primal. Instinctual. Two souls made of stardust finding their way home.

Us.

There may be things we're still uncovering from the time between the relationship we once had and what we have now, but I don't regret our decision to take things to this level already. And hours later, when we lie together in bed, Phoenix holding me, his body curved around mine, I take comfort in the once-familiar sound of his deep and even breathing as he falls asleep.

For my part, I'm almost afraid to close my eyes in case I wake up to find myself at home in LA and discover that this night and the weeks that led up to it were only a dream. But eventually my eyes shut on their own, and slumber pulls me into its dreamless depths. When my eyes next open and wakeful reality comes into focus again, Phoenix's arm is still draped across me. He must see or feel me stir, because he holds me closer and buries his face in my hair.

"Good afternoon." His voice is muffled, but I hear the softness in how he speaks. My heart is already dangerously close to bursting right out of my chest. Waking up in Vegas has never been like this.

"It really is."

It's a cheesy answer, but it's the truth. I could stay like this for an eternity, snuggled into him, our legs and arms tangled together, with nothing else we need to do and nowhere we have to be. That's exactly what we do for a few tranquil minutes, neither of us speaking, with only the sound of the fan from the central air and muted daytime noises from outside as a backdrop to the quiet.

"What time is it?" I ask.

"It was noon when I woke up, so later than that."

His lips glide over my ear and then find my neck. I sink even more into the feeling of him and the cocoon of his body against mine, torn between staying positioned as I am and letting him continue, or taking bolder physical action driven by the fire he's already managed to spark at my core. We may never leave this bed.

My stomach turns out to be the decisive third party in the situation when it quietly growls. I nearly laugh at how it's this, of all things, breaking into the moment, but I'm also not self-conscious about it. Everything about right now has the comfort of the years we already knew each other this way. Lord, this is bliss.

"Should I make us something to eat?" Phoenix's hand drifts down to rest on my stomach.

"Mmmm. Would that mean we have to get up?"

"Just for a while, so we don't get too hungry, or hangry. Then we can do whatever you'd like."

"I never get hangry," I protest.

"There was that one time driving back from San Francis—"

"Out of bounds, mister. We promised we'd never speak of that drive again." I try to sound stern, but laughter bubbles into my words. "Let's not forget you were also hangry and ready to abandon the car in favor of walking through the ice and snow in the Grapevine until we found a rest stop."

"I will never deny I was hangry. That drive turned out okay in the end, though, or it did after we had food."

"I remember," I say softly.

We'd been stuck on the section of the 5 freeway that was just outside of the Grapevine mountain pass for close to three hours. Our drive from San Francisco had started almost eight hours earlier, and we'd skipped stopping for lunch since we'd had a late breakfast and should have made it home in five hours. We didn't think to check on road conditions, which means we also didn't expect a winter storm.

The longer we remained in one place, the hungrier I became. I tried to distract myself by thinking through scenes in the manuscript I was working on. Phoenix interrupted my thoughts as he wondered aloud about turning off the car to conserve gas. He was worried we would get cold.

"Do whatever," I muttered, not intending to sound as short-tempered as I did. But I'd lost my train of thought, and I was already frustrated and starting to feel like we'd be stranded there for the rest of our lives.

Phoenix didn't get testy about my response or our plight. He only touched my arm, then took my hand and apologized for not thinking to check the forecast for the Grapevine, as if it was his sole responsibility to do so. That's who he was during that part of our relationship, before the drinking and the drugs.

The highway patrol eventually detoured vehicles off the interstate as parts of it remained closed due to accidents and dangerous conditions caused by snow, graupel, and icy roads. Phoenix and I decided to find somewhere to stay the night. The diner we stopped at along the way could have been a top-rated gourmet restaurant as far as we were concerned. As grumpy as I was after hours of being stuck in the car, barely moving, the food and being out of the car made me feel human again. Our moods were lighter by the time we left the diner.

When we found an out-of-the-way mountain inn, and Phoenix went inside to ask about a room, I had no idea he would return with the keys to a suite that included a jacuzzi tub. I also didn't know that when he'd left our table at the diner to use the restroom, he'd stopped our server and asked about getting slices of strawberry cheesecake to go. He'd picked them up at the cash register after telling me to go ahead of him to the car while he paid our bill at the register, then put them in the bag with our takeout boxes of food we hadn't finished.

That night was another one that continued past dawn. When we checked out and hit the road after having a late brunch, the fumes of sleep we were both existing on didn't matter. Then, much like now, our world was pure afterglow.

Amusement sparkles in Phoenix's eyes. "Is that a yes or a no for food?"

There's no reason for me to wish we could live on air and stay here forever, and so the pang I feel at the thought of untangling ourselves from one another for an hour or two is silly. We have the rest of the weekend together to do more of this, or anything else we want to.

"It's yes," I say. "Thank you."

Phoenix presses his mouth to my forehead, then releases me from his arms. My eyes sweep over every visible inch of his body when he gets out of bed, as though I'm memorizing him and everything about the present moment. As he moves through the room, my resistance to greeting the day transforms into gratitude for the journey we've been on so far, and for what's still to come. If the last few weeks have proven anything to me, it's that the most magical things in life happen in unexpected ways.

I remain where I am for a few more minutes, listening to water run from the sink faucet in the bathroom while he brushes his teeth, and then his footsteps as he makes his way downstairs. After I summon the willpower to sit up, I take in the halo of daylight trying to peek around the window shades and reorient myself to the world beyond this house.

That's when I remember not saying goodbye to Ava last night. We left the bar without a word to her or anyone else. Now I'm curious if something happened between her and Nash after the show, and what led to the unmistakable flirting I witnessed between them.

I lean over to grab my phone from the bedside table and unlock the screen. There are no new texts from Ava, so I type a message to her.

*Sooooo... did you have a good night?*

My question isn't specific to her and Nash, but she'll know exactly what it means when she reads it. If all went well, she could be having lunch or a late brunch with him now. Whatever happened, I'm looking forward to being the one to cross-examine her this time.

When there's no sign of her typing a reply, I abandon my phone and finally climb out of bed. By the time I've put on clothes, splashed water on my face, brushed my teeth, and returned to the bedroom, Ava has answered my text with a long one of her own.

*Ugh, no. We all went to Torin's house after the show and I passed out in his guest bedroom. I didn't think I had that much to drink, but he didn't think I was in any shape to decide about leaving with Nash. I doubt I'd remember anything if I had gone home with him, so it's probably for the best. I texted him earlier to ask what his plans are after I'm done with my event tonight, but he's leaving for a couple of days of session work at a studio somewhere that isn't close to Vegas.*

I send her a quick reply, sympathizing with her night and asking how she's feeling, then set my phone on the table. Phoenix's phone lights up as I do this, and so I see a missed call and voicemail notification, and a text that pops up on the screen.

*Listen to your messages and call me when you get this.*

The name above the text is Dalton Petaluma. It isn't familiar to me, but I'm guessing it's someone connected to what Phoenix is working on out here, or maybe it's his agent. We haven't talked about his plans for his acting career, or if he has any outside of what he's currently on location for, except for what he mentioned about the script his agent sent him for the adaptation of my book. He'll see Dalton's message when he checks his phone. Maybe he'll bring it up then.

The aroma of eggs and bacon cooking greets me as I head downstairs, and so does chatter from what sounds like a news program. When I get to the kitchen, I spot a TV mounted on one of the walls. Phoenix is at the stove, but he puts down the spatula he's holding and picks up a mug from the counter when he sees me.

"Coffee?" he asks.

"What's the most enthusiastic way I can say yes to that?"

He chuckles and places a pod in the coffee maker that's on the counter, then returns to the stove to check on the bacon and eggs while the coffee brews. I'm about to approach the counter to retrieve the mug when the coffee maker finishes, but Phoenix beats me to it with a smooth sequence of movements that first involves a stop at the fridge for a carton of vanilla creamer. I hang back, watching him stir just the right amount of sweetened liquid into the steaming coffee, then he picks up the mug and brings it to me.

"Find yourself someone who remembers how you take your coffee *and* delivers it to you." I take the mug from him.

"Does that mean I passed the afternoon-after test?" The smile he beams at me is enough to light up a small city on its own.

"It's looking good for you, but I'm withholding final judgment until after I taste the food," I joke.

"The food is coming right up."

"Want a hand with anything?"

"Nope." He pecks my cheek, then steps back over to the counter and retrieves plates from a cupboard. I take a seat at the table while he transfers food from the frying pans onto the plates.

As he does this, a voice on the television announces a breaking news story. The news anchor's change in tone from lighthearted to serious is swift and so much of a contrast that it commands my attention, even though the TV audio was previously only background noise to me.

*"A source with connections to the Orange County Sheriff's Department in California has revealed there are new developments surrounding the investigation into Elenna Paseo's disappearance from her Aliso Viejo neighborhood several years ago. Authorities are reportedly close to making an announcement about a major break in the case, but our calls to law enforcement officials have yet to be returned. The source also cited the name of someone alleged to be involved in these developments. Since we haven't yet been able to confirm the involvement of this person, and for the safety of everyone involved, we are not disclosing the name we were given at this time."*

My gaze shifts from the screen to Phoenix. He's motionless, nearly suspended in time while I watch him, and he forgets to blink as his eyes remain focused on the television. The news anchor moves on to a story about wildfires in northern California, but he doesn't appear to notice. He finally does blink when scenes of a fiery hillside fill the screen, but other than that, he still doesn't move.

After what must be a full minute of him standing in the center of the kitchen, holding a forgotten plate in his hands, I get up from my chair and approach him.

"Are you okay?"

I touch his shoulder. He startles, and a tremor runs through him, but then he focuses on me. Recognition and awareness return to his eyes.

"Sorry. I didn't mean to let the food get cold." He continues to the table and sets the plate down. I follow him there and am about to sit again, but he places a hand on my shoulder this time. "I'm fine. I just didn't expect that."

He holds my gaze for a few beats, almost like he's trying to convince me, or maybe he's convincing himself. Then his hand falls away. He returns to the counter to grab the other plate, along with forks and knives. I lower myself into the chair.

He seems present and collected now, despite what I just witnessed, and even though there has been a detectable shift in his mood since a few minutes ago. But when he joins me at the table and passes me the cutlery, there's the slightest tremble in his fingers. It reminds me of when I asked him if he thought Len was alive during our coastline cruise on my birthday. No, he isn't fine. Not totally. He must be wondering what the break in the case is and what it means.

I set my fork and knife beside my plate, then reach across the table to cover his hand with mine. He looks at our hands, and then at me. What I glimpse in his eyes now isn't what I saw before. His hand is steady again when he flips it under mine so we're palm to palm.

"Have you heard from Ava since last night?" he asks.

It takes me a second to follow the change in subject. When I grasp that we're talking about Ava, and presumably about her well-being, something in me softens even more. Here we are, confronted with the announcement about a break in Len's case. It's clearly brought up raw feelings and unanswered questions, and yet he still wants to check on Ava. It wasn't that long ago when she would have volunteered to pour concrete into his shoes if someone had wanted to throw him off a bridge, and she still isn't sunshine and warmth in his presence, but he cares.

"You really are concerned about her, aren't you?" There's something oddly sweet about this, and it's why I hold back on repeating what I said last night about Ava knowing what she's getting into if something happens between her and Nash.

"I am. It might end up being my fatal flaw."

I can't help but laugh. "You and me both. Yes, though. We texted earlier. She stayed at Torin's house last night. She said she passed out in his guest bedroom, even though she didn't think she had that much to drink."

His eyebrows lift at that. This and his clenched jaw are peculiar responses, since he should be happy to learn Ava didn't hook up with Nash. Is it a reaction to hearing Torin's name?

"She's okay today?"

"She seems to be, but all I know is what she put in her message. I'll get the full story from her later. I'm glad she was somewhere safe with people she trusts. It sounded like Torin decided for her about not leaving with Nash, since he didn't think she was in any kind of shape to make a decision." I pause for a moment, then give him a teasing smile. "It's proof he isn't only protective of me."

"That's not always a bad thing. I think Torin and I agree on something in this case." It's difficult to tell if it's relief that eases the crease between his eyebrows, or approval, or both.

"Careful. Next thing you know, you two will be best friends."

My joke gets a smile out of him while he reaches for a slice of toast. "I'd settle for him not wanting to tear me limb from limb when he sees me with you." The smile fades when he takes a bite and chews, and his eyes hint that he's retreated into more serious thoughts. It's hard to tell if he's thinking about the news again, or about Torin's attitude about us being together.

"Hey." I touch his arm. "Torin has to get through me if he wants to lay a hand on you. I'm pretty invested in your body staying in one piece."

A sparkle of mischief returns to Phoenix's eyes. "Any parts of my body in particular?" He nudges my foot under the table.

"We could go through them one by one after we eat." I rest my elbow on the table and prop my chin up with my hand.

"Tempting. Are we going to make it out of the house today?"

A sultry smile tugs at my lips. "We'll see where the day takes us."

# Chapter Twenty-One

PHOENIX DECLINES MY OFFER to help clear the dishes or wash the pans he used after we've eaten, even when I point out that cleanup would take half the time. I wait until his hands are submerged in sudsy dishwater before grabbing the carton of coffee creamer from the counter to put away.

"You shouldn't be lifting a finger," he chides.

"And why is that?" I stop behind him on my way to the fridge and place a gentle kiss on the back of his neck.

"Because I can take care of this, and it's your weekend away. Pretend this house is an all-inclusive resort."

"I'd still put the creamer back in my room's mini-fridge at a resort. But I'll let you wait on me hand and foot after that, if you insist."

"I do insist." He stops scrubbing a pan for long enough to lean over and kiss my cheek. I catch his smile before I continue on my way.

Cool air wafts over my skin when I open the fridge and scan the shelves for a place to put the carton. My eyes land on a yellow can, and they stop there while I process what I'm seeing and read the small text printed on it. No, I'm not mistaken, because it isn't a mocktail. It's a 50-proof whiskey sour, and it's one of five unopened cans.

Phoenix told me he's sober, so why does he have alcohol in his fridge? They aren't for me, because I don't drink whiskey, and he should remember that I hate these particular drinks with a passion. They're what he used to drink to get wrecked.

"There should be room for that on one of the shelves inside the door," Phoenix says over the sound of water spraying from the faucet.

"Uh, yeah. I see one next to the whiskey drinks."

I put the carton on the shelf and shut the door. The water stops running.

"Nash left those here the last time he was over. I forgot they were there."

"You're okay with keeping alcohol in the house?" I turn around to look at him.

"Del, I—" He pauses, wiping his hands with a dish towel. His chest rises as he takes a breath, then falls again when he releases it. "I haven't touched whiskey or any other alcohol in over two years. I promise."

"Okay." I search his face for any sign that he isn't telling the truth. His gaze doesn't waver from me.

"We can empty those into the sink if you'd like."

"Nash might mind," I point out.

"He probably doesn't remember leaving them here. I'll give him money to buy more if he does."

"It's fine. If you can handle seeing them when you open your fridge and aren't tempted to drink one, then we don't need to pour them down the drain."

Phoenix puts the dish towel on the counter. "Are you okay with seeing them? I know how much you hate them, and why."

"Yeah, well."

"I can move them to the other fridge in the garage."

He's definitely moving the drinks, but I'm coming with him. Since we parked in the driveway after getting home from the airport and again after the helicopter ride, I haven't been in the garage and wasn't aware there's another fridge there. I would like to see what's in it.

"That's an excellent idea. I'll help you so it only takes one trip."

I take two cans out of the fridge. If he refuses my help with another excuse about not lifting a finger, then I'll know there's something he doesn't want me to see.

He nods and walks over to where I am. His hand brushes my shoulder before he reaches for the other three cans that are still on the shelf, then he shuts the door.

"Lead the way," I tell him.

He walks ahead of me out of the kitchen and to the door that leads to the garage. But when we're inside the garage, he pauses.

"Could you open the fridge?" he asks.

It's his way of saying he knows what I'm looking for, without actually voicing the words. But he doesn't sound upset, or smug, or even sad that I want to take inventory of what he has in this refrigerator.

"Sure." I step past him.

There are no yellow cans inside this fridge, or anything else that looks incriminating. Instead, it's filled with bottled water, vitamin water, and a few cans of soda. I put the cans I'm holding on a shelf, then step back to let Phoenix do the same.

There's a part of me that's compelled to apologize, but the words die in my throat before I say them. No. That's what the old me would have done. I had every reason to question what I found, especially with our history.

Phoenix puts his arm around me and touches his mouth to my hair. Then he pulls back and tilts his head to look into my eyes.

"You can look in any fridge or cupboard or drawer in this house, and I'll understand why. I want you to feel safe with me."

"I do. I just—" I stop, searching for the right words. They don't come.

"I know."

"I feel foolish for questioning it."

"Don't. We should be able to have the hard conversations."

His reassurance doesn't stop me from breaking eye contact with him, or from burying my face in his shoulder. "I think now would be a good time for me to go upstairs and shower."

"I'll show you where the towels are." He slips his hand around mine.

I let him lead me out of the garage and back into the house, where he walks with me up the stairs. Once he's shown me where the towels are in his bedroom's walk-in closet, I retreat into the bathroom and close the door. But as I take my shampoo, conditioner, and body wash out of my toiletry bag, I hear him speak.

"What was that?" I ask, then wait. He says something else, but it doesn't sound like he's talking to me. He must be on the phone.

"What's going on? Is everything still cool, or should I be worried?" There's a pause, like he's listening, and then he speaks again. "Today isn't good. My girlfriend is visiting from LA. Can we try for Tuesday, or is that too much of a risk?"

That's when I remember the text I saw earlier. He probably saw the message and called Dalton, since this sounds like a business conversation. He'd better not be jeopardizing a job by postponing something because I'm here.

I debate waiting for him to wrap things up on the phone and telling him this, or mentioning it after I shower, but then decide against it. Only he knows what's best for him and his career, and he doesn't know I saw the message or that I'm eavesdropping on his phone call. Besides, we just got through one uncomfortable conversation. The last thing I should do now is question his decisions about what he does for a living.

❧

When I finish showering, steam still curls through the air, but my thoughts are clearer than they were when I stepped in. Somewhere between rinsing my hair and drying off, an idea comes to me for my book that could help bring together the loose ends I've been struggling with. It percolates while I get dressed and after I hand the bathroom over to Phoenix, until I can't ignore it.

I need to map this out. When this happens at home, I grab sticky notes and a pen, scribble out one plot point or thought per page, then arrange them on the wall in front of my desk to look at. Sometimes I reorder them, until the flow feels right. When I'm in a bind and don't have the sticky notes and my wall, like when I'm in my car and can park somewhere for a few minutes, I grab a notepad and pen and map things out with bubbles and arrows. It's messier, but it still works.

I didn't bring sticky notes with me, and I somehow left my notebook at home, even though I meant to put it in my carry-on bag. Since Phoenix is in the shower, I can't ask him if he has either of those things here. But he knows my writing process, and he did say I could look in any drawer or cupboard. Maybe he has something I can use before the idea disappears.

The drawers of both bedside tables don't turn up anything, so I head downstairs to the kitchen and rummage through the drawers there until I open one that contains a few pens, a manila envelope, and a stack of pages that might be a script. I lift up the envelope and pages, and find a Moleskine notebook below them. If the notebook has blank pages I can tear out and use, it will do.

I pull it out from the drawer and open its teal cover. Handwriting on the first page gives me pause, because the unfamiliar looping cursive isn't Phoenix's writing. The name scrawled there confirms it isn't his notebook.

The machine-printed text at the top of the page reads "*In case of loss, please return to:*" The name written on the line below that is *Elenna Paseo*. Len.

I flip through a few pages, each one covered from top to bottom in the same handwriting. Every page in this notebook is full. Then I notice dates at the top of some of the pages. This looks like a journal.

Curious, I skim the text on the page in front of me. My eyes land on a paragraph that has Phoenix's name.

> *I drove Phoenix to LAX today. He resisted when I offered, saying the round trip from Laguna was out of my way and that he could call a car service. I wouldn't let him. Maybe it's because I needed to see him walk inside the airport terminal myself. His last crash out was bad. He texted me later, claiming he boarded the plane. I have to trust he did. I couldn't walk him past security to make sure he didn't get wasted in the lounge or at one of the terminal bars. His text sounded sober,*

*but who knows?*

*Everyone tells me I have to stop worrying about him and that there's only so much I can do. That I should give up trying and stop being there for him if he refuses to help himself. But I keep thinking of his phone call from the hospital, collecting him there, and the way he looked. How empty and defeated he seemed, like he'd lost a piece of his soul. It still haunts me.*

"Del?" Phoenix's voice carries down the stairs.

I shut the notebook and shove it back in the drawer like it's burning my fingertips. I don't know why, but I feel like I just saw something I wasn't meant to. Why does he have Len's journal? And why is it here with him in Las Vegas?

"I'm down here," I call back. "I was about to look for paper or sticky notes I could use for a book idea I had. Do you have something I can use?"

There's the sound of his footsteps on the stairs, then Phoenix walks into the kitchen with damp hair and his cheeks still flushed from the shower. "I think so. Hang on."

He opens the drawer next to the one I found Len's journal in and pulls out a slim notepad and pen. "Will these work?"

"Perfect," I say, forcing a smile.

"Use whatever you need."

"Thanks."

I retreat to the table with the notepad, but my focus is gone. The ideas that felt urgent a few minutes ago scatter like paper in the wind. It doesn't help that Phoenix is here, tapping at his phone. Does he sense something is off, or suspect I was already rummaging through drawers and found Len's journal?

I could mention it, but we just got through an awkward and serious moment with the alcohol in the fridge. Asking about the journal now doesn't feel right. Instead, I flip the notepad open and stare at the blank page, trying to summon my idea back. It doesn't come, so I jot down random points from other parts of my book, in case Phoenix is watching me.

He's quiet, and it's probably to let me write and think, but the silence puts me more on edge. I have to say something to break it. Then I remember Ava's text from earlier today. He'd probably like knowing Nash won't be getting romantic with her after last night's disaster, if he doesn't know already.

"I forgot to tell you earlier. Ava said she won't be seeing Nash again while she's here. He left town today for a studio session."

"He did?" Phoenix sounds surprised.

"You haven't heard from him today?"

He shakes his head. "No. What makes you ask?"

"I thought you might have if he also heard about the update in Len's case. He told me last night that he's still desperate for answers about what happened. He must be beside himself if he's heard the news."

There's a pause as Phoenix considers my words, and I swear

there's another shift in his energy. I want to kick myself. Bringing Len up again so soon after the news we heard probably wasn't my best idea. I'm about to backpedal out of the topic, but he beats me to speaking.

"He talked to you about Len? I missed that."

"It was when you were getting the third degree from Torin. He also overheard what Ava told Torin about my book and asked if it was based on Len's disappearance, and if I had any theories about what happened. He said to get in touch if I feel like bouncing ideas off him, or if I have questions about Len."

Silence greets my words. There's a crease along Phoenix's forehead now, and his mouth parts, almost as though his jaw muscles have gone slack.

"You look stunned," I say.

"I'm shocked he brought her up. He almost never talks about her." Phoenix rubs the back of his neck, his eyes fixed somewhere over my shoulder. But then he looks at me. "What Nash said goes for me too. You can bounce ideas off me or ask me questions about Len. I'll support your book in any way I can."

I smile faintly, grateful for the shift away from everything that still feels raw. "Careful," I joke. "You're starting to sound like my biggest cheerleader."

His eyes brighten a little. "Starting to? I guess I need to level up my game. Would pom-poms or a megaphone help?"

I laugh, shaking my head. "You're doing fine."

The light in his eyes holds steady as he crosses the room and joins me at the table, brushing his thumb over my hand as he sits down. "If it doesn't interrupt your writing time, how do you feel about a sunset and moonlight kayak tour through the Black Canyon and Emerald Cave tonight?"

His question takes me by surprise, but in the best way. After everything this afternoon brought, the idea of gliding across water under the fading sun and a sky full of stars feels like exactly what we need.

"It sounds perfect," I tell him. And it does.

# Chapter Twenty-Two

A*RE YOU STILL IN town or are you back in LA?*

My gut feeling is to ignore the text from Torin that my car's voice assistant reads as I steer onto Hollywood Way, leaving the Burbank airport in the distance. The blue Prius I spot in my rearview mirror seconds this instinct since its license plate ends in *111*, the angel number for trusting your intuition and listening to your heart. Monday morning has been challenging enough after getting on a plane, departing Las Vegas, and landing back in my LA life, and it isn't because of the physical distance that's once more between Phoenix and me.

Saturday evening was a peaceful escape from how our weekend began. My thoughts of Len's journal and how Phoenix felt about the break in her case were cast aside the moment we pushed away from the shore in our kayak. Nothing could have been more romantic than paddling together as we watched the sunset. Later, we sat hand-in-hand by a crackling bonfire under the moon and stars. Then there was the sweet simplicity of yesterday, waking up to rumbling thunder while sheets of rain fell from the sky. We stayed curled up under a blanket indoors, watched movies, ordered takeout, and simply existed. I should be "all glowy" as Ava once observed, yet the rose-tinged hue of most of the weekend has already faded.

It could be the text from Ava that popped up on my phone the moment I turned airplane mode off after landing. It was a link to a short video of Phoenix and me at The Auriga on Friday night that someone posted on social media. My guess would be the girl who took our photo that night, who appeared to recognize Phoenix. Ava sifts through a lot of entertainment news for her job, which explains why she found it. But my mom often scrolls TikTok and Instagram and stumbles across posts about my books. It's only a matter of time before she sees the video. I haven't figured out how to explain the events of the last few weeks to my family yet. Torin and Ava's concerns about Phoenix returning to my life have been enough to deal with.

Fatigue could be a culprit too. Lord knows I didn't sleep much this weekend, which is another reason I should put off answering Torin. I'm not physically or emotionally equipped to rehash Friday or to get into another disagreement with him about Phoenix while I'm running on fumes.

But Torin has been my friend and protector since well before I knew Phoenix. He's always had my back, and he and Ava took care of me when I was at my lowest point. The thought of leaving things with friction between us winds my insides into knots. For this reason, I dictate a reply to his message.

*I'm driving home from the airport. It was good to see you this weekend.*

My phone immediately rings. I just told Torin I'm driving, so he knows I'm in my car and not somewhere I can't talk to him. There's no reason for me to ignore his call.

"Hey."

"Hi. I'm happy you're home safe."

There are a couple of ways I could take that, whether it's that my flight landed safely, or that I'm home and "safely" away from Phoenix. I opt for the former and don't question it, mostly because I'd like to restore the peace between us.

"It was a little windy leaving Vegas, but when isn't it? I hope Ava's flight is smoother."

I actually don't know if Ava flew to Vegas or drove, or when she's coming home, but it gives me something to say that seems relatively safe. Keeping this a surface-level conversation and not diving into our conflicting points of view about my love life might smooth things over for now.

"I'm sorry to hear about the flight, but I'm relieved you're home and far away from whatever mind manipulation Phoenix has done on you."

So much for the hoped-for truce. "Excuse me?"

"We should talk, Del. Like, really talk."

"It sounds like some talking already happened. Did you really say you'd take out Phoenix's kneecaps with your drumsticks?"

I expect him to say this was overembellished or only a joke. But Torin chuckles, almost as if he's proud of saying this and that I know about it.

"One wrong move, and he'll be a lucky man if I stop there. He should already consider himself blessed since I haven't shown up at his door today to have a word."

"You will not do that." I use my most firm, mess-around-and-find-out tone, but it's met with another faint chuckle.

"We'll see."

*Deep breaths.* Losing my patience isn't worth it, but damn. It's difficult to be the bigger person.

"I know you can't stand him, and that's fair. But I need you to trust me and my choices, and to respect that I'm capable of making decisions for myself."

"My trust in you isn't the issue."

"Other than things from the fairly distant past, has Phoenix given you any reason not to trust him recently?"

"I could start with what he's doing in Vegas. Has he told you how long he's allegedly been working here for?"

Allegedly? The urge to roll my eyes is fierce. "I haven't asked him."

"Maybe you should."

"Or you could tell me, since it sounds like you know."

"He's been here for the last eight months. Doesn't that seem like a long time to be filming something on location?"

My only points of reference are the films he worked on the last time we dated, but every production has its own schedule and set of circumstances. I don't even know if what he's working on in Vegas is a film, because he hasn't said much about it. A multi-episode series for a cable network or streaming service would take longer to shoot. Without facts or context from Phoenix himself, I'm not ready to jump to conclusions or to feed into whatever Torin is accusing him of.

"Have you asked him about it?" I counter.

"Once. He said something vague about starts and stops and production delays."

"And?"

There's a pause, then a loud exhale. "Just hear me out. For someone who claims he's here to work, his schedule is open enough that he's with Nash on weekday mornings and afternoons a lot. You don't think that's suspicious?"

I don't. Phoenix had some odd late-night hours on other productions, especially when scenes called for filming outdoors at night. But pointing this out won't do much when Torin is determined to see anything he does as shady.

"What is it you suspect?" I ask instead.

"I don't know," he admits. "I haven't put my finger on it, but something doesn't add up. Even Nash has said his job seems to barely require him to be on set. I want you to be careful."

"I always am." The cheer in my voice is forced, and I'm sure he hears it. "I'll even ask him about it if having an answer will help you sleep at night."

"I'd sleep better if you cut him off and never gave him the power to hurt you again."

"You've made that clear. Can we move on to something else?"

Torin is silent. I mirror him while slowing my car to a stop at a red light, but then run out of willpower.

"Your heart is in the right place, and I love you for it, but I'm not in this with blinders on. Now, can we talk about why Ava and Nash are all flirty? She hasn't told me what led up to it."

"Nash hasn't told me, either. I was as surprised as you are."

"You aren't concerned?" I ask, thinking of Phoenix's reservations about Nash.

"Nah, Ava can hold her own. I'd be more worried about what she'll plot to destroy Nash's ego if he does something she doesn't like."

"That's valid. I hope he knows what he's getting into."

Our conversation loses its tension after that. Torin mentions a show his band has in Huntington Beach on Saturday, and I promise to make it out with Ava in tow. Neither of us brings up Phoenix again, but my thoughts still return to him and our weekend once I'm home.

What is it still nagging at me, and why? It could be the journal, but it feels like something else. I search my brain, but only the most benign items rise to the surface. I sift through them anyway.

Is it because Phoenix ignored what sounded like a slew of text messages this morning while he drove me to the airport? His phone chimed a bunch of times, but he must have turned message announcements off because there were no notifications on the console of his SUV. The last time I saw any notification light up the console screen was Friday night.

But no, being bothered about that would be silly. He was giving me his full attention at the time, and I was a few minutes away from leaving. In his place, I also wouldn't spend that time checking messages. It doesn't explain why nothing came up on the console, but who knows? Maybe a setting changed, or he didn't want the interruption while we were together.

I squeeze my eyes shut and think again, but nothing else stands out. This still doesn't put me at ease.

# Chapter Twenty-Three

"What's on your mind, chica?" Ava asks.

Her voice is surprisingly serious and quiet. I almost miss her question over the din of the restaurant patio at Granville and the motorcycle brigade roaring along Beverly Boulevard.

"Hmmm?" I stop stirring the ice cubes in my lemonade with what's fast becoming a soggy paper straw and glance across the table, but I avoid meeting her gaze. "Why do you think I have something on my mind?"

She inches her sunglasses down her nose and narrows her eyes. "Because I know you. For a woman who's in the honeymoon phase of a relationship, you sure seem preoccupied about something. Based on your face and your annoyed sighs, it isn't lust and butterflies."

She isn't wrong, and she knows me inside out. Dodging the question is futile, but I try anyway.

"Book stuff."

"Lies." She tosses a fry at me. It lands on my arm and leaves dots of oil and salt on my skin when it slides down to the table. "Are you having second thoughts about Phoenix now that you've done the deed again and it's out of your system?"

"How do you know we—"

"Please. You stayed with him all of last weekend, and I'd have questions if you hadn't. This isn't your first rodeo together, even if he still gives me clown bullfighter vibes. Respectfully."

I had a feeling the ceasefire last weekend was too good to last. "You seemed okay with him in Vegas?"

"I was siding with your sex life in Vegas, not with him. I was also more focused on where I thought my night was going with Nash. So?"

"What?"

She holds up another fry. I pull my arm off the table and shrink back in my chair, but she doesn't send this one sailing in my direction. "Was the sex a letdown after building it up in your imagination?"

"Not at all."

It's the truth, but Ava harping on this doesn't help my mood or my mental state. I already wish I could physically return to Friday night after the helicopter ride and stay in those hours forever.

"Then what are you stewing over?"

"Respectfully," I begin, enunciating each syllable of the word so she can't miss the undertone, "what makes you think I'm stewing?"

"Your crankiness, your energy, and your aura." Her own undertone is smug and matter-of-fact.

"You read auras now? Do your clients know, or is it a new service you're testing out on me?"

She glances up at the sky and makes a show of appearing put out. "Don't change the subject, and don't get all sarcastic with me. That's my thing."

"I learned from the best."

Ava gives me a disbelieving look and pushes her sunglasses back up her nose. "Can you make it through the day without killing someone, or do I need to put you on a plane back to Vegas for more vitamin D?"

"You did not just say that."

"Oh, but I did. Have you listened to yourself today?"

She sits back in her chair, both of her eyebrows arched. Guilt floods through me almost instantly, because yes, I'm cranky, and she's bearing the brunt of it. She shouldn't have to. This time when I speak, I do my best to lighten my tone.

"I'm not getting on a plane to go anywhere. We have Torin and Nash's show in Huntington Beach tomorrow, remember? And then you're going to have the night you should have had last weekend."

"Don't get ahead of yourself. There are no after-show plans yet." Ava's mouth turns up at the corners, though, which means the same thought has crossed her mind. Maybe I can distract her with this and segue into something less triggering to me.

"Let's drive there separately, just in case," I suggest. "You never know where the night will take you, although it better be back to your place with Nash in tow if those guys aren't staying somewhere decent."

"We weren't already driving separately? I thought you'd be in Laguna with Phoenix and arriving with him."

I say a silent goodbye to my plans for diverting her attention and switching topics. It was nice for the minute it lasted.

"He can't make it here this weekend, but it's probably better for keeping things civil with Torin."

"Finally. That, right there, is what you're so bothered about." She straightens in her chair, which is a sign I'm in trouble. It's time to deflect.

"I'm bothered because I've written exactly five usable pages since getting back on Monday, and I have deadlines. Calling myself a novelist is laughable at this point."

"Uh-huh. You aren't writing because your mind is occupied by Phoenix. Did he say what he's doing instead, or is he chickening out about facing Torin again?"

"He isn't chickening out. He has to work."

"And you decided not to go there to see him when he's off for the night?"

Ava is in interrogation mode. This needs immediate interception before it gets out of hand.

"I told Torin I would come to his show, and I'm looking forward to it. I'm not going to bail on my friends." There. She can't argue with loyalty and not canceling my plans.

It turns out she can, because she's already spotted the loophole. "You could go to the show on Saturday and drive to Vegas after. There's no traffic at that time of night. Or Phoenix could fly you there Sunday morning and you could stay for a few days and write while he works. He hasn't offered to do that?"

"It would involve talking to him and arranging it, so no."

I didn't mean for that to slip out, but Ava has a knack for getting me to divulge things I don't intend to. If she ever wants to exit public relations, I'm certain she could land a job with the FBI or CIA, or start a career as a private investigator. Torin and I have told her this plenty of times.

The lack of communication between Phoenix and me is out there for her to mull over and voice her opinion on now, so maybe she'll talk sense into me and insist I'm making something out of nothing. His texts and calls likely tapered off this week because he's working long hours. It's temporary.

Ava purses her lips and studies me for what feels like an eternity. Then she calmly picks up her iced tea, takes a sip, and returns the glass to the table.

"If you're telling me he pumped and dumped, then I may be the one going to Vegas on Sunday and showing up at his door. Have you heard from him since getting home?"

"I have. I'm probably overthinking and reading into something that isn't there."

"Let me be the judge of that. When did you last hear from him?"

"Monday morning. I texted that I'd landed in Burbank, and he replied."

A muscle twitches in Ava's jaw. "Monday. That was days ago."

"He said he'd be pulling long hours this week and weekend. I hoped all that work would mean he'd have a clearer picture of when everything will wrap up so he can be back here full-time."

"Did he send the last message or did you?"

"I did. I sent a text on Tuesday to ask if I left a necklace at his place. He didn't answer, so I sent another message yesterday to check on him."

"Have you tried calling him?"

"Yes," I admit. "I tried before I left my place to come here. It went straight to voicemail."

"May I try calling him?" Although Ava sounds relaxed and phrases this as a question, we're both aware it's a thinly veiled threat.

"Absolutely not. Forget I mentioned it."

"It's too late for that."

"I'm sure he's busy. You know how filming goes, and it's only been a few days. Besides, I need to concentrate on finishing the draft of my book. He's aware of my deadlines, so he could be letting me focus."

The side-eye coming from across the table stops me from saying anything else.

"I agree you need to focus on writing, but you will not make excuses for him. It takes two seconds to check in by text, especially when you've just reached that level of intimacy for the first time since you last dated. He should know better. I also have a crazy schedule this week, and a client with the emotional maturity of a twelve-year-old causing chaos all over social media and starting online wars with diss tracks, but I'm having lunch with you right now."

"Thank you for having lunch today. I love and appreciate you for making time for me."

I do love and appreciate her, but telling her this is also an attempt to defuse what I've started. She's visibly riled up on my behalf, which means there's a chance she'll call or text Phoenix and let him have it anyway. If she knew all the reasons for my mood and why I think he hasn't been entirely forthcoming about other things, she'd be livid with him and disappointed in me for not loving myself enough to walk away now.

Phoenix falling off the map this week brought me back to my birthday, when I raised the idea of going to Vegas to see him. While he agreed in the end, he was resistant at first. Now I wonder if there was more to it than what he claimed about not wanting me to have to travel to see him. Are there other reasons he didn't want me to pop up there, and do they have anything to do with why he's so quiet now?

I haven't told Ava about this yet, or about how Phoenix mentally checked out for parts of last weekend after the news about Len, or about the whiskey sours in the fridge and the journal I found. She would only point out what I'm painfully aware of, since I haven't stopped dwelling on those things and his communication break. As much as I've been the avoidant one with other men I've tried to date over the years, I'm creeping back into old patterns.

I was anxiously attached by the time our relationship blew up the first time. My therapist suggested Phoenix's hot-and-cold behavior had a lot to do with it. He showed nothing but adoration for me on his sober days, but descended into drama, misery, and occasional silence when he drank. I never knew which version of him to expect by the end. My therapist said I held on because of dopamine spikes when he showered me with affection. She explained it as a psychological addiction from intermittent reinforcement, even if Phoenix didn't do it intentionally.

Echoes of that anxiety have returned this week. It's troubling, but my eyes are open to it this time. That should count for something. Or am I lying to myself again because of how Phoenix behaved at the start and my craving to return to that sugary high?

"Promise me you'll walk away if he breadcrumbs you now that he's physically gratified. It would be one thing if he'd presented it as a hookup situation only. He doesn't get to lead you on after nearly destroying you once before. Not with me as your best friend."

Ava isn't a fool. She's already clocked this without knowing the rest of it.

"I know, but it's complicated. I'm worried about him."

She raises an eyebrow. The sun catches on her sunglasses, and she tilts her chin to block the glare. "You're worried about someone who might have ghosted you?"

"I found alcohol in his fridge—the infamous whiskey sour drinks. He claimed Nash left them there."

Ava stills, her fingers tightening around her glass before she sets it back down. "So you think he's still drinking and went on a bender after you left?" She leans back and folds her arms over her chest.

"I don't know. I want to believe he told me the truth and that he really is sober." I twist the napkin in my lap, winding the fabric between my fingers. "But if he has been drinking this week, I remember what he was like. When I think about that, and his reaction to news we heard about a break in Len's case, it's hard to say what his frame of mind would be. Now he's not answering calls or texts. What am I supposed to think?"

"Maybe you dodged a bullet and it's a blessing."

"I should have stayed longer and made sure he was fine, even if he had to work."

"Del." She leans forward again, her forearms braced against the table. "I love you, but you aren't his mother. He's a grown man with a fully developed frontal lobe. If he wasn't fine, and if he felt like he needed someone there, he should have told you."

"It's more than that. I also found Len's journal in a drawer."

"Why would he have—" Ava stops. "No, I'm not even going there. This is already a mess you don't need. You need to look out for yourself, not him."

My phone vibrates as I start to answer, rattling against the table.

I glance down and see a message from Phoenix. Talk about timing.

*I'm so sorry for not answering you before today. The reception is bad where I am and I didn't see your texts until now. Your necklace is at my place. I'll bring it to you when I see you, which will be the second I'm done here. Love you and miss you.*

Ava probably can't see my screen from where she is, but I feel her eyes boring holes into my head as I read the message twice. She coughs when I keep my head angled down and don't say anything.

"Let me guess. He finally broke his silence and you're reading a text from him?" She doesn't sound impressed, but I don't expect her to be.

"Yup."

"And?" she prompts. "Did he say why he disappeared?"

"He has spotty reception where he's been and didn't see my texts."

Ava's scowl tells me she doesn't buy it. "Is he working from the moon?"

"Nevada is the desert," I remind her. "He could have been somewhere far outside of Vegas, which might as well be the moon. I'll give him grace this time."

Ava almost never loses her cool, but I've seen her come close a few times. This is one of them. She plucks her napkin from her lap and crumples it into a ball, then tosses it on her plate and eyeballs me. "You've given him more grace in his lifetime than ten people deserve."

"That's fair. He knows it, though."

It's her turn to sigh. "Does he?"

Her question hangs in the air while I spear a tomato from my salad and focus on chewing. I don't have a good answer.

"Actions over words, Del. You know this. Promise me he gets one chance this time and that's it, because it's one too many extra chances with the history you two have. Believe someone when they show you who they are. This isn't his first or even second strike, and I can't watch you become a ghost of yourself again."

She removes her sunglasses to pinch the bridge of her nose. One glimpse at her eyes haunts me. As much as I went through after the first time with Phoenix, it wasn't only me. Ava did too, as she stuck by my side and pulled me back from the precipice I teetered on for months. While she may have encouraged me to see him again for one weekend to tie up loose ends, she didn't sign up for another round of me diving right in and it ending in more heartbreak.

"I promise this is his only shot. Pinky swear. I won't put you or me through that again."

I hold out my pinky finger. Ava remains stone-faced while she hooks her finger with mine, but then she smiles and chucks another fry at me.

"Lord help him if he botches this, even if it's self-sabotage, because he doesn't know what he's up against when I'm not holding back for your sake. He'll relocate to Siberia before he sets foot in Southern California again."

I have no reason to believe she's exaggerating.

# Chapter Twenty-Four

After Ava and I part ways on the sidewalk outside Granville, I spot a blue Prius parked a few cars down from mine. It's the same one I noticed driving behind me when I left the airport on Monday. The plate and its repeating numbers catch my eye again, and for a second I just stand there, taking in the coincidence.

That small jolt of recognition is enough to pull me out of the loop of thoughts about Phoenix and back into real life and what I have planned for the rest of today. I unlock my car and get inside, already thinking about the pages waiting for me at home.

A few songs from my latest writing playlist fill the short dri-ve, helping me shift into work mode. I'm determined to make progress on the book and keep my focus where it belongs. Reply-ing to Phoenix's message can wait until later. Another conversa-tion with him will only pull me off track.

By the time I get home, I'm in the right mindset again. My

laptop goes on, the playlist keeps running, and the words start to come. Since I don't have Ava to confiscate my phone from me when I'm at home, stuffing it under a sofa cushion becomes the magic formula for keeping it out of sight. Hiding it works. Thoughts about Phoenix's vanishing act and his message are demoted to the outer fringes of my mind until much later that night, after I've retrieved my phone and brought it with me to bed. It's almost as if its movement sends out a signal, because that's when it rings and the screen lights up with Phoenix's name.

Seeing his call is a crash landing back into reality after a few productive hours of writing and thinking about characters and plot. Do I answer, or do I let it go to voicemail and talk to him tomorrow? Ava would probably tell me to ignore my phone for now. It's late, and I've exhausted my brain for the day. But do I want this on my mind all night? I know myself, and I'll lie awake having imaginary conversations with him.

I grit my teeth and tap the screen. "Hey."

Loud static answers me. That's my first clue he's driving. His voice cuts in and out when he says hello and asks how my week has been.

"Your connection isn't great," I say, even though he'll have an equally hard time hearing me.

"Give—" He fades out again for a beat, then comes back. "...m inute."

Road sounds and crackles break the silence. I should tell him to call back once he has better service. But it's almost eleven o'clock, and I'm cozily enveloped in my duvet. I was about to start reading a book I agreed to blurb, so my quote about it can be included on the back cover when it's released next year. If we hang up now and I begin reading, it's only a matter of time before the paragraphs on the pages swim in front of me, my eyes close, and I fall asleep. My phone's ringtone would wake me up, but it's better if I'm fully alert for this conversation. I need to be.

The static subsides after another minute. Phoenix's voice is clear when he speaks this time. "I thought I was out of the dead zone when I called. I should have waited another few minutes."

"Things sound good now. Where are you?"

"On my way home for the night." It isn't his actual location, but he keeps talking before I can ask how far away he is. "How much trouble am I in?"

"Trouble? What do you mean?"

My teasing tone isn't completely sincere, but it hides the doubt I've wrestled with all week. Not that I'm trying to spare him. This is about staying in control and doing what Ava suggested. I want to watch his actions instead of only listening to his words. Diving into my feelings will distract from that.

"I didn't mean to leave you on delivered," Phoenix says. "I really didn't see your text until I went to send you one today."

Without having him on video or seeing him in person, there's no way to read his face or body language for signs of him bending the truth. All I have is his voice and the trace of worry in it. A past version of me would have heard his tone and let the subject drop.

Not this time.

"Do you think I'd be quiet for that long and not check in?" I ask.

"I thought you were deep into writing. I know you have deadlines. Still, I wish I'd tried to check in with you sooner or double-checked to make sure I hadn't missed a message. Things have been a little crazy."

That's what I told Ava. She thought I was making excuses for him, and maybe I was. But it could also be an excuse he made up on the spot. We just slept together for the first time in years, and he had to know what his silence could make me think. He also knew I was concerned about him after the news about Len's case. He should have at least tried to communicate with me before today, but he didn't attempt to send a message or check if I had tried to reach him. We both had other things going on, but typing out a quick hello is a less than thirty-second effort.

A darker thought also seizes control of my brain and won't let go. *A few days of silence is much less time than he's proven he's capable of. Remember how easily he left without a word before, and how he disappeared and stayed away for years.* Blind trust in him this time is hard.

"I'm sure you'll find a way to make it up to me." There's an edge to my voice. This is a challenge, not me teasing him. He controls his own fate by what he does next.

"I wish I was there with you right now and spending the weekend making it up to you, but I'm coming to see you as soon as I'm done here."

"When will that be?" Either the signal cuts out and he misses my question, or he ignores it.

"What are you up to this weekend?"

Repeating my question is an option, but what he asked is an opening to tell him something he may not like. It's actually perfect.

"Ava and I are seeing Torin and Nash. Their band has a show in Huntington Beach tomorrow night."

"They do?"

"You sound surprised." He also sounds less than thrilled, as I suspected he might.

"Nash didn't mention it to me. I'm sure it will be a good time."

It sounds like an attempt at enthusiasm, but I barely hear him. *Nash didn't mention it.* The words echo. Nash went out of town on Sunday, or he told Ava he did. Phoenix said he was working all week in a place with horrible reception. When would they have talked that Nash could have mentioned the show?

"Where are they playing?" Phoenix asks.

"The Ocean Floor, near Pacific City."

"Do you and Ava want to stay at my house? It's closer than driving back to LA after the show. I can text you the lock code."

"Ava might have plans with Nash." He's silent, so I continue. "Have you mentioned your concerns to him about starting something with her? It sounds like you talked to him recently."

He's quiet for a beat too long, which confirms he didn't miss the subtext of what I said and how it throws his claim of poor service into question.

"I talked to him on Monday. It was before I texted you."

Nice save, if it's true. Nash told Ava he was in the studio on Monday. Considering Phoenix was with me from the time we woke up until we parted ways at the airport, he's limited himself to a small window of time.

"You talked to him before my flight landed?" I ask. "Wasn't he in the studio, or did Ava misunderstand his text?"

"It was right before he went in, while you were in flight." When I don't reply, he pivots. "How has writing been going?"

I could ignore his question and keep pushing, but I'll see Nash tomorrow night and can get the general time of their conversation from him. If I can't think of an offhanded way to bring it up by then, I'm certain Ava can.

"Writing was slow earlier in the week, but I made up for it today. I think I'm through what I was stuck on. How is everything you've been working on?"

"It's getting there. I'm looking forward to closing this chapter and moving on."

In the weeks we've been seeing each other again, Phoenix hasn't disclosed a single thing about the project he's working on, other than it taking longer than expected and not having a firm date for when it will end. I didn't think much of it before, but Torin's words from Monday come to mind now. Phoenix used to tell me every detail about his days on set.

"How long have you been working on this?"

"It feels like forever at this point." Another non-answer.

"Torin said you've been in Vegas for eight months."

There's a pause before he speaks. "I didn't realize he'd been counting, but yes. As I said, it feels like forever. I'd like to be home and with you."

"That's a long time. You were never on location for more than a few weeks at a time that I remember."

"I hope nothing ever takes me away for this long again, especially now."

A new wave of static crackles through the phone speaker. After asking if I can still hear him, Phoenix says something about a restaurant in Laguna Beach he'd like to take me to when he's home again. He describes it for me, and I make brief comments in the appropriate places, but my heart isn't in it tonight.

I could be overthinking, but this feels a lot like last weekend when I told him Nash talked to me about Len, after the announcement about developments in Len's case. Is Phoenix still speculating about what we heard that day, and could that be why he doesn't sound like himself?

I test my hunch. "I've been checking the news but haven't seen anything else about Len. Have you?"

"No. There hasn't been anything." His voice is strained. Have I hit a nerve?

"Are you doing okay?"

"I'm—wow. Hang on a second."

His end of the call sounds like a million marbles scattering across the floor. Then there's a loud boom.

"Nix?"

"The sky just opened up. The rain and thunder and lightning are wild."

"How far do you still have to drive?"

He says something, but his voice cuts out. My phone beeps three times, and then there's nothing. Our call dropped.

Maybe that's my sign to let things be for the night. Our conversation was more of an effort than it should have been, and I can't shake the feeling that he's still holding something back. I should sleep on it and decide how I feel in the morning.

I start a new text to him. *I'm zonked, so I'm going to bed now. Focus on driving and making it home safely. Let me know when you get there, and let's talk again tomorrow or Sunday. Love you.*

After sending the message, I set my phone to silent and place it on the table next to my bed. If he answers me, it can wait.

# Chapter Twenty-Five

It feels like déjà vu when the Ocean Floor doorman checks my name off a list. He hands me a wristband and sends me inside the bar, where the thumping drumbeat and thrashing guitars of the opening band have already taken over. Until a few weeks ago, I hadn't seen one of Torin's shows in practically an eon. Now, hanging out at his gigs seems like a regular occurrence, like it was in our college days.

Ava's text that she's already here landed on my phone a few minutes ago. It doesn't take long to spot her in the darkened room, chatting with Torin near the bar. Nash is here too. He sits on a barstool, off by himself, with his eyes glued to his phone.

The atmosphere of the Ocean Floor is entirely different from Nebula. It's beachy and aquatic-themed, features a floor-to-ceiling water wall, and has a distinctly laid-back vibe. The contrast between Nebula and here reminds me that tonight should be less of an ordeal than the last two times I've been in a room with Torin and his band, but my shoulders tense up when I get close to the bar.

"She's alone!" Ava announces to Torin with a wink. She's loud enough for me to hear her over the music.

Torin hugs me, then he makes a show of looking to my left, looking to my right, and then looking behind me.

"What are you trying to see?" I ask.

"Not what, but who, and I'm glad I don't. Did you come to your senses and ditch him?"

So it's going to be like this tonight. I wiggle out of Torin's arms. "Comedians, both of you. Phoenix had to work this weekend, which Ava already knew."

"What a shame," he quips. "At least he's finally working, or so he says. Has he explained what he's been doing in Vegas the rest of the time?"

Ava squints at him, and then at me. Her entire face is a question mark. Wonderful. This is not the time to get into Torin's suspicions about how long Phoenix has been in Las Vegas for and if he's really working there. She's wary enough after him disappearing for a few days and claiming reception issues.

"He isn't here, so why is he still living rent-free in your head?" I give Torin a tight smile.

"Dude, Del came here to have a good time and not for you to hassle her. Save your energy for the stage." I recognize Nash's voice before I turn around and see that he's vacated his barstool. He's now next to Ava, his arm around her waist.

How Nash turned out to be the peacemaker in all of this is a puzzle, but I'm grateful for his words and am more convinced than ever that Phoenix has no reason to be concerned about anything romantic developing between him and Ava. He's so far the only voice of reason in this group.

"Thank you," I tell him. "I came for the fun and not to be ambushed."

Torin squeezes my shoulder. "You know I adore you. What kind of friend would I be if I wasn't watching out for you?"

As nice as it would be to not always feel like I'm on the defensive about my personal life, I can't argue. Torin has always been on my side, even if it sometimes seems like tough love. Like Ava, he doesn't want me to get burned again, but I wish both of them would stop acting like they expect it to happen.

"Jacob is giving us the bat signal," Nash tells Torin. He nods his head at a far corner of the room. "We should see what's up before we go on."

He presses his mouth to the side of Ava's hair and smiles at her before heading off across the bar. Torin follows him. That leaves me with Ava and a bar that's suddenly much quieter. The opening band must have finished their set.

"I'm sorry if you feel attacked," she says. "We did come on a little strong."

"It's nothing I haven't helped to bring on by being open about dating Phoenix again, or by complaining to you when I didn't hear from him."

"Are you still ignoring his text, or have you spoken to him since?"

"He called me last night."

Ava watches me like she's waiting for more, but it's better if we let the subject rest. My mind needs the break, and not every chat we have needs to dissect his behavior or turn into a therapy session.

"What did Torin mean when he asked if you knew—" she starts to ask, but then stops. Her lips remain parted.

"What's wrong?"

She doesn't answer. I'm about to turn around to see what she's gaping at, but the brush of someone's hand against my arm stops me.

"Mind if I join you?"

It's Phoenix's voice. Now I do turn around. He gazes at me with an affectionate twinkle in his eyes.

"You aren't working." Do I look as astonished as I sound?

His smile brightens by a few megawatts. "I was, but we ended early today. I grabbed the next flight here after we finished."

"You don't need to work tomorrow?"

"I'm a free man until Monday."

He takes my hand in his and leans in for a kiss. The room spins around me when his lips touch mine, as though I'm trying to balance on a beach-themed Tilt-A-Whirl until the shock of him being here melts away. Then something magical happens. My mouth parts under his, and instinct takes over, and the energy between us that seemed so off this week is suddenly like sunshine. But when our kiss ends, a glimpse of Ava glowering at Phoenix dims it again. She arches an eyebrow and fixes me with a stern look.

Right. Whatever brain chemicals he just triggered don't change his vague answers from last night, or the niggling sense I've had that he's keeping something from me. Logic and clarity still have a place here, even if him showing up and surprising me has my heart waging a war with my head. So what are the facts?

First, he's here. He got on a plane and came to me when he finished working today. That's the definition of him showing his commitment with an action, isn't it? Ava probably can't disagree with that, but Torin might. There's still the question about exactly what kind of work Phoenix has been doing in Vegas for the last eight months, if he's working there at all, where he was for a few days this week with supposedly poor cellular service, and why his hours are all over the place enough that Torin has seen him with Nash a lot during daytime hours. Definitive answers and solid alibis are needed.

Second, his signal truly was bad during the start of our phone conversation last night, and our call ended because it dropped. It would be hard for him to fake that, unless he intentionally drove somewhere with poor service. Which, if he was trying to cover his tracks, he could have. Phoenix pays attention to detail, so I can't rule this out.

Third, there's something he still isn't telling me about Len. That much is clear. As his girlfriend, I deserve to know why.

Motion on the stage pauses my thoughts. My gaze shifts in that direction, and I catch Torin glaring at Phoenix from behind his drum kit. He sends a bewildered look my way, which is understandable. I just told him that Phoenix had to work this weekend, and now here he is at the show, with his arm around me. Something tells me I should plan for a quick exit tonight to avoid another clash between the two of them.

The band is four songs into their set when it strikes me that Ava has remained quiet this whole time. She hasn't said a word to Phoenix since he got here, and her silence and failure to greet him with her signature sarcasm is out of character. I sneak a glance at her and catch her doing the same with me. We lock eyes until she vacates her spot a few feet away and walks over to us.

"Come to the restroom with me?" she asks, still not acknowledging Phoenix.

Ava is never reserved about letting him hear what she thinks of him or something he's done. Her wanting to take me somewhere else and speak in private sets off alarm bells.

"Sure." I touch Phoenix's arm. "I'll be right back."

Ava grabs my elbow and almost hauls me to the other side of the bar and down a corridor. Once we're inside the women's restroom, she spins around to face me.

"He didn't tell you he was coming, did he?" It sounds more like an accusation than a question.

"I had no idea he'd be here. He said things wrapped up early, so he grabbed the next flight out."

"How did he know to come to the Ocean Floor? Did you tell

him about the show and that you'd be here, or did Nash?"

"I mentioned our plans to him last night when he called."

"That's what I figured." Ava raises a hand to her temple and rubs it.

"What's wrong? Isn't this him showing me how he feels with an action? Getting on a plane and surprising me is sweet."

"Sure, if possessive and territorial men are your thing," she mutters.

"I'm not following. I thought you'd be relieved to see he hasn't pumped and dumped, as you put it yesterday."

"It's giving energy of him not wanting Torin to get in your ear in his absence. Or that he's aware he messed up by ghosting you for a few days and knows you can pull someone ten times better than him in a second when you're out at a bar and don't have him hovering at your side."

The first thing she said elicits a memory from last weekend. I offered to talk to Torin on my own, but Phoenix wanted us to face him together. Could that have been the real reason behind why he was so willing to jeopardize the peace of our night out? Was he worried that Torin would say something to change my mind about dating him again if he wasn't there to run interference? It seems far-fetched, but Ava may be seeing this more objectively than I'm able to.

He's innocent until proven guilty, though. No matter what happened earlier this week, I can't completely rule out taking him at his word.

"For the sake of playing devil's advocate, he could be telling the truth," I point out. "Maybe he did feel bad about disappearing this week and then made a last-minute decision to get on a plane when work wrapped up early."

"Do you believe that?"

It's an excellent question. "I don't know what to believe," I admit.

"Then you have one job this weekend." Ava grips my shoulders and peers into my eyes. "Leave this bar with him tonight, and don't let him go back to Vegas until you have answers you're satisfied with for everything you haven't asked him about yet. Something feels weird, and I don't like it."

She makes digging for the truth sound easy. If only it were.

# Chapter Twenty-Six

When the band's last song is announced, I lean closer to Ava and cup my hands around her ear. "Come to the stage with me?"

She nods and follows me as I weave past the people who are between us and the front row. I didn't tell Phoenix where I'm going, but I'll let him assume I want to finish out the night dancing by the stage with Ava while cheering Torin on. My true motive is to catch Torin as soon as he's done playing, say goodbye, and make a clean getaway ahead of any chance for barbs to be exchanged and tempers to rise.

Torin may not appreciate the hasty exit, but I'll chat with him later. It's better if I'm the one asking Phoenix questions tonight. Torin bulldozing him won't accomplish much other than resistance and having to dodge a fight.

Anyone watching me in front of the stage with Ava would think the two of us are having a blast, with nothing weighing on our minds. Maybe that's true of Ava, but I should be nominated for an Academy Award with the way I keep a smile plastered on my face through the end of the song and while Jacob thanks us all for coming. I wave Torin over as soon as he gets up from behind his drums.

"Great show!" I exclaim, once he's in front of Ava and me. "I need to get out of here, but I wanted to say goodbye first."

"I'm heading out with her," Ava adds. "I'm sure you guys want to get on the road as soon as you can tonight."

There's no protest from Torin, nor does he show even a glimmer of surprise that we're leaving so soon. He only mops his forehead with a bar towel he has in his hand, says how great it was to see us and how much he appreciates us coming, and agrees with Ava that he and the rest of the band want to pack up and load out as fast as they can. He doesn't mention Phoenix, and that's a positive sign. This is Torin on his best behavior.

I wait for Ava to give Nash a hug and a kiss goodbye. He whispers something in her ear that brings a sly smile to her lips and a tinge of pink to her cheeks.

"They're not staying in town overnight?" I ask her as we make our way back across the bar.

"Nope. They have a private pool party gig in Vegas tomorrow that came up at the last minute. From what Nash told me, Phoenix recommended them to a friend when the first band canceled. Sound check is at noon, so they're driving back tonight."

If she's disappointed about not having a do-over of her missed connection last weekend, she's hiding it well. Perhaps it's whatever Nash just said to her, and they have other plans on the horizon she's keeping under wraps. It's not the time to ask with Phoenix only a few steps away.

His gaze lingers on me as we approach, but Ava nudges me with her elbow and brings me back to our earlier conversation in the restroom, and the one we had yesterday over lunch. Right. Tonight isn't about getting caught up in his affectionate glances or sweet words. He still has a few things to answer for.

"Let's get out of here," I declare, linking arms with him.

Ava all but ignores his existence while we amble out of the bar and walk to the parking garage. "My car is on the main level," she says once we get there, but she only addresses me. "I'll call you tomorrow."

"Drive safely," I tell her. We hug for a few seconds, and then she's off, stalking away impressively fast for someone wearing the shoes she has on.

"It was good to see you," Phoenix calls after her.

"Yep." She continues walking and disappears around a corner.

Ava's departure leaves us alone together, next to an elevator. Phoenix doesn't ask why she ignored him all night and dismissed him just now, even though she was polite to him at Nebula last weekend. Maybe he expected it after going missing for a few days.

I press the button for the elevator, but then something occurs to me. Did he drive here, or take a taxi or an Uber? We haven't talked about where we're going next.

"How did you get here from the airport?" I ask.

"With a rental car. I'm parked on level four."

"I'm on three."

He's quiet until I glance up at him. After I meet his eyes, he cradles the side of my face in his hand and strokes his thumb along my cheek. "Stay with me tonight?"

Spending the night at his house is the opening I need. I can ask him questions there, and read his body language when I do. This conversation won't be interrupted by reception issues.

"I'd like that. I'll meet you at your place?"

He drops a kiss on the top of my head, then on my eyebrow, and rests his forehead against mine. We remain that way, our heads together and his arms around me, until the elevator dings and the doors open.

Phoenix is already parked in his driveway when I turn onto his street. He waits for me to park, then he opens my car door for me and helps me out, keeping hold of my hand while he leads me up the front steps. I was a bundle of nerves the first time I walked into this house. It's the same feeling I have now when I step inside and he shuts the door behind us, but for a different reason.

"Are you hungry?" he asks.

His question may have a double meaning, since he brushes my hair to the side and touches his mouth to the back of my neck. He starts with soft kisses that become delicate nibbles, and it's already enough to bring goosebumps to my arms.

"Is there food here?" I ask, struggling to stay focused. He hasn't been home in two weeks that I know of.

"There are a few things in the freezer I could heat up, or I can see if anything is still open and will deliver." His breath tickles my skin, and lord, here we go again. I need to concentrate.

"I'm good for now, as long as there's water."

Except I should have requested food, because that would take a few minutes to prepare. It would give me a break and some time to mentally reset. How does the slightest touch from him threaten to torpedo my willpower this way?

"I have water in the fridge. Would you like some?"

At the slight bob of my head, he places one last kiss on my neck and then stops. Thank God. I have a fighting chance at forming sensible thoughts again.

I follow him into the kitchen, watching while he opens the fridge and retrieves two bottles of water. He sets the bottles on the counter. I cautiously join him there, all the while sifting through my brain for a way to ease into the conversation I came here to have.

My brainpower doesn't last long, because Phoenix picks up where he left off in the foyer. His caresses and butterfly kisses send a cascade of tingles through my body, and my head feels like it's filled with glitter and cotton candy. The situation becomes more hopeless as he reaches my earlobe. When his arm circles my waist and he draws me in closer, and when his free hand slips under the hem of my halter top, I'm tempted to cast all of my questions aside for the night and figure the rest out tomorrow. There are important facts I need to uncover and things I'm not happy about after last week and our phone call last night, but it doesn't change the physical pull he has on me.

Another part of me has more self-respect than that. This part of me also has some willpower left to summon.

"Where were you working last week?" I ask.

"Hmmm?"

His hand moves lower now, playing with the zipper on my skirt. I squeeze my eyes shut, trying to block out the desire rising inside of me.

"The place with bad phone reception." I take hold of his hand before it roams anywhere else.

"It was way out in the desert. Why do you ask?"

His reply took a few seconds. Was the pause for him to collect himself, or did he have to think about what to say?

"Isn't it brutally hot there right now?"

The counter stool next to me presents an opportunity to create more space between us. I let go of his hand, take a seat, and wait for him to answer.

"It was insanely hot. I've never felt an inferno like that before, even in Las Vegas."

"And you stayed there for a few nights?"

He sits on the stool next to mine and reaches for his water. "We had an RV with air conditioning, and it cooled down a bit at night.

I still wouldn't ever want to do that again."

"Do you think you'll have to?"

"No. We got what we needed."

The "what" in "what we needed" is still a riddle. I reach for the other water and take my time twisting off its cap.

"I'd love to hear more about what you're working on. I miss the days when you told me stories about what happened on set."

"I wish I could say more right now." He glances at a spot on the counter, and then at me again.

There it is. He can act, but he can't lie to me. His eyes just gave it away.

"Why can't you say more?"

"There's a non-disclosure agreement. I probably shouldn't have even said I was in the desert." Peeling the label off of his bottle suddenly becomes an all-consuming task.

"That sounds pretty locked down."

He puts the bottle back on the counter. "Promise me you won't mention where I was this week to anyone? Not even to Ava, please."

Why would disclosing such a general location to my closest friend be a problem? Most of Nevada is the desert, but I'll play along for now. He doesn't need to know I was with Ava when his text came through and he claimed phone service problems, or that I'd speculated about him being in the desert when she asked if he was working from the moon.

"There's a lot riding on this," he adds when I don't answer. "I wouldn't ask you to keep it to yourself if it wasn't important."

"Whatever you're working on must be top secret if you can't give me even a little hint." It's tempting to point out that he works in the film industry, and that sharing a few details won't compromise national security or change the fate of the world, but this probably won't help me.

He leans forward and covers my hand with his. "I promise I'll tell you everything when I can. I swear that on my life, because I don't ever want you to think I'm keeping things from you. We've been through too much together for me to risk that."

"Would you also swear on my life?"

"Yes."

In spite of what he said and how serious he seems, he rubs his chin and blinks a few times. Rapid blinking is a sign of someone dodging the truth, which I learned while researching body language for one of my past novels. Is he lying to me?

Whether he is or isn't, I note it and move on for now. I have other questions to ask. "Since you can't say much about work, there's something else I'd like to talk about."

"What's that?" He offers me an apologetic smile. "If I haven't signed an NDA about it, then I'm an open book."

We'll see about that. I tip my head to the side and look him straight in the eyes.

"I want to know everything you haven't told me about Len."

# Chapter Twenty-Seven

"YOU WANT TO TALK about Len?"

Phoenix couldn't appear more dumbfounded if dancing kittens barged into his kitchen and tangoed across the counter. It could be the lighting, but his face looks a shade paler than usual.

"Yes. You said I could ask you questions about her last weekend, remember? It was after I told you Nash offered the same thing."

A vein in his forehead pulses. The only sounds in the room while I wait for him to speak are a quiet buzz from the refrigerator and the hum of a fan powering his central air.

"Is it background for your book?" he finally asks.

"It's background for me, the person dating you."

"I'm not sure I'm following."

He fiddles with his watchband and keeps his eyes focused somewhere to the left of me. Is he sincere in his confusion, or is he buying time?

"I've felt your energy shift any time Len's name has come up over the last week, ever since you heard that news report. It makes me wonder what I don't know."

"About her case?" He squints, and I don't think it's from the overhead lights. This seems more like acting.

"You tell me. It's like you space out into another world and get tense and distant in this one. Is it something about how she disappeared, or being reminded of her, or something else? I want to understand where you go and what I can do when you go there."

I also want to understand more about why he was so stunned when he learned Nash spoke to me about Len. He said it was because Nash rarely talks about her, but is that truly it? Is there something about Len he's keeping close to his chest and thinks Nash might expose, or that would explain why he has her journal? I don't know how to ask without sounding jealous of someone I've never met. Mostly, I'm confused and missing the information I need to help me connect all the dots.

"I'm sorry I haven't been myself this week. Knowing there could be an answer any day to what happened brings up a lot."

"Is that all it is?"

"Is there a reason you don't believe that's all it is?"

I should be annoyed that he's answered my question with a question, but something in his voice doesn't let me. He doesn't sound angry or defensive. He sounds sad.

"You hid things you felt the first time we dated, and those were important things that sent your life spiraling. Our relationship ended because of it. You may have healthier ways of coping now, but I'm not about to get shut out a second time. I promise I will walk out of this house, block your number, and not look back unless you tell me the truth. That means all of it."

His shoulders and neck stiffen, and he hardly blinks during the long silence that follows. Then he nods. "Where would you like me to start?"

"At the beginning. Or with why losing Len was the incentive you needed to get and stay sober when salvaging our relationship wasn't. Why did she mean more to you?"

I didn't intend for the last part to come out, but there it is. I've steered this exactly where I didn't want to go before we've even started.

"Del."

There's pain in his voice when he says my name. Now I'm the one who can't meet his eyes.

"Motion to strike my last question," I mumble.

"Look at me, please."

I'm frozen, though, unable to move a muscle until Phoenix tilts my chin toward him. Heat rises to my neck and cheeks. I want to hop off this stool, crawl under the table in the corner, and hide.

"I told you I met Len while working on a film. She was a makeup artist and did my makeup every day, so naturally we talked. She was the one who hid my dark circles and bloated face. She also knew when I was hungover or drinking on the set. She alluded to it, asking if everything was okay. I could tell she cared, but I didn't know why until later."

Phoenix rubs the back of his neck. He keeps his gaze fixed on the counter.

"Some of the cast and crew went out to a bar after work one night. Len didn't drink, but she came—probably to keep an eye on me. We ended up at a tavern in the Valley. I didn't know Torin's old band had a gig there until they took the stage after I'd had a few drinks. The booze and my attitude kept me there until the bartender cut me off. I didn't know it, but Len had asked him to. I was already in a mood and getting ready to leave. Torin was between sets, and he saw me and approached. Things got heated and Len followed us outside. Torin was about to deck me, and she threatened to call the cops. He cooled it. She offered to drive me home. I tried to decline, but she lived in Aliso Viejo and knew I lived in Laguna Beach. She was already going that way. The next time I was on set, she asked about you."

"About me?" This already doesn't make sense. Unless Len was also a fan of his from his earliest film roles, how would she know about me or my connection to him?

"She heard Torin mention your name before he was about to punch me, and then she listened to me talk about you the entire drive home. I'd had so much to drink that she couldn't understand most of it."

"What did she want to know? If I was your girlfriend, or if we'd recently broken up?"

"She wanted to know where to find you." I'm so in my head that

Phoenix's reply might as well come from a different dimension.

"Where to find me?" I repeat.

"She thought you should know how sick I'd made myself over the things I'd done and that I really did love you. Somewhere in that drunken mess of a conversation, I'd told her a few halfway understandable things about why I left and why I wouldn't reach out to you. She thought it would help for us to talk and for me to come clean, even if it only meant closure."

There's a piece of the story missing here. There has to be. "Len cared that much about the broken relationship of someone whose film makeup she did?"

"She cared because I said something else during the drive about it not mattering if I lived or died. Her brother once said the same thing. He was a recovering alcoholic who didn't make it. His body finally shut down. She said it would haunt her forever if she didn't try to do something before I met the same end, and she was convinced her brother's spirit played a role in making sure our paths would cross. She'd gotten the job because another makeup artist had backed out right before filming started."

"Oh."

My less-than-adequate answer slips out without me meaning for it to, and then I'm fumbling in the dark for something else to say. It turns out I don't need to, because Phoenix keeps talking.

"I wouldn't tell her your last name or anything else that would help her find you. Why would you want to hear from her about me after everything I did? You deserved peace. So she let it drop and asked me if I'd considered getting help for what she already recognized was a drinking problem. I tried to downplay her concerns and changed the subject, but she didn't give up. She knew your first name and did some online sleuthing. Older entertainment articles helped her figure out the Del I'd sobbed about was you, author Delaney Sharpe. She'd read your debut novel, and she was a fan. The next time I showed up to set after downing a liquid breakfast, she gave me an ultimatum. I could claim I had food poisoning, let her fiancé drive me home, and show up to work sober the next day. Or, I could show up drunk again, and she would message your social media accounts to tell you about me and everything I still felt for you."

Len followed me on social media, so I believe that part. I'm stuck on what came before it, about her fiancé. Nothing I've come across while researching her case mentioned she was engaged.

"Why didn't her fiancé come up in any of the news stories? I don't remember reading or hearing anything about him."

"She and Matt ended their engagement before she went missing, but it was on good terms. They wanted different things. It happened the same week as everything with Chaz and me in Newport, and then I checked into rehab in Antigua. Len didn't tell me they'd broken up until near the end of my program. I pretty much existed in a bubble at the facility, with most outside news never filtering through. The few people who knew I was there wanted me focused on getting and staying sober."

He pauses for a drink of water. I mirror him while piecing

everything together. Len wanted to help because he reminded her of her brother. She had a fiancé for much of the time they knew each other. Phoenix agreed to rehab as part of a deal with Chaz that kept my name out of the tabloids, and somehow this program worked when the one before it didn't.

"The program in Antigua just worked for you, even after the one you tried before it didn't?"

"It was a good program, and being in another country made it harder to walk out and go home. My agreement with Chaz was the main reason I saw it through. In a lot of ways, I wanted to do it for you and be the person I should have been when we were together, even though I thought it was too late for us."

His hand drifts closer to where mine rests on the counter. He curls his fingers around one of mine, but it's not where my attention is.

"You told me weeks ago that losing Len was your wake-up call to get your life together. Now you're saying she was still present and talking to you when you were in rehab, and that it was your agreement with Chaz and wanting to do it for me that made you stay. Am I missing something?"

"No." His voice is soft, and he keeps his hold on my finger. "All of that is true. Len disappeared a few days after I finished rehab. It gave me one more reason to stay sober and not relapse on top of everything else, because I promised her family I would do everything I could to help them find her. I couldn't do that if I was drunk all the time. The shock of her being gone and not knowing what happened shook me out of my pity party. My focus became bringing her home. I spent a long time convincing myself that we'd find her alive, until months passed, and then a year, and then longer."

He's gone from linked fingers to covering my hand with his again, like he did a few minutes ago when he said he would tell me everything about what he's working on in Vegas when he's able to. The tremble I noticed in his hand the other times he's talked about Len is back now. It doesn't flood me with sympathy or prompt me to move on to another subject. Not yet.

"You told me once that you accepted she might not be alive, and you still don't know either way. But you tensed up when I told you Nash talked to me about her, and the same thing happened last night when I asked if you'd seen anything else about her in the news. I heard it in your voice. Both times felt like you didn't want to open up to me about what you were thinking and feeling, and I'd like to know why."

"I did tense up," he admits. "I thought I'd accepted it, but it was easier when there weren't updates on the news. Deep down, I still had hope she was alive, and that all of us looking for her didn't fail her. Hearing something changed in her case made everything real again. It forced me to realize I'll finally need to face the truth, whatever it is. That's where my head has been this week, and I'm sorry. I didn't want any of this to make you question things about you and me."

He moves his hand off of mine and strokes my hair, then runs his fingers along my cheek. The tremble is still there.

# Chapter Twenty-Eight

"You met Len once." Phoenix's hand settles on my shoulder.

"You told me I didn't know her the first time her name came up and I asked, before I knew Len and Elenna are the same person."

It could be Ava or Torin's influence, or my self-protective instincts, or my natural inclination to look for plot holes thanks to my career, but I'm on high alert for inconsistencies in his answers.

"You didn't know her, but you met her. She went to a book signing you had at The Grove. I didn't find out until later, because she didn't tell me until one of the last times we talked while I was in Antigua. She thought I would ask her not to go."

"Why would you have asked her not to go?" It's not like Len would have walked up to me and introduced herself as Phoenix's girlfriend if they were only friends, and there's a chance she would have brought her fiancé if she was still with him at the time.

"Because of her reason for going. She wanted to tell you everything. How I felt about what I did to you, that I was still in love with you, and that I'd stayed away because I didn't want to keep hurting you and knew you deserved more. That I had planned to propose to you. That I was in rehab and cleaning up my life. She also wanted to ask you to see me in person when I got back from Antigua, but without me knowing so I couldn't be a coward about it. She was trying to reunite us."

Except none of that ever happened. "I think I would remember someone telling me all of this at a book signing."

"She had you sign a book for her, but she didn't go through with the rest of it. When she saw you in person and heard you speak, she knew she couldn't. It was your moment to shine, and she thought you seemed so genuinely happy to be there. She realized it was the wrong place for it."

That's for sure. Back then, the mere mention of Phoenix's name at my book signing would have had me asking her to leave, never mind the rest of it. I may have appeared happy—and I'm sure I was in that moment, doing what I'd worked so hard for and loved—but it took everything I had in me to get to that point after he walked out.

In the present, in his kitchen, I'm at a loss for how to respond to the possibility this could have happened. It might be how quiet I've become, or because the mood between us now is far from fireworks and physical chemistry, but he carefully lowers his hand from my shoulder, like I've become fragile glass he's afraid will shatter if he keeps it there.

"I know you said you weren't hungry before, but should I try to find us something?"

The gentle way he asks nearly breaks me. I came here intending to fire off every question on my mind, but now, as parts of me fray at the edges, I'm willing to let things rest. I shake my head.

"I'm still fine. Let's just go to bed."

"Of course. Thank you for still staying here tonight."

I search his face for any sign that his gratitude is a mask, or that he's only playing the part of the caring boyfriend who's trying to empathize with how I feel. I can't find one. All he radiates is something so tender, it now floods me with guilt. Have I been assuming the worst for no reason?

The man can pull off a scripted performance like no other, but to fool me with this would be next level. It would be pure evil for him to waltz back into my life just to take me down again. No matter what happened between us years ago, and no matter how strange this week has been, he wouldn't do that. Phoenix might be my personal brand of kryptonite, but he isn't the devil.

"I'm going to brush my teeth and get ready for bed." I break eye contact and slide off the stool.

"Your toothbrush from the last time you stayed is in the holder. I'll be right there after shutting things down out here."

"Okay."

It's a relief to make my escape from the kitchen and the heightened emotions I hope we can leave there.

Later, when we're in bed next to each other, it seems like we can.

Snuggled together, with Phoenix holding me, it's like the kitchen conversation happened on another planet, on a different day.

"Want the TV on?" he asks.

"Sure."

He must use the arm that isn't around me to press a button on the remote, because the television flickers to life a few seconds later. I don't know what we're watching, but it doesn't matter. All I want is to fully forget about the earlier part of the night and start over fresh when my eyes open in the morning. I assume Phoenix wants the same thing, until he speaks again.

"What you said tonight, about Len meaning more to me. I didn't ever want to make you feel that way. You're everything to me."

I flinch at the flashback before I can stop myself. He holds me closer and continues.

"If I could go back in time and stop every wrong turn and bad decision I made, I would do it in a heartbeat. I would make sure you never questioned how much I love you or how much you mean. Not then, and not now."

Here in the secure hold of his arms, and with the hindsight of knowing all that I didn't before tonight, the conclusions I came to during the last few days now seem overblown and driven by the ghost of who I once was. I shift in Phoenix's arms, turning so I can see his face in the faint light from the TV.

"I shouldn't have said that before. It wasn't fair."

"It was very fair," he says gently. "Always be honest with me about how you feel. I don't want to risk losing you again."

I nod, acknowledging his request. I've been asking the same thing of him, but have I been just as guilty of holding back? I could have said something after I found Len's journal. But I kept it inside, not wanting to rock the boat right after discovering the cans of whiskey sour in his fridge and having him prove he wasn't hiding alcohol in his garage. I wanted the perfect weekend. Then I took my anxiety and fears out on Ava.

"Promise me the same?" I ask.

"Always."

For a long moment, he just looks into my eyes. His thumb traces along my jaw, like he's memorizing the contours of my face. The tenderness in his gaze and touch undoes something in me. When he bends his head over mine and our lips meet, I'm ready for him.

My hands tangle in his hair and the weight of the evening lifts. But Phoenix's lips pressed against mine, and his tongue exploring my mouth, aren't enough for long. My hands glide over his body, moving lower, until he catches my wrists, holding them gently.

"Del," he murmurs. But he doesn't move, and he doesn't release his hold.

I pull back slightly so I can glance at his face, in search of why he stopped kissing me, and why he stopped me from touching him. What I see in his eyes steals the air from my lungs.

"It isn't just about this for me. I need you to know that, especially after me being out of touch this week. Just because we took it there last weekend, doesn't mean I expect to tonight. That's not the reason I came here, or why I asked you to spend the night."

The vulnerability I hear in his voice has meaning beyond anything he could say. Any remaining doubts hidden in the shadows of my mind and heart slip away.

"I know it isn't. It's not just about this for me either. It never was."

His hands are still circled around my wrists, so I can't touch him while I speak. The yearning to almost has me unraveling, because there's only so much words can say. But then something shifts in his expression, making me forget everything else I wish I could express. His hands loosen, letting go.

Then it's pure instinct. His kiss finds me again. The sweetness of it leaves me breathless and dizzy. My body curves into his, craving his warmth and his weight as my anchor. I need to melt into him, until he ends where I begin and I begin where he ends.

It's as if he hears what I'm thinking. His hands slide to my back, his palms pressing against the thin cotton T-shirt I have on. It's loose on me because it's his shirt, but fabric has never felt more constricting. He finds the hem, and I help him pull it over my head. The slow glide of his fingers against my bare skin ignites a fire. But he doesn't rush, and neither do I.

My lips find his neck, and then his ear. His breath hitches when my teeth graze his earlobe. A soft sound escapes him as his hands travel down my sides to my waist. His fingers splay across my skin as he rolls us gently, shifting his weight until I'm beneath him.

He looks down at me, his hair falling forward, the light from the

TV casting a muted glow over him. His thumb brushes along my cheek as if he still can't believe I'm here, or that we belong to each other again. For a moment, everything stills.

Then he lowers himself, his body settling against me. I press into him, my arms winding around his neck, a quiet sigh escaping me as his mouth finds mine. He doesn't stay there for long. Soon his lips brush the curve of my throat, then my collarbone. His hand traces over my breast, my ribs, and my stomach, stopping to draw light circles at my hip, then along my thigh. His kisses follow the same path.

My hands roam the smooth lines of his back until a shift of his body and weight brings us closer. I hook my leg around his, our hips flush, trying to tell him without words that I want more. But he chuckles softly, his breath tickling my ear before I feel his gentle nibbles along my neck.

"We'll get there," he murmurs, the words vibrating against my throat. And we will. Arouse and retreat, give and receive—it's an artful dance we perfected years ago that will take me to the edge of a supernova waiting to explode.

He doesn't have to ask what I want, because he already knows. It's the way his hand moves over me, the slight change in pressure, the teasing pause before he touches me where I most want him to. He moves with a deliberate rhythm, until my soft moan and quiet plea dissolves the last of the restraint between us. Then there's only trust.

# Chapter Twenty-Nine

It feels like reliving a moment when I wake up in Phoenix's bed. There's an empty space beside me, the pillow indentation is still fresh, and the sound of running water comes from the bathroom. But it's light outside, and my phone reveals it's almost noon, and Phoenix is fully dressed in jeans and a T-shirt when he emerges from the bathroom. My eyes follow him as he crosses the room and grabs his wallet from the top of the dresser.

"Are you sneaking out of your own house?" My eyelids might be open, but my voice is still hoarse from the hours I was asleep. I sit up and reach for the water on the bedside table.

"I was hoping to be out and back before you woke up and to surprise you with brunch." He walks to my side of the bed and sits next to me. Again with the similarities to the last time I woke up here.

"In that case, this is a dream and it never happened, unless you're taking food orders."

"Do breakfast burritos sound good?" he asks. "If not, I can get whatever you'd like."

I intentionally stare at him for a few drawn-out seconds, careful to keep a straight face. My silence and memories of last night's conversation must make him nervous, because he speaks again.

"I thought since they used to be your favorite and—"

I raise a finger to my lips, still looking at him. He immediately stops talking. After a dramatic pause, I lower my hand. "You're trying to seduce me again, aren't you?"

If relief could be a person, it would be Phoenix in this instant. "Is it working?"

"I'll decide when you return with the breakfast burritos. Bonus points if you also get churros."

He tousles a strand of my hair, then leans in to kiss my forehead. "Consider it done. Would you like me to make you coffee before I go?"

I scrunch my nose. "That's sweet of you, but it will delay the breakfast burritos, so no."

"Good point. I'll be on my way, then." He gets to his feet and gives me his puppy-dog look before leaving the bedroom, which means I'm in the best kind of trouble when he gets back.

The front door of the house opening and closing is soon followed by the sound of an engine starting. I reach over to the floor and retrieve the T-shirt I wore to bed from where it landed last night. Then I slip it over my head, get to my feet, and head into the bathroom to splash water on my face. Phoenix left his phone on the counter, so I pick it up and move it to keep water from getting on the screen.

The phone lights up when it's in my hand. I shouldn't snoop, but it's a reflex to glance down, and I see the message there. Temptation to read it takes over when I realize it's from Dalton Petaluma, the same person who called and texted him last weekend. Phoenix won't tell me about what he's working on, but maybe Dalton's message contains a clue.

*Trying to reach you. I need you to come to the station. Call me when you get this.*

Does "the station" mean a TV station? That seems like an odd way to phrase it, since a studio lot or soundstage would be more likely for Phoenix's line of work.

Then an idea hits me. Would finding out who Dalton is and what films or TV shows he's worked on offer more hints about the top-secret project in Vegas, without Phoenix having to breach his NDA? Knowing this could turn up information about the project itself. Surely not everyone involved has kept their vow of silence. No one ever does these days, and some people are always ready to post entertainment gossip online.

I put Phoenix's phone down and return to the bedroom to retrieve mine, so I can search for Dalton's name. I expect an IMDb page with his film or TV credits, some social media profiles, and possibly a few articles where his name is cited or where he's been quoted. That isn't what comes up at all.

According to what's in front of me, Dalton Petaluma is a homicide detective. Which means the station he needs Phoenix to go to is probably a police station.

The snatches of a conversation I heard while Phoenix was on the phone last weekend replay in my mind. He asked someone, whom I'd assumed to be Dalton, if he should be worried. With the context I now have about who Dalton is and what he does for a living, I'm more puzzled than ever what the call was about and why Phoenix reacted that way to what he was told.

Why would he be in regular contact with a homicide detective? Does it have something to do with the investigation into Len's disappearance? The text from Dalton and the phone call happened the same afternoon the news broke about developments in her case. Presuming these were about her, then what did the conversation I heard mean?

*Stop. Don't jump to conclusions or make assumptions yet.*

Dalton's messages may have nothing to do with Len, although I'd love to know what else Phoenix could be talking to a homicide detective about. Do I ask him after he gets back with our food, or would that end up with me on the defensive, trying to explain why I was looking at his phone in the first place? We're in a good place today after last night's tension. Bringing this up could highlight my trust issues again. My anxiety needs to take a backseat for a while.

With that conclusion, I set my phone back on the table, knocking one of my earrings to the floor in the process. It rolls under the bed, out of view.

Great. I get on my hands and knees to peer under the bed. It doesn't take long to spot my earring, but it's rolled too far for me to reach. I'll need to find something to push it with. A clothes hanger might work.

I stand up again and cross the room to Phoenix's closet, where I retrieve an empty clothes hanger, then return to the bed. This time I'm able to reach the earring and slide it toward me with the hanger. Halfway to me, it drops into a knothole I didn't notice in one of the floor's wood planks. The plank is close enough that I should be able to reach it with my hand and feel for the dip my earring fell into.

I find the knothole easily enough, but digging my earring out of it with my finger causes a piece of the plank to move. Curious, I curl my fingers around the edge of the knothole and try to lift the loose section up. It moves with hardly any effort. There's a space below it, and something in that space.

No, not just something. Unless my eyes are playing tricks on me, it's a handgun, and I can't tell if it's loaded from here. I'm also not about to touch it.

Why is Phoenix hiding a gun beneath a floorboard under his bed? Why isn't it locked up in a case, and when did he even get a gun? He was one of the most anti-firearms people I knew during the first time we dated.

The gun isn't a figment of my imagination, though. It's right here, and it's real. There has to be a logical explanation for this, and for Dalton's message. What I need to do is put the plank back where it was, wash my face and brush my teeth, and sweep the last sleepy cobwebs from my brain with coffee and food when Phoenix returns.

But when I'm in the bathroom again, cupping my hands under the running water, another thought barges into my mind. It's about the guest bedroom downstairs, and how it's completely gutted. The floor is torn out, with new flooring half installed. There's new, unpainted drywall. Wires dangle from the ceiling where a light fixture should be. I didn't get a close enough look at the windows to see if they're also new.

In that moment, my brain connects everything. What I've seen this morning, Len's journal, Phoenix's secrecy about his trip to the desert, his near-total disappearance from public view for several years, and his unexpected re-entry into my life. I turn the water off and study Phoenix's phone, even though the screen is dark now.

Oh my God.

# Chapter Thirty

IF SOMEONE WANTED TO remove gunshot residue, blood, and other DNA from a room, what would be the most effective way to do it with the lowest risk of missing something? Get rid of every surface that could hold a trace of anything, that's how.

I can't prove that's why the guest room is torn apart. I also can't prove that the gun hidden under the floorboard has any connection. Maybe paranoia is creeping in. But when those things are stacked up with everything else that's happened over the past few weeks, how can it not?

Phoenix came to Torin and Nash's show on the night this all began, knowing I would be there. He intentionally kept himself off of Torin's radar until he was inside the bar so he could seek me out, then he pushed to reconnect. All of this took place after he overheard Ava tell Torin that my latest book is based on Len's disappearance. He had six years before then to reach out. Locating me wouldn't have been hard, but he only did it then.

Even if sobriety delayed him, there's a big gap to account for between when he finished rehab and when he surfaced in my life again. The timing is questionable. Did he want to know what I'd uncovered about Len's case, and what theories I'd formed? He knows how deep I go when I research. Maybe that scared him.

Then there's the homicide detective who has contacted him multiple times, possibly about Len. Could Phoenix be a person of interest connected to her disappearance?

The first text I saw from Dalton Petaluma was sent the same day the news came out about a break in Len's case. Not long after the announcement, and soon after I returned to LA, Phoenix took off into the desert for days and went dark. It could be all the true-crime documentaries I've watched, but my imagination is volcanic now, erupting with theories and questions. Was he actually working there, or was he hiding out somewhere he couldn't be located to decide on his next steps?

A shudder runs through me at my next thought: Did he visit Len's burial site to see if she'd been found, and could he be capable of murder?

My mind wants to protest this at every turn. He's the man who makes me romantic playlists, carefully plans dates, remembers how I take my coffee, and keeps a running list of my favorite foods. But how much do I really know about who he became during our years apart?

Phoenix was out of control when he walked out on me, and every tabloid story after that said he only got worse. There's no telling what he could have done when he was drunk beyond reason and using drugs on top of it. He said he's been sober since his rehab stint in Antigua, but was it that easy? Or did he do something later that scared him into sobriety and kept him that way so he could cover his tracks?

Torin said Phoenix has been in Las Vegas for about eight months, and Phoenix hasn't denied it. Torin also said he's with Nash a lot. Phoenix met Nash through Len, and it's a safe bet Nash knew about his drinking and behavior back then. The paragraphs I read in Len's journal were about Phoenix's addiction, and she noted a crash out that was worse than she'd ever seen him. I didn't get a chance to read what came after that.

Did something happen that made Phoenix want to stay close to Nash once Nash moved to Vegas? Could Nash have seen or heard something, or did Len confide in him about something that has Phoenix worried? Maybe she wrote about it in her journal. That would explain why Phoenix doesn't want Nash and Ava to be romantically involved. They'd spend hours or days alone together, and Nash might say something to her. It could also be why he showed up at the Ocean Floor last night, unannounced.

Only Phoenix has the answers, but I'm not sticking around to ask him. Every instinct I have screams at me to leave. If the break in Len's case means authorities finally know what happened, and if Phoenix is involved, who knows what he'll do if I say the wrong thing? His behavior has been off all week, and he could turn dangerous when he sees Dalton's message.

Realizing this propels me out of the bathroom and into the bedroom. My reflection blurs in the mirror as I grab my clothes. Panic lodges in my throat while I change out of Phoenix's T-shirt, shove my feet into my shoes, and grab my phone and purse.

I'm in the foyer and a few feet away from escaping when a car door shuts outside. Phoenix is home.

The front door opens, and his face lights up when he sees me. He extends the takeout bag he's holding out to me, but then his gaze lands on the purse slung over my shoulder and the keys in my hands. His smile fades.

"You're leaving now? I thought we were having brunch?"

My heart pounds so hard, it feels like it's rattling my ribs. What if he suspects what I've pieced together?

"I—I forgot about an appointment," I stammer. "If I don't go now, I'll be late."

"Okay. Do you want your food for the road?" He keeps his eyes trained on me, as though he's searching for the truth in what I said.

It's doubtful he's tampered with the food, but not impossible. I've also lost my appetite. But refusing to take it home would be a sign that something is very wrong.

"That would be great. Thank you."

Phoenix doesn't reach into the bag to separate our burritos and churros. He just keeps watching me. A chill takes over my body.

"Are you all right to drive? You're pale as a ghost, and your hands are shaking."

He reaches for one of my clammy hands. I recoil and back away before I can stop myself. Now I really have his attention.

"Is everything okay?" he asks.

"I need to go." I move to pass him, but his hand lands on my shoulder.

"Del?"

"Let go of me." I try shrugging him away, but his hold is firm.

"I will when you tell me what's going on. You don't seem like yourself."

The room spins around me, a blurry collage of objects and colors. It's all I can do to stay standing. My inner voice shouts to push Phoenix away and run, but my body won't cooperate and it's difficult to breathe.

Words tumble from my mouth, wild and uncontrollable. "I'm not myself? You're the one hiding Len's journal in a house in Las Vegas, and hiding a gun in the floor under your bed here, and who has a homicide detective blowing up your phone."

Phoenix's eyes widen. "How do you—"

I cut him off. "You've been acting weird since the news about Len's case, and since you found out Nash talked to me about her. You said you had to work this weekend, but then miraculously finished so early that you made it here last night, after I told you Torin and Nash had a show and that I'd be there. Torin thinks you aren't working in Vegas at all, and now I think he's right. You stayed away for years, then suddenly needed to see me after you heard my book was based on Len's disappearance. But you're asking me what's going on?"

Adrenaline is the only thing powering me now, but it clears the fog from my brain and the molasses from my limbs. I twist out of Phoenix's grasp.

"What are you saying?" he asks.

I hear his question as I reach for the door and pull it open, but I don't answer and I don't look back. Some higher force carries me down the steps and into my car. Phoenix calls after me, but I don't process what he says. I lock the doors, start the engine, and go.

My rearview mirror reveals Phoenix in his driveway, watching me leave. For a second, I wonder if it's divine protection keeping him from getting in his rental car and chasing after me. But then I remember he doesn't need to. He knows where I live.

Bile rises to the back of my throat. I can't throw up. There's no time to pull over, and I need to figure out where to head next. Going home might not be safe.

I check the rearview mirror again, and my heart skips at least two beats. The blue Prius I've noticed lately is behind me. It's the same one I saw leaving the airport, and after lunch with Ava two days ago. Now it's in Laguna Beach and driving in the same direction as me.

This isn't a coincidence. I'm being watched, and I'm being followed.

# Chapter Thirty-One

PHOENIX MUST HAVE HIRED the driver to keep an eye on me. Nothing else makes sense. I don't want the Prius tailing me to wherever I end up, which means I need to make the driver lose sight of my car. But I'm not familiar with the side streets around here, stunt driving isn't my forte, and the panic surging through me makes it hard to focus on both my next move and the road signs. What do I do?

*Inhale, exhale, and think. Inhale—*

I brake hard before I zip through an intersection with a stop sign. My tires screech against the road, then the car comes to a stop. That was close. Now is not the time to let my thoughts consume me.

After checking all sides of the intersection for traffic, I lift my foot from the brake and apply it to the gas pedal with more pressure than I mean to. My car jerks forward again. A quick mirror check reveals the Prius still following me at a distance. A plan to help me make it somewhere in one piece needs to come from someone else, because I'm in no shape to drive and think at the same time. There's one person I can always count on when I need advice or a problem solved, and I sure hope she's near her phone.

"Call Ava Sinclair," I tell my car's voice assistant.

There's confirmation, then a pause. One ring. Two.

"You're psychic," Ava says when she answers. "I was about to text you to ask if you got answers last night, since I hadn't heard from you."

"I'm being followed," I blurt out.

"What?"

"A blue Prius has been lurking around since I got back from Vegas. It was behind me when I left the airport after I came home, and it was parked near Granville on Friday while we were there. It's following me home from Laguna Beach now. I'm panicking and I need your help."

"Wait, slow down. You sound like you're about to hyperventilate. You're certain it's the same car? Breathe first, and then answer."

I gulp air into my lungs, but my breath is shaky, and it makes me cough. My eyes water, blurring the road in front of me. "It's been the same license plate each time."

"Do you have any idea why someone is following you?"

I swipe at my watery eyes with one hand. "It might involve Phoenix."

"What?" she sputters.

"I think you were right about him showing up last night to keep an eye on me, but not because he was worried about Torin getting in my ear. I have reasons to believe he was involved in Elenna Paseo's disappearance and didn't want me talking to Nash about her again."

It takes Ava a few seconds to speak. "Are you saying... I mean, you think that Phoenix..." she trails off. "Start at the beginning?"

"He got weird after hearing something on the news about developments in Len's case last weekend, and again when he found out Nash talked to me about her and my book. He's also been opposed to you getting involved with Nash. My guess is Nash knows or suspects something, and Phoenix thinks he might say something to one of us that would help me connect him with Len's disappearance because of how much research I've done."

Ava says something else, but my call waiting tone beeps multiple times and drowns her out. My stomach lurches when I see the name on my caller ID.

"He's trying to call me. I left his place a few minutes ago." I swallow the excess saliva in my mouth. Nausea is back in full force.

"What else happened that has you like this? Did he try to hurt you?" Now Ava is the one who sounds distraught.

"I found a gun hidden in the floor under his bed this morning, and there's this whole thing with his guest room I'll explain later. When I put that together with the last week and other things that have seemed off since he popped up in my life again, it all made sense."

*Don't puke. Listen to Ava and focus on the road. Everything will be fine.*

"Does he know what you suspect?"

"Yes, and now I don't know what to do or where to go. He knows where I live, and so does the guy in the Prius. I don't feel safe going home, but I won't feel safe anywhere with someone following me."

One of my hands slides off the steering wheel. My palms are slick with sweat, and my whole body trembles.

"You should still go home," Ava advises. "I doubt you'll lose whoever is following you, so you may as well stop there first. There might even be an AirTag or another tracking device on your car."

"Wonderful." I force my hand to grip the steering wheel again.

"Park your car in your garage. Then you need to get up to your place as quickly as you can, pack a bag, and go somewhere else for a few days. I'll join you there."

I do need to go somewhere else, but there's a problem with that. "How will I get out of my building or drive anywhere else without being followed?"

Poor Ava. I just told her Phoenix may have killed someone and that I'm probably in danger, and now I'm looking to her for answers about what to do without time to process it all. What if she's in danger now, too, just for being my best friend and for being close with Nash?

"Another car," she instructs me. "Have an Uber get you, and give them your garage's gate code to pick you up by the elevator so you won't be seen getting in from the street. Change your clothes, put your hair back, cover your head with a hat, and wear sunglasses just in case. You'll be harder to identify if someone sees you for a second or two."

"How did you come up with that so fast?"

"A lot of my career is getting celebrities out of jams, remember? Sometimes that means sneaking them out of places without anyone recognizing them."

Right. She's spent most of her adult life cleaning up messes and thinking on her feet. It's a good thing one of us has those skills.

"Where will we go?" I ask.

"A hotel is probably the best place for tonight. Somewhere with security and that needs a room key to access the elevators. It will buy some time so we can decide what to do and if you should call the police."

"The police already know about Phoenix. A homicide detective told him he needs to come to a police station. I'll tell you the rest at the hotel."

"Do you want me to stay on the phone with you until you're home?"

"No. I'm going to do what you said. Pray I can make it out of my building undetected."

"I'll find us a hotel. Call me when you're home."

"I will. Be careful, though. Since you're close with Nash, I'm worried Phoenix might have someone following you."

The call waiting tone beeps again as I'm about to end the call with Ava. I let it go to voicemail this time, too. By the time I turn onto my street nearly an hour later, Phoenix has attempted to call me nine more times and has left a message, and the Prius is still in my rear view. I almost expect it to zoom in behind me when I enter my parking garage.

While I wait to see if the Prius appears, I go into my phone's contacts and block Phoenix, then put the phone in my purse. The Prius doesn't enter the garage, but my fight-or-flight instinct is still amped all the way up when I climb out of my car with the pepper spray I normally keep in my glove box gripped in my hand. I keep a tight hold on it while I creep across the garage to the elevator, and when the doors open after the elevator reaches my floor.

There's still no relief when I enter my condo and lock the door behind me, since I'm listening for footsteps in the hallway or any other movement. I've just put my purse on the kitchen counter and am about to head to my bedroom to throw clothes in a bag when a sickening thought takes hold. How does the Prius driver know when I leave home?

Yes, he recognizes my car, but there are other ways out of the building that don't involve the parking garage. Is he only following me when I'm driving somewhere and keeping constant vigil over the garage's exit for every vehicle that drives out? Or is something else alerting him whenever I leave, so he can watch all the exits?

My creative brain must be on autopilot, because two scenarios I'd consider for a situation like this in my books spring to mind. The first is that someone has hacked into the security cameras that monitor the elevators on each floor of my building. While unlikely, I still have to consider it, but there's another idea I want to investigate. It means going back into the hallway. I also need to be doing something that looks natural, like taking a trash bag to the garbage chute, in case my movements are seen.

A minute later, I have the half-full bag from my kitchen trash can in my hand and have opened my door. It's a challenge to be low-key about scanning the walls and ceiling while I walk to the chute, but I can't call attention to myself in case there's a hidden camera somewhere. Nothing stands out on the way to the chute or for most of the short walk back, but then I glance at a potted silk plant across the hall from my condo. There's a small black square attached to the pot's rim, and it's angled at my door.

It's too risky for me to inspect the square object up close, but I'd bet every one of my book advances and my next five years of sales that it's a camera, and that it's either connected to a hotspot somewhere close by or that the signal for the open Wi-Fi at the pool is strong enough to reach here. If I'm correct, then this makes the plan Ava came up with a lot harder to pull off.

I hurry back inside and dig my phone out of my purse. Ava answers my FaceTime on the first ring.

"You're home. Thank God."

"I'm here, and so is the Prius. There's also what looks like a tiny camera attached to the plant in my hallway, and it's pointed at my door."

"Noooooo." The way she draws this out would be comical in

any other circumstance, but not this one. Her mouth hangs open after she's finished saying it.

"Check around your door, too, just in case. The one here is a small black square. I have no idea how to get out of here without being followed."

"Can you cover the camera?"

"Not without it showing me leaving and then covering it."

"Make it look accidental?" she suggests. "Is there a big box or something you don't mind leaving out there that could block it? You can pretend you're taking it to the elevator and put it where it obstructs the camera's view. Or if that's too suspicious, could you walk by with something that knocks it off the plant so it isn't facing your door?"

She sounds calm, but the way she twists a strand of hair around her finger tells me otherwise. It's her nervous habit, and it rarely makes an appearance.

"I can try," I say.

"Be ready to change your clothes, put on your hat and sunglasses, and make a run for it right after you do."

I nod. "Did you find a hotel, or do you want me to work on that?"

"We have an early check-in at Loews Hollywood. I'll call an Uber and head over after I check for cameras here."

"Okay. I'll meet you there."

Ava is saving me from the fallout of Phoenix again. This time, I might owe her my life.

# Chapter Thirty-Two

If I've ever needed a sign that guardian angels exist, arriving at the hotel without another Prius sighting is it. Tunnel vision takes over after I meet Ava in the lobby, with the other people there fading into the background now that I'm no longer keeping constant vigil over my surroundings. The chatter around us quiets to a muted buzz as we casually stroll to the elevators and adopt a carefree air, as though it's a perfectly normal Sunday afternoon in Hollywood. We should be applauded for our award-worthy act.

Once we're in our room, with the privacy hanger on the doorknob and the deadbolt in place, it all changes. Ava has questions.

I tell her everything I pieced together this morning after finding the gun, including the details about the gutted guest room. She listens, nodding at times. When I've finished explaining my theories, she doesn't challenge my conclusion. She simply hugs me.

"We'll figure out what to do," she promises.

"What can we do? The police already want to see Phoenix. What if the message on his phone and me confronting him spooked him into hiding? Or worse—what if he's lurking around my place until my guard is down and I go home? We can't stay here forever."

"We can stay here today and tonight, though, and tomorrow night if we have to. It gives us time to come up with something."

"Yeah." It's tough to envision a way out of this, even if we had all the time in the world.

Ava reaches for a canvas shopping bag she set on the desk upon entering our room. "I brought wine and a cheesecake I had in my freezer. I wasn't really thinking when I left and I just grabbed what was in sight. A reality break for sugar might help us think."

The last meal I ate was a late dinner before heading to the Ocean Floor last night. My appetite vanished with the events at Phoenix's house today. But I should try to eat, and the wine could help mellow me out. I give Ava a weak smile.

"We've come up with some of our best ideas over cheesecake and wine."

"Exactly. We can pretend we're back in the dorms in college, plastic cups and all."

"It would be nice to rewind our lives back to those days." It was a time before Phoenix and I dated, when I only knew of him from afar. There have been times over the years when I've wished I had stayed at a distance and had let my college crush fade after graduation. I would have spared myself years of heartache and all the peril I'm in now.

Ava picks up the TV remote and presses a button. "Up for a

movie marathon?" she asks.

"Only if it's all comedies. Our lives have enough drama right now."

"Agreed." She stops changing channels when a teenage Alicia Silverstone appears on the screen.

The distraction works for a couple of hours. It's unhinged to be watching *Clueless* in a hotel room, while picking at a slice of strawberry cheesecake and sipping Valpolicella, when Phoenix might have killed a woman and has someone following me. I try not to think about it. For brief snatches of time here and there, I even succeed.

It's during the movie's closing credits, when the aftermath of today's adrenaline kicks in and every cell in my body feels like it's been rolled over by a cement mixer, that my emotions take over. Not the ones driven by fear or survival, because that would be understandable. No, what sets me off is so inconsequential by comparison, it's laughable. I'm aware of this, but once the first tear rolls down my cheek, the rest flow like a waterfall.

I truly wanted to believe every word Phoenix said. How he realized he couldn't stay away, how he loved me the whole time we were apart, and how he loves me now. I wanted to believe in us and that working through our tumultuous past would be worth it in the end. I was upset with myself last night for doubting him and thinking he had something to hide, when my doubts were valid all along. And yes, I'm thankful to be safe in this hotel room with Ava, but other parts of me are broken.

What is it about the human need for romantic love? It's blinded me twice, yet it's still such an instinctual desire to want to belong with someone else. Phoenix had my heart and soul once. I nearly gave it to him again, and all I'm left with are questions and doubts.

Did he mean any of what he said or showed me this time around, or was he only playing a character and watching his own back? If my book was about something else, or if Ava and Torin hadn't discussed it that day and he hadn't overheard them, would he have kept his distance from me for the rest of our lives?

I may never know. Once upon a time, I thought seeing him again would be the final curtain call for our story and help me reclaim the pieces of myself I'd lost, so I could move on with someone else. Then he made me wonder if he was the right person all along. Now he's left me with another gaping hole to mend as my tears continue to fall.

"Are you holding up okay?" Ava's tone is soft and almost maternal.

I bite down on my bottom lip and shake my head.

"Do you need anything?" she asks.

"My heart in one piece and to trust my judgment again, but that's my fault."

"It isn't."

I wipe my cheek with my sleeve. "I let him in again when I should have known better. Believe someone the first time they show you who they are, right? You tried to warn me, but he even had me fooled again last night."

"I was his biggest skeptic, but I didn't see this coming. You can't blame yourself. I won't let you."

Ava gets up from her bed and joins me on mine. She hugs me again, like she did before the movie.

We don't brainstorm a single solution that night. Instead, we watch two more movies and order overpriced room service food for dinner and another bottle of wine. The growing alcohol buzz gradually numbs my mind and emotions, until the early hour when my eyelids become too heavy to stay open.

Ava's voice is the next thing I'm aware of.

"Del, wake up."

She sounds frantic. My eyes fly open, because frantic isn't something Ava ever is. Did someone find us? Are we trapped here?

"I'm awake. What's going on?"

Daylight spills into the room from the window, but I have to blink a few times for Ava's face to come into focus. It's drained of color. She passes me her phone.

"Read it. I can't—just read it."

She sinks onto her bed, then reaches for a pillow and hugs it to her chest. Am I mentally prepared for what she wants me to read? I glance at the phone and scan a news article she left open on its screen.

"No," I whisper.

A familiar face stares up at me, but the person in the mug shot below the article's headline isn't Phoenix. It's Nash.

## Arrest made in death of missing Orange County woman

*LAS VEGAS (AP) — A 31-year-old man has been charged with second-degree murder in the death of former Aliso Viejo resident Elenna Paseo. The man, also a former Aliso Viejo resident, is being held without bail.*

*Nathaniel "Nash" Larviksen was taken into police custody in Las Vegas early Monday morning. Sources say Larviksen was a longtime friend of Paseo. The two grew up as neighbors and attended school together. Paseo and Larviksen reportedly remained close friends until Paseo went missing.*

*A source connected to both the Las Vegas Metropolitan Police Department and the Orange County Sheriff's Department, who spoke on condition of anonymity, claimed Hollywood actor Phoenix Alden worked closely with authorities in Nevada and California to obtain information and evidence that led to the arrest. Alden was said to be a friend of both Paseo and Larviksen.*

*A police spokesperson confirmed Paseo's body has been recovered, but would not disclose further details. Unconfirmed rumors allege her body was found in the Mojave Desert last week.*

*This story will be updated as more information becomes available.*

The phone slips out of my hand and lands on the bed. I look at Ava. She stares at me. Neither of us speaks. We don't have to.

Of the two of us, Ava is the closest to Nash. She kissed him in front of me two days ago and would have spent the night alone with him last weekend if she hadn't been in a physical state that caused Torin to intervene. It's no wonder she looks haunted.

What I just read about Phoenix working with authorities on Nash's arrest flips everything upside down. Was he trying to protect Ava and me from Nash this entire time? Is that why he came to Nebula after hearing her and Torin talk about my book? And was his work with the police why he's been in Las Vegas for the last eight months and couldn't tell me what he was working on or when it would wrap up?

The possibility sheds new light on his behavior. Could he have been helping police find Len's body in the desert when he went off the grid for a few days? And did he turn up at the show in Huntington Beach to make sure Ava and I remained safe?

It doesn't explain the guest room and the gun, but what if the guest room really was under renovation for no other reason than giving it a facelift? And what if I came to a horrible conclusion based on finding a gun that was legally owned, even if having a gun is completely out of character for Phoenix? If there was enough evidence to charge Nash with second-degree murder this morning, then it means the firearm I discovered isn't what killed Len.

That leaves being followed. Was Phoenix behind it, or was Nash, or is something else going on? With Nash now in police custody, and Phoenix seemingly innocent of any crime, my sense is that I'm not in danger. But only Phoenix can tell me if he had anything to do with me being followed, and only he can answer the new questions I have.

"This probably means we can leave the hotel today." Ava's voice is hollow.

"I should talk to Phoenix. I'll ask if he knows about the Prius."

I don't know if I'm replying to Ava as much as I'm trying to motivate myself to have the most uncomfortable conversation of my life, a day after I pretty much accused Phoenix of murder. Will he even talk to me now? I wouldn't if the roles were reversed and he thought I was capable of a heinous crime.

"You should talk to him at some point, but it doesn't have to be today if you aren't ready. I'll call him to ask about you being followed if you want. Or we can take a chance, go home, and see if the Prius is still around."

"I appreciate that, but no. I'm responsible for this mess and need to face up to it."

"Okay." Ava releases the pillow in her arms and sets it beside her. "In that case, I'm taking a shower."

She hoists herself up from the bed and shuffles into the bathroom. I can't tell if she wants to be alone with her thoughts, or if she's giving me privacy to call Phoenix.

I pick my phone up from the table between the two beds. Phoenix's voicemail from yesterday is still waiting to be heard. Now is probably the time to listen to it, even if the message makes me want to shrivel up in a corner more than I already do.

My finger hovers over the play button. I jab at the screen and squeeze my eyes shut.

*"Please call me, Del. As bad as everything looks, it isn't what it seems like. I can understand why you think I—"* There's the muffled sound of him clearing his throat. *"I can't say more than that in a message. There are reasons I haven't been able to tell you more than I have. I promise it will all be clear soon. Just... I need to talk to you."*

The message ends there.

He was right. It is clear now. I rub a hand over my face and contemplate my phone. How do I even start to apologize for the assumption I made and what it means about my trust in him until this point? All he's done is try to win it back, and I wouldn't let him.

I open my contact list and unblock him, then tap the call icon under his name. After five rings, there's a click. My heart sinks when Phoenix's recorded voice asks me to leave a message. My brain fumbles for appropriate words to speak. It doesn't come up with much.

"Hi. I heard about Nash. Saying I owe you an apology doesn't really cover it, but I do. I'm so sorry—more than I have words for." I pause for a few seconds, collecting my thoughts. "There's something else, too. I'm being followed and I don't know if I'm safe or what's going on. Do you know if Nash has anything to do with that?"

I stop there, since I don't know what else to say. It's an awkward lull while the voicemail records my silence, until I ask him to call me when he can and end the call.

All I can do now is wait. I put my phone screen-side down on the table so I'm not staring at it and willing it to light up with a call, then reach for my laptop. There's bound to be more out there about Nash's arrest and potentially about Phoenix's role in it.

While I brought my laptop with me to the hotel, I haven't opened its lid since Saturday afternoon. When I do, I wish I'd left it shut. I blocked Phoenix on my phone yesterday, but I signed in to send and receive messages from my laptop on Saturday when I was discussing the evening's plans with Ava. It's either a glitch or by design, but texts Phoenix sent me yesterday that were blocked from my phone are in front of me now on the screen. One in particular is a slap in the face.

*I was still in Antigua the day Len vanished. I was out of rehab, but I stayed there for another ten days to explore the island. I didn't find out she was gone until after I got home. Police confirmed all of this during their investigation. There were multiple video recordings from my hotel and the airport in Antigua to confirm I was where I said I was when Len went missing.*

There's a photo below the message. It shows a laptop screen displaying a check-in confirmation email for a flight from V. C. Bird International Airport in Antigua to LAX, with a layover and connecting flight in Miami. Phoenix's name, flight date, flight numbers, departure times, and seat numbers are listed in the email. His departure was four days after the date Len was recorded walking down her street by a neighbor's security camera and wasn't seen again.

He wasn't even in the United States. If I'd given him a chance to explain that and show me the check-in email yesterday, I wouldn't be holed up in a hotel room with Ava right now, feeling like I've made the worst mistake of my life.

My phone chimes. A message from Phoenix pops up on my laptop screen at the same time.

*The guy following you was security I hired. There was someone else protecting Ava. I hired them after Nash was trying to get with her and he asked you for theories about Len.*

I read the message three times, and each time deflates me more. All Phoenix wanted to do was protect Ava and me. No one would pay for private security to make sure we were safe unless they truly cared.

*Are you okay?*

The three dots that tell me he's replying appear on my screen. They stay there for a full minute, then disappear, like he's stopped or is reconsidering what he was going to say.

*The truth, please.*

The dots appear again. This time, a message comes through. *I'm not. But I will be.*

I type another question. *Can we talk?*

Minutes pass while I stare at my message. No answer comes.

# Chapter Thirty-Three

Ava and I don't speak much while we pack up our things and head down to the hotel lobby. I keep checking my phone, pretending to read a news article about Nash's arrest, but the words blur until I give up and open my messages again. There's still nothing.

Ava touches my shoulder. "Stop. You'll make yourself crazy."

"I think I'm there." I slip my phone into my purse and glance at her.

"Torin texted me while you were in the shower. He's coming here for a few days and staying with me."

Fresh guilt surges through me. I've been so consumed by wanting to make things right with Phoenix, I didn't even think to check on Torin.

"How's he holding up?" I ask.

Ava shrugs. "It's hard to tell. I'll have a better sense when I see him. But he did say, and I quote, 'Tell Phoenix I'll still break his kneecaps if he does anything to hurt Del. Otherwise, he's solid in my book.' So I'm passing his message along for you to deliver."

I manage a small smile, even though it's taking everything I have not to dissolve into tears. "That mostly hinges on him ever wanting to see or hear from me again. I don't know that I would, if I were him."

"He'll talk to you."

"Should he?"

Ava doesn't answer right away. Then she steps forward and wraps her arms around me. I lean into her hug and rest my head on her shoulder. Exhaustion and defeat have taken over my body, so I say nothing.

"You know I'm still working through how I feel about the past and what his choices did to you, so bear that in mind when I say this. I'm normally the last person who'd come to his defense, but my take is he's dealing with a lot right now and needs some time to himself. Lord knows I do, and I didn't even know Len. He has his grief about her, whatever his role in Nash's arrest was, and what happened between the two of you to process."

"Yeah," I whisper.

She's probably correct, but it doesn't help the sick feeling in the pit of my stomach, or the headache taking hold at my temples.

"Are you sure you don't want to come to my place for a while? Torin's flight gets in this afternoon, and then we can all commiserate together."

My phone dings, alerting me that my Uber is close by. I raise my head again and she slowly releases me from her arms.

"I mostly want a nap, but I'll text you later if I feel up to coming by. I'm glad you'll have his company."

"Me too."

I study her. She's been putting on a brave face since showing me the first news article about Nash this morning, but something in her eyes looks empty.

"Are you doing okay?" I ask.

She bites her bottom lip and gives a tiny shake of her head just as my ride pulls up at the curb.

"Not really, but I'll get there. So will you. Call me later, okay?"

"Okay."

I hug her again, then walk over to the car that's waiting for me.

Once I'm home, locked away from the outside world, I head straight for my bed. But I'm still awake more than an hour after I've settled my head against a pillow and pulled the duvet around my shoulders. I wanted to be alone, but now there's only silence, and my brain won't turn off. It's like someone poured ten cans of energy drinks into it, but the rest of me feels like I'm sinking in quicksand.

Every time I close my eyes, I see Phoenix's face and hear his voice calling after me. The more I relive our last minutes together, the heavier the guilt becomes. How did I get all of this so wrong?

I flip onto my side, but the change in position doesn't help. Nothing will until I can talk to him, so I sit up in bed and reach for my phone. He doesn't pick up when I call, and I don't leave another message.

Logic says to leave him alone and give him space. My heart refuses. By the time I realize what I'm doing, I'm already out of bed and gathering my purse and car keys. I need to see him, even if I've destroyed everything and he turns me away.

The drive to Laguna Beach takes me more than two hours, thanks to the afternoon traffic and an accident on the freeway. I try calling Phoenix again twice from the car. My calls go to voicemail both times, so I don't try again.

His rental car is parked in the driveway when I pull up, which tells me he's likely at home. But the sight of it reminds me that the last time I was here, I was running away from him in sheer terror. Will he open the door when he sees it's me? Am I even welcome here now?

I don't know how I get from my car to the front steps, but I do. Some invisible push helps me raise my hand to ring the doorbell. Then I wait. My heart leaps into my throat when the door opens and I see him.

Phoenix looks like he hasn't slept in days. His eyes are tired and glassy, and the faintest red blotches dot his cheeks. Stubble covers his face, his hair looks like a hurricane swept through it, and his T-shirt is creased. For a long moment, he just stares at me, one hand braced against the doorframe. I should say something, but there isn't a single word in any language that seems adequate.

"Hi." His voice is quiet and rough, like he hasn't used it in days.

"I'm sorry." My words come out in a choked whisper.

His grip tightens on the doorframe. The pain in his eyes lands like a knife to my heart. But what did I expect to find when I came here? I wouldn't be overjoyed to see me if I were in his place.

"Can we talk?" I ask.

It's the question he didn't reply to hours ago, and I see his hesitation to answer it now. He shuts his eyes for a moment.

"Come inside." His eyes open again and he releases his hold on the doorframe.

Phoenix waits for me to walk past him, then closes the door. I walk ahead of him to the living room, but stop when I see another person already there, sitting in a chair. The older man's face and salt-and-pepper hair seem familiar, but I can't place him. His gaze bounces from me to Phoenix.

"Del, this is Owen—Len's uncle and my AA sponsor."

Now I know where I've seen him before. He was interviewed for some of the stories about Len's disappearance that I came across while doing research for my book.

Owen rises from his chair and steps forward, extending his hand to me. "I've heard a lot about you from Phoenix. It's good to finally meet you."

"Likewise," I say, even though this is the first I've heard of Owen's involvement in Phoenix's life. "I'm sorry, I didn't know you were here or mean to interrupt. I can come back another time."

"You aren't interrupting. I was about to leave."

"I'll walk you out," Phoenix tells him.

Owen says goodbye to me, and then I'm alone while their voices become quieter and more distant. The living room feels smaller than the last time I was here. Dim light filters through half-closed blinds. It brushes across the sofa, a folded blanket, and an untouched mug filled with coffee on the table. An unopened bottle of water is next to the mug.

I don't know what else to do, so I sink onto the sofa and wait for Phoenix to return. When he does, it's with the same hesitation I sensed from him at his front door. He takes a seat next to me, but the gap he leaves between us might as well be a flashing red caution sign.

He doesn't speak, so I do. "I didn't know Len's uncle is your sponsor."

I don't mean for it to sound like I'm accusing him of withholding information, but something tells me it's another piece in the jigsaw puzzle that's led us here. Len's brother was an alcoholic who didn't make it, and I've just learned her uncle was one who recovered. Addiction was in her family. She'd witnessed firsthand what ongoing recovery looked like and what happened when someone couldn't recover. Maybe she was correct about what she'd told Phoenix—that the spirit of her brother brought them together as friends. Len was the friend he needed then.

"She introduced us before I left for Antigua. Like the rest of the world, he'd heard about the fight Chaz and I had and my stint in the emergency room, and he knew I was Len's friend. He offered to be my sponsor if I was serious about recovery. He couldn't help her brother, but he wanted to try to help me."

Phoenix goes quiet again. His hands rest on his lap like he's using them to ground himself. I so badly want to reach over and touch him, but I don't.

"How is he handling everything?" I ask instead.

"About as well as anyone could, I guess. He came by to check on me."

"You said you weren't okay earlier."

He lifts his hand, palm up, and lets it fall. His gaze flickers to the window. "Everything is a lot right now."

I nod, unsure if he wants me to stay or leave. If there's one thing about him I've learned to recognize, it's when there's a storm behind his calm he's trying not to let me see. He holds it back until it's too late. But I see it, and I'll let him sit with it on his own if that's what he needs. I don't want this to end in a fight we'll both regret.

"I'm sorry," I say softly. "I can go if it's a bad time for me to be here."

"Please stop saying you're sorry. It's destroying me every time you do." He presses his lips together and runs a hand over his jaw, then exhales. "I don't even know what I'm feeling right now. Angry, sad, guilty... all of it, probably."

I'm about to apologize for saying sorry and him feeling that way, but I catch myself before I do. "I don't know what else to say. I did some inexcusable and hurtful things yesterday, and I won't blame you if you're angry or kick me out of your house."

"I'm not angry with you, and I'm not asking you to leave. I just—I don't know what to do. It's like being run over by a truck. I'm grieving, and I'm relieved Nash is behind bars, and I'm coming to terms with exactly how much I shattered your trust and what that means for us now. My head is swimming."

It's my turn to get quiet. He starts to reach his arm out to me, but then catches himself and rubs his cheek instead. How have we gone from candlelight dances and the most intimate acts, to second-guessing touching one another? This is misery.

"I've been replaying everything," he says. "Not just what happened lately. All of it. The way I left before and how I thought I could come back and earn your full trust again in the short time we've had together. I don't blame you for thinking what you did. It kept me awake some nights because I couldn't tell you everything."

"You could have, you know. I wouldn't have told anyone." I clasp my hands together to also keep from reaching out to him. "I hate that you felt like you couldn't confide in me and had to deal with everything on your own while pretending you were fine. Yesterday aside, when have I ever done something to make you think I can't be trusted?"

If he'd explained why he was in the desert when I asked him on Saturday night, instead of giving the vague answer about his project being top secret, then I might not have reached the verdict

I did yesterday morning. I would have stayed and made sure he was emotionally okay. We wouldn't be having this conversation now.

"I trust you," he says, his voice low. "That wasn't it."

"Then tell me what stopped you from saying something, because I don't understand."

He twists a silver ring on one of his fingers. His chest rises and falls, then rises and falls again, keeping pace with my own breathing. It may be the only thing in sync between the two of us.

"I didn't want you to worry about Ava's safety, and the same thing with Torin. I know you wouldn't have said a word to either of them, but I also know your heart. You would have blamed yourself if something had happened and you hadn't warned them. I also couldn't risk putting you in harm's way if Nash had detected even the slightest change in your energy when he was around. You didn't ask to get caught up in all of this, and I didn't want you to be. I thought I was doing the right thing. I was wrong."

There's a saying about how the road to hell is paved with good intentions. Never before in my life has it made more sense than now. I also can't argue with his reasons, because the points he made are correct. I would have been out of my mind about Ava spending time alone with Nash, and I would have been equally as concerned about Torin. Could I have hidden that from Nash in his presence? Even I don't know.

"We were both wrong in some ways."

I unclasp my hands and roll my shoulders, moving my head from side to side and stretching my neck as I do. Phoenix twists his ring again and stares at his hands. Every second of silence is like a thousand tiny paper cuts to my soul.

"How long did you know Nash was a suspect?"

Can he tell me this before it comes out in Nash's trial? I don't know, but he needs to say something before the quiet bleeds me dry.

"Since about a month after Len went missing." His voice is dull and thick with something I can't pinpoint.

"Can you tell me how you knew and got involved?"

He doesn't look up right away. His thumb drags over the ring again, a nervous reflex he doesn't seem to notice. When he finally meets my eyes, there's a long pause, like he's still debating how to answer.

"Where would you like me to start?" he asks.

# Chapter Thirty-Four

"WHERE IT MAKES SENSE to," I answer. "I only know what was in the news, and there wasn't anything about you or Nash, or even about her ex-fiancé. I've watched enough true crime to know it's usually the ex under suspicion."

Phoenix studies me for a second, as if weighing what to say. His expression tightens, and I can tell he's choosing his words carefully.

"Matt had an alibi. He was in Ohio visiting his family, and neighbors of his parents had recordings from their home security camera of him taking the family dog for a walk every afternoon. He was also on video at different stores there starting before Len's last sighting, and during the days he said he was out of town."

"Where did Nash say he was?" I reach for the bottle of water on the table. My mouth is dry, even though I'm not the one doing most of the talking.

"He never told me. We weren't close at the time, but he joined a search party Len's family organized to scour her favorite hiking spot. He seemed pretty upset that she was missing, and I assumed he'd also been cleared."

Phoenix stops, his Adam's apple bobbing once. He leans back slightly, and the couch creaks in the quiet.

"Water?" I offer the bottle to him.

His fingers brush over mine when he takes it. Our accidental touch makes me want to clutch his hand and never let go, but I don't have the courage to do it. Phoenix takes a drink, then hands the bottle back to me. Our fingers don't touch this time.

"I was surprised when a homicide detective called me a couple of weeks after the hiking spot search and brought up Nash's name. The detective knew I was a professional actor, and he had an unusual request. Long story short, I agreed to try to become closer friends with Nash and to keep an eye on him while watching for certain things. The detective thought my acting background could help me be convincing."

Phoenix says all of this like it's the most normal thing in the world now. Maybe it is, considering how long ago Len disappeared and how long he's known Nash was the prime suspect. But how is he so calm about the potentially life-risking position he put himself in the whole time?

"You weren't worried about Nash catching on, and what that could mean for you?"

"I was, and so was the detective. The gun you found under my bed was issued to me. I was trained to use it in case he suspected what I was doing and came after me. I kept it close to where I slept, but not somewhere Nash was likely to find it if he broke in to search for evidence I had against him or to harm me. There's another one at the house in Vegas."

The gun I found was for self-defense, not murder. The realization lands like a punch to my chest. Even if I didn't know what was going on with Nash and the investigation, Phoenix was prominently in the public eye after we ended things the first time. For all I knew, he could have received threats or even had a stalker during our years apart. Protection should have been one of the first things I considered, but it wasn't.

*It was hidden under a floorboard, though.* Can I justify blaming myself for the path my discovery sent me down, especially when I'd also found Len's journal in Vegas and saw what she'd written about Phoenix? I only knew what I knew, and there's still more to learn.

"Did Nash ever seem like he was catching on?" I ask.

"Not that I could tell. He didn't think me reaching out to him was odd, because I was a friend of Len's and he and I had already met a few times. We became better friends, and I was also his driver for when he wanted to party, because of my sobriety. That meant I was with him during times he had a few drinks and let down his guard. Over time, he talked to me about out-of-the-way places in the Mojave Desert that he thought were scenic drives, and I shared those locations with investigators in case they turned up anything."

"Is that what broke the case?"

"Not at first. The turning point was when Nash asked me to go with him to meet a guy interested in buying a car he'd listed for sale. There was something in the news around that time about someone who was robbed after setting up a similar meeting to sell a van, so he wanted to be safe. I didn't know he had another car. He told me it belonged to his brother and was still registered in his brother's name in another state, since his brother took a cruise ship job and asked Nash to store it for him. He said his brother decided to sell it. When investigators used the info I gave them to track down the car after it was sold, they found Len's DNA in the trunk."

My hand flies up to my mouth. "Oh my God. He had her in the trunk?"

"That's what the prosecution will try to prove. When the DNA results came back, there still wasn't a body to confirm she had died. Investigators continued combing through the routes in the desert Nash told me about. One finally turned up a discarded shovel that looked like a shovel a hardware store had video of Nash purchasing the same day Len was last seen. They also found remnants of trash bags that had drops of Len's blood. That's what the break in the case was that we heard about last weekend, and I hadn't been made aware yet. They thought they were close to finding her body. The morning after you left Vegas, I went with them into the desert, to help them look for landmarks Nash had described to me in case it could help with the search. They found bones and a skull while we were out there. I had a feeling it was her, but they had to confirm it with dental records."

"You saw her body?" Whatever kept me from touching him before splinters apart and slips away. I instinctively reach for his hand.

"Yeah. Well, her skeletal remains."

He presses his lips together and shuts his eyes. There's a tremor in his fingers. For a moment, neither of us speaks. The only sound is the faint hum of the refrigerator down the hall in the kitchen.

I can't even fathom what he went through that day. While I was safe and comfortable at home, irritated that I hadn't heard from him, he was out in the sweltering desert, watching people dig up the bones of his friend. I don't know if he senses what I'm thinking, or if he simply appreciates my hold on his hand, because he puts his other hand on top of mine.

When the trembling in his fingers stops, I feel safe asking another question. "Do you know why Nash killed her?"

"I do, and it's why I was concerned about Ava. Nash wanted to be more than friends with Len. He was infatuated with her and had been for years. She thought it was innocent, and even cute, until it started to seem obsessive."

Images flash through my mind as he says this. I thought the way Nash kept looking at Ava when we were at Torin's house was cute, even though she seemed oblivious to it then. How long had he wanted to turn their friendship into something more? And if she had rejected whatever advances led to her nearly hooking up with him, what would the outcome have been? I tighten my hold on Phoenix's hand.

"I was afraid something similar would happen with Ava," he says, echoing my thoughts. "Especially if they had taken things further and she changed her mind later. It also didn't help that Ava resembles Len. They could have passed as sisters. That's another reason why even Nash and Ava's friendship bothered me."

If blood can actually run cold, then mine does at hearing this. I grab the blanket that's beside me and pull it around my shoulders. "I understand that now. I didn't then."

"Len kept a journal," he continues. "She wrote a few things in it about Nash's behavior after she and Matt broke their engagement off. She also told me he'd been acting pretty intense when she called me the day before I left rehab. The case being built for his trial will try to prove it was a crime of passion after Len kept turning him down romantically."

Here I was, teasing Ava about Nash and encouraging her to date him, thinking they were perfect for each other. I thought Phoenix was overreacting, when he was really worried about her safety. My thoughts must be written on my face, or maybe I shudder, because Phoenix rubs his hands over my arms like he's trying to restore warmth to my body.

"The journal I found at your house in Vegas—is that the one she wrote all of that in?"

He shakes his head. "The police have that one locked up with other evidence. The one you saw was one she filled the pages of before that happened. They didn't think it contained anything that would help the case, but I asked if I could review it anyway. I was looking for something that might align with things Nash had said to help us find her."

He keeps rubbing my arms, but my thoughts are colder than anything his hands or the blanket can warm. I knew Len had a striking resemblance to Ava. It was one of the first things I noticed when the posters and billboards with Len's face began popping up in LA. Is that why Nash was drawn to her? If it was, what could have happened to Ava if they had become intimate and she only viewed it as a one-night stand with no strings attached? It's too sickening to think about.

"Are you okay?" Phoenix asks.

"Not really," I admit. "I'm realizing a lot all at once. When did Len know that Nash wanted more than friendship?"

"He wanted to date her in high school, and again during college. She thought it ended there since she only saw him as her childhood best friend and treated him like a brother, and Nash seemed to like and get along with Matt. But the day he found out she and Matt broke up, he was already trying to put the moves on her. She didn't think turning him down again would be a big deal, since she'd done it before. She told him she'd just ended her engagement and wasn't ready for anything new."

"Was that when he...?" I can't finish the sentence out loud. *Was that when he killed her?*

"Not that day, but that's when the red flags started. The last time I talked to her, she was rattled by something that had happened earlier in the week. She'd been out with friends to see a band, and

Nash showed up at the same bar. She was drinking plain ginger ale, and Nash bought her another one she didn't ask for. It was the only drink she didn't keep in sight from the time it was poured. Later, she felt sick and woozy, and then she couldn't stand without help. Nash insisted on taking her home, but one of her friends claimed Len was staying at her place that night and it made more sense to bring Len there. Nash got more aggressive about it, but he was outnumbered by her other friends. Len said she had been putting distance between the two of them since that night, and that he seemed agitated and was getting bolder about showing up at her house unannounced. He refused to take no for an answer if she didn't want to go somewhere with him. She documented all of it in her journal, which her family turned over to the police."

"You didn't say anything to him when he joined the search party for her?"

"No. I saw him as a guy whose lifelong friend was missing. It didn't seem right to bring it up under the circumstances. I didn't like what Len had told me about what happened at the bar, and how he behaved after that, but I thought he'd been cleared by police at the time."

Something he mentioned about Len and Nash's night at the bar is stuck in my brain. We need to go back to that. "What you said about how Len got sick when she was out at the bar—did he drug her ginger ale?"

"She thought he might have. She wrote about it in her journal but knew that even if she had been drugged, she couldn't prove if it was him or the bartender or someone else who did it, or if she'd gotten sick from something she ate."

"Ava was in bad shape after a night out with Nash, even though she didn't drink that much."

It's as much a question as it is an observation, even if the inflection in my voice makes it a statement of fact. Did Nash have something to do with why she felt so out of it that night and passed out, and did Phoenix make the connection when I told him about Ava's text? It would explain a lot about his shift in mood at the time.

"It was too similar to be a coincidence," he agrees. "I'm grateful Torin was there. He can't stand me these days, but he's always been the kind of guy who watches out for you and Ava."

Phoenix's voice trails off. For a few seconds, neither of us speaks. The heaviness between us isn't anger or hesitation anymore—it's the weight of everything he's told me. I search his face, expecting to see the tension that was there earlier when he saw me at his door. All I find now is exhaustion.

"I don't even know what to say."

He gives me a small, tired smile. "You don't need to. Just being here is enough."

Then we're silent again. Phoenix absently twists his ring, a return to his nervous reflex from a few minutes ago.

"What are you thinking about?"

My question is barely above a whisper. His gaze flickers to his hands before coming back to me.

"Are we okay?" he asks.

My lungs constrict at the question. "I want to be."

We both hear the catch in my voice. He covers my hand with his. "So do I."

Heaven knows we still have things to work through. But in this moment, there's nothing else but the two of us and the gratitude for forgiveness and second chances that floods me from head to toe.

Phoenix sits back against the sofa cushions, like he's finally allowing himself to relax. His eyes search mine.

"Stay here with me tonight. Please." His voice is soft.

I swallow the lump in my throat and nod. "It's the only place I want to be."

The space between us feels thin enough to disappear with one more breath. And then it does. When his lips brush mine and I press my mouth to his, our kiss doesn't make me feel like twenty-two or twenty-three-year-old me, and I'm not transported to a memory from our earlier days. There's something in this kiss that's different. It's less giddy and less infatuated, because it goes deeper than either of those feelings. It's wiser, stronger, and filled with possibility and hope. More than that, it feels like coming home.

Like all the best moments that should be suspended in time, our kiss also has its natural end. My eyelids flutter open the instant our lips no longer touch. Phoenix's eyes open, too. There's a depth in them that feels like he's staring straight into my soul.

He traces my bottom lip with his finger. "I really do love you with all of me. I'm sorry for all the times I've made you doubt that."

I believe him. I can feel it in the way he stays close, and in the quiet steadiness between us.

"Please stop saying you're sorry," I tell him, repeating his words from before. My mouth curves as I say it, and the heaviness that's shadowed us for days begins to lift. I meet his eyes. "I love you too. Let's start again with that."

When he kisses me again, it's slower and deeper, full of promise and a rhythm we're discovering again.

# Chapter Thirty-Five

A WEEK AGO, I would have believed there were better odds of it raining jellyfish in LA than of Phoenix and me receiving a text from Torin, asking if we could have dinner with him and Ava while he's in town. But our worlds have spun upside down and back again since the last time we were all in the same room. Perhaps I shouldn't have been surprised by the invitation that lit up our phones yesterday afternoon, or to now be turning into the same parking lot in Marina del Rey that we did on my birthday, which seems like a lifetime ago.

Like that day, Phoenix helps me out of the vehicle, only this time it's his rental car instead of his SUV. Once I'm on my feet and he's shut the car door, his fingers find a knot in my shoulder. He gently kneads it.

"Are you worried about dinner?" he asks.

Nothing I said or did on the drive here should've tipped him off to my apprehension about tonight, even with everything that's changed since the last time he and Torin came face to face. He still reads me like a book.

"I'm hoping for peace tonight, that's all. You've been through enough this week."

"We all have. I think everything will be fine." His hand falls away from my shoulder and rests against my back as we make our way along the boardwalk to the same Italian bistro where we celebrated Torin's birthday so many years ago.

Ava and Torin are already seated, waiting for us, when we walk inside the restaurant. Our table is next to a window with a stunning marina view. The evening sun hangs over the ocean, making the water sparkle. The backdrop for our night is like something out of a movie. I only wish Torin's reason for being in LA wasn't so unsettling.

But Torin seems relaxed when he sees us. He pushes his chair back from the table and is the first to pull me into a hug. Ava also greets Phoenix with a hug, which is a sight I haven't witnessed in more than six years. It's almost beyond my comprehension, and it fills me with hope at the same time. The real test is what happens between Phoenix and Torin.

I don't have to wait long to find out. As soon as Torin releases me, he extends his hand out to Phoenix, then leans in to clap him on the back.

"Thanks for coming, man. It's good to see you."

Watching the two of them takes me back in time to when this would have been a normal interaction. Now, though? As much as I love Torin and understood his attitude about Phoenix and me and what his intentions were, his open hostility at Nebula wasn't necessary. In Phoenix's shoes, I might be tempted to trot out my inner pettiness and respond to "it's good to see you" in the same way Torin did to him then. Phoenix answers with equal camaraderie, though, and the two of them sit down at the table together, across from each other.

I manage to rip my gaze away from this display of goodwill for long enough to return Ava's embrace. "Miracles really do happen," I say, at a low enough volume that only she hears.

Her mouth quirks up at the corners. "I told you he feels differently after... well, you know. He's aware Phoenix probably risked his own life and protected all of us."

It's something I haven't stopped thinking about since Monday. What if Nash had found out what Phoenix was doing, or even suspected? Would he have tried to harm or even kill him, or would he have gone into hiding, lurking as a danger in the shadows? Ava and Torin's conclusion that Phoenix risked his life to bring Nash to justice for Len's death, while also protecting us, really doesn't overstate the danger he put himself in.

If what's happening at the table is any indication, then Phoenix was right that everything will be fine tonight. He and Torin are already deep in conversation as Ava and I take our seats.

"Are you here permanently now, or do you need to go back to Vegas?" Torin asks him.

"I have to make one more trip there to get my stuff from the house and turn in the keys," Phoenix replies. "After that, I'm here for good."

"Let me know if you need a hand packing up."

"Should I be there to supervise, or will you leave your drumsticks at home?" I crinkle my nose at Torin. He's been friendly so far, but I'm only half kidding. I don't want him pulling any more stand-in big brother bravado if he's left alone with Phoenix.

Torin clutches his chest. "That hurts. I want to help get him back here to you, not maim him."

"Uh-huh." I turn to Ava. "Up for another Vegas trip to make sure they behave?"

"Only if we stick to gambling and supervising, and don't get tangled up with any musicians." She throws an apologetic glance Torin's way. "No offense."

He leans over and gives her a side hug. "None taken."

Ava smiles, but it doesn't quite reach her eyes. There's an uneasiness there I can't miss. Her usual spark isn't in her tonight, but I can't blame her. The last few days have taken a toll, and she and I haven't talked much aside from a few texts. I assumed she was busy with Torin and working through the complicated emotions she no doubt has about Nash, and she likely assumed Phoenix and I were busy making up. Which, admittedly, we have spent a lot of time doing. Tonight is the first time we've truly come out of the bubble of him and me since Monday.

Our server arrives at our table to ask about appetizers and drinks. When he leaves, Torin turns to Phoenix again and says something about a Raiders preseason football game. It's my chance to get Ava alone.

"Come with me to the restroom?" I ask her.

"Sure."

"We'll be right back," I tell Phoenix and Torin as I get up from the table. They both nod and continue their conversation.

I lead Ava to the back of the restaurant and into the women's restroom. We're the only people in here, thankfully. Since this may not be the case for long, I don't wait to speak.

"How are you doing?" I lock eyes with her. "Be honest, please."

She shrugs, picking at a piece of fuzz on her sleeve. "I was doing better than I was on Monday, but then Nash tried to call me today."

Something icy grips my insides when I register what she said. "He isn't out, is he? I thought he was being held without bail."

Nash being outside of prison walls anytime soon hadn't crossed my mind as a possibility. Wouldn't someone have told Phoenix?

"No, thank God," she replies. "I looked up the number of a missed call, and it was from the jail he's at. It shook me up a little."

"I understand why. Does Torin know?" All our small group has been doing tonight is hugging, but it doesn't stop me from putting my arms around Ava again now.

"Yeah. I had a meltdown when I realized who the call was from. Of all people and with the limited phone calls he probably has, why contact me? Torin did what he could to calm me down and swore he'd make sure Nash would never be able to touch me, even if he somehow ends up out on bail or is found innocent at his trial, but I don't know how he'd be able to stop it."

"Sometimes I think he actually does have friends with mob connections, if that helps." My stomach still flutters at the thought of Nash on the loose, despite my words.

"Let's hope."

Ava gives me one last squeeze and lets go. It's my signal to do the same. Once she's out of my arms, she steps up to a sink and stares into the mirror on the wall in front of it, then fusses with a strand of her hair. The moisture shining in her eyes tells me she's fighting back tears.

"I've always thought I could read people. How do I trust my judgment after this?" She meets my gaze in the mirror's reflection.

"This isn't your fault or something you missed. You weren't even interested in him that way a few weeks ago, remember? Your intuition is fine."

"I let his sweet-talking get out of control and played right into it. I thought he was harmless, and that maybe it was worth exploring. But to think he might have drugged my drink, and that he abducted and murdered another woman who was his friend." She trails off and looks down at the sink. "I don't understand how someone can do that and still seem so normal the rest of the time."

I could try to soothe her with words, but it doesn't seem like the best time to explain that not being able to understand what Nash did is a good thing, and that it means nothing is wrong with her. She already knows that on some level, and she'll accept it in time.

"I know," I say instead. "None of us understand it. We all love you, though. I'm here for whatever you need, no matter what time it is or what I'm doing, and I'm sure Torin and Phoenix would say the same."

Ava nods and sets her purse on the edge of the sink. She rummages through it and pulls out a lip gloss, then applies it to her lips with a shaky hand.

"I'll be okay," she assures me, putting the tube back in her purse. "It takes more than this to keep me down."

She will be, because she's one of the strongest people I know. But it doesn't change the fact that she's struggling with this and needs time to work through it. I only hope she doesn't try to hide how she feels from me.

By the time we return to the table, no onlooker would guess she was holding back tears, or that she's afraid for her physical safety. Ava hates to let her vulnerability show, or to ever be seen as fragile. Still, I'm aware. I won't let her brush this off later, or face any of it alone, no matter what brave front she shows.

Our appetizers arrive moments after we sit, along with a bottle of sparkling water and the soft drinks and iced teas we ordered. It's unclear if Torin and Ava passed on wine or another alcoholic beverage out of respect for Phoenix's sobriety, or if neither of them feels much like having a drink. Recent events have been a lot to process even for me, and clearly for Ava as well. Of all of us, though, Torin spent the most time with Nash, and his band is now without a guitar player. That means canceled shows. Ava may have insight into how he's handling everything, but he and I have yet to talk about it.

"How long are you here for?" I ask him, after our server has taken our entrée orders and has left the table.

"Just through the weekend. We have another band filling in for us at Nebula on Saturday. Jacob has been talking with someone he knows about playing with us, so we'll be rehearsing next week, then back to regular gigs."

"Do you think you'll be ready for that?"

"Ready or not, the show must go on. My rent certainly does. Besides, Ava will be more than happy for me to be out of her hair."

"Don't listen to him," she chides. "He made dinner the last two nights and was a willing participant in our face masks and movie night, so he can stay as long as he wants."

Ava genuinely means what she says. It's in her voice and in the grateful look she casts Torin's way. What she told me in the restroom echoes through my mind. It may take some time for her to feel safe again. For her sake and Torin's, I wish he could stay longer. When he goes home, I'll make sure she and I have weekly girls' nights and plans lined up with our other friends. She can depend on me to be there for her in the same way she's always been there for me.

# Chapter Thirty-Six

AFTER DINNER AND LINGERING over dessert, the four of us leave the restaurant together. Outside, the air is soft with the scent of salt and summer. We part ways, with Ava and Torin headed in the opposite direction of where Phoenix and I parked.

He and I pause a few steps away from the restaurant doors so I can rummage through my purse. Once I unearth the tin of mints I was looking for, I pop one in my mouth, then offer the tin to him.

"It's a beautiful night," I comment. "Do you want to walk for a bit?"

"I'd like that."

He slips his hand in mine and we stroll the boardwalk, retracing the same steps we took on the night we left Torin's birthday dinner here. Neither of us breaks into song this time, but the familiar surroundings and actions still tug at my heart.

The Del and Phoenix of years ago didn't know what was ahead, but we know what's behind us now. Tonight, we're older and arguably wiser. We're in love again and less naive, and we have the potential to become so much stronger than we were. Does he also feel it? He may, because he touches my elbow and stops walking. I stop, too.

"I realize there isn't music, and maybe I'm being sentimental, but..." He opens his arms to me. Even without the rest of the sentence, I know what he's asking.

"We'll make our own," I say.

He loops his arms around me and holds me close. His chin brushes the top of my head until I lean it against his shoulder and we begin swaying to a beat only we can hear.

Then, as if by magic, quiet chords from an acoustic guitar fill my ears. A violin chimes in a few bars later, playing the melody of Pachelbel's "Canon in D." I open my eyes and notice what I didn't before. A man and a woman stand at the side of the boardwalk, with an open guitar and violin case on the ground in front of them. The two buskers smile at us, and I smile back, then I raise my head to look at Phoenix.

Pure love radiates from him as he gazes at me, a smile also on his lips. Even though people pass by in clusters, it feels like a private concert meant only for us. And as our bodies and hearts keep time under the lights and stars, nothing has ever felt in more perfect harmony to me than Phoenix and I and this moment do now.

When the notes fade into the night, he pulls back slightly to look at me. "One more dance, and then I'll take us home?"

I nod, expecting another classical song to begin. But Phoenix steps away and murmurs something to the buskers before pulling his wallet from his pocket and tucking a few bills into the violin case. He thanks them, then comes back to me.

"What did you ask them?"

"If they take requests."

He draws me into his arms again as a familiar song fills the air. It's music without words, but I don't need them. I'd know "Thinking Out Loud" anywhere, in any lifetime.

I tilt my head, smiling. "Pulling out all the stops tonight, aren't you?"

"Just setting the mood," he says, grinning.

"For the dance or for when we get home?"

"Both," he replies. I laugh, resting my forehead against his chest as the music swells around us.

"Careful," I tease. "Keep this up and I might think you're trying to seduce me."

"Might?"

His grin widens and he twirls me once, the boardwalk lights blurring into gold and white around us. Laughter tumbles past my lips, and then he pulls me close again and presses a soft kiss to my temple. For a few perfect seconds, the world feels still, but also vibrantly alive. Then it's in motion again, a symphony of footsteps on the ground, chatter drifting from nearby patios, and the music that plays on.

Phoenix and I are living proof that what's meant to be will always be, no matter the odds. Whatever the future holds, and whatever comes our way, we're in this together.

It's the cadence of us, and it's the most beautiful melody I know.

# Acknowledgments

Del and Phoenix's story began with a rush of ideas one winter day while I was in Canada visiting my parents. I quickly wrote them down and set them aside. A month later, back home in LA, an announcement for an annual novella contest on a social writing platform inspired me to revisit my ideas and bring them to life. But I soon realized *On the Way Down* wasn't a novella. It was a full-length novel, and it demanded to be written that way. So many people had a role in helping it become the book you've just read.

First, thank you to Fay Sunday. You stood by the first draft of this story from its first chapter. Your comments and support propelled me through writing and completing that draft and truly bringing Del and Phoenix to life. I'm grateful beyond words.

Next, thank you to Jodie Reyes and Jessica Fadness. You've both been so supportive of my writing goals and of the breaks I took while drafting *On the Way Down*—even the ones that stretched into months before I found my way back to this book. (If you know, you know. Friends of the century, both of you.)

My heartfelt thanks and appreciation goes to the TrueHearts Collective, and to Allie Larkin for founding this incredible group of creative souls and bringing us together. Meeting all of you, and discussing so many creative topics in a safe, judgment-free, and friendly space gave me the inspiration and motivation I needed to make the leap back to the path I wanted to follow with my writing. I am so thankful for the time we've spent together, and for our conversations and connection. It's a gift to know each of you.

Taking a book from draft to reader-ready is a climb. Thank you to Lexi Batsides for your insightful developmental review and feedback. You helped me focus on what needed work and how I could strengthen this story, and your thoughtful guidance has been invaluable.

As always, thank you to my mom and dad. You've let my creative imagination run wild since my earliest memories and have always been my biggest and most supportive fans.

To all my friends who understood when I needed to write or edit and disappeared for days at a time, and when messages were left unanswered for hours or days—I appreciate you. Thank you for your support, for being in my life, for your messages, for checking in on my writing, and for your likes and comments on my book-related social posts. I'm thankful for all of you.

And finally, to everyone who's read this book: I am f
grateful for the time you invested into Del and Phoenix'
Thank you for being here.

# Author Newsletter

Keep up with the latest book news from Jennifer Farwell! When you sign up for her author newsletter, you'll receive six bonus chapters of her latest teen celebrity romance, *One Night Only*, as your welcome gift.

Go to **jenniferfarwell.com/newsletter** for more information and to subscribe to the no-spam newsletter. If you choose to sign up and get the bonus chapters, you may unsubscribe at any time.

# *Preview of One Night Only*

*One Night Only* is Jennifer Farwell's latest teen romance, and it's available now! Here's more about the first book in a swoony new series that explores fame, trauma, and the power of being truly seen.

**She was born for the spotlight. Until it nearly destroyed her.**

Cayden "Deni" Indigo is the hottest teen pop star on the charts, until an explosion at her concert shatters everything. Now she can't step on stage without panicking, and people blame her for the deaths at her show.

When her mom decides she needs a summer away from the spotlight, Deni ends up at a lake in Northwestern Ontario, Canada, where no one recognizes her without her stage makeup and wigs. That includes Hunter Gray, her new neighbor. As her life shifts from red carpets and award shows to boats and bonfires, she starts to fall for Hunter—and he starts to fall for her. There's just one problem: Hunter *hates* celebrities. And Deni hasn't told him the truth.

But secrets never stay hidden for long. And when Deni's catches up with her, it's not just her heart on the line—it could be their lives.

**A scene from *One Night Only*:**

Twigs snap, and leaves crunch, and then a person emerges from the brush. He's tall, my age, and holding a camera. But he doesn't aim it at me. If anything, he looks surprised that I'm here.

"Morning," he says.

"Hey," I reply, watching as he plucks a leaf from his golden-brown waves of hair. Being an LA girl, I expect this exchange to be the end of it and for him to continue on his way. That's what happens most of the time when I encounter a neighbor while out walking Alfie at home, if we acknowledge one another at all.

Apparently, that's not how things work at this lake.

"You're not from here, right?" he asks.

How did he pick that up in the approximately thirty seconds he's been in front of me? I'm not wearing a neon sign that says I'm from Hollywood, and there's nothing about my clothing or makeup-free face that shouldn't blend in with cottage life. My suspicions about his camera come creeping back. Would the tabloids employ a teenager?

"What do you mean?" I keep my tone casual.

"I know everyone at this lake, and I haven't seen you before. Did you walk over from Loon?"

"Loon?" I repeat, confused.

"Loon Lake." He examines me more closely. I stare back at him, noticing the dark amber color of his eyes. "I'll take that as no. Are you visiting someone?"

It's hard to tell if he's truly curious or just being nosy, but something in his expression is genuine and friendly. It disarms me in spite of myself.

"My mom rented a cottage here."

"Cottage," he repeats. His mouth twitches.

"What about it?" He's ribbing me about something, but I don't get the joke.

A merry glint dances in his eyes. "We call it a camp around here. You 'cottage' people automatically give away not being from this part of the province."

"Oh, really?" I put the hand that's not holding Alfie's leash on my hip. "Where do you think I'm from?"

He contemplates me for a moment, pressing his lips together. We don't break eye contact once. "Back east or down south," he finally answers. "Probably the GTA, though."

"What's the GTA?"

My question elicits a chuckle. "Greater Toronto Area. You must be from out west."

"You could say that." It's true, after all. Los Angeles is about as west coast as it gets in North America.

"B.C.?" he guesses.

"Nope."

"Alberta?" he tries again.

"Do you always interrogate people like this?"

"Only people who seem interesting and worth the time," he replies. "Am I right about Alberta?"

"You aren't even close."

"Wait!" His face lights up.

"Waiting." There's a look of recognition on his face that makes me nervous. Was that "wait" as in he's realized I seem familiar, or something else?

"You're staying at the Wilson's camp, aren't you? You're one of the *Californians.*" He says "Californians" like he's announcing the name of an old *Saturday Night Live* sketch. If we talk again after today, I'll need him to stop doing that.

"You got me. Is there a Nextdoor for lake gossip or something?" I pray there is not, and that no other information about Mom and me has made the rounds ahead of our arrival.

"The Wilsons texted my parents to let them know someone would be staying at their camp in case you needed something. My family's camp is the next one over."

"So we're neighbors?"

"Yup, and I'm out here for the rest of the summer with my

parents and sister. You're stuck with running into us for however long you're staying." His lips curve into a grin.

I have to be jet-lagged from yesterday, because my mind goes blank. All I can concentrate on is the dimple in his cheek and how real his smile seems.

"I'm Hunter, by the way." He extends his hand. The touch of his fingers against mine jars me from my haze.

"Deni."

The second syllable has barely slipped out when I realize what I've done and want to kick myself. I should have made up a different name. Hunter, his family, and who knows who else around here already know I'm from California. I'm assuming Mom had to share her full name, including our last name, to arrange the rental and payment. If I want a quiet summer to heal and time away from prying eyes, I have to limit the clues about who I am.

"What else did the Wilsons tell your mom?" I try to sound unconcerned.

"Wouldn't you like to know?" Hunter waggles his eyebrows and gives me a sly look.

"Well, yeah. I do like to know what someone knows about me when I meet them."

"Do you meet many people who already know a lot of things about you?" I think he's teasing me, but I can't be sure.

"Not before today," I lie.

# *About the Author*

Love, laughter, and happily ever after are what you'll find in the celebrity and teen romance novels penned by Jennifer Farwell, whose writing has been featured by *Publishers Weekly*, *Cosmopolitan* on Cosmopolitan.com, Wattpad, Marriott, and more. She's been writing since the day she picked up a navy blue crayon as a toddler and began scribbling on her parents' freshly painted white walls, and this led to her completing an MA in English, a journalism degree, and all of her novels to date. Jennifer grew up in Thunder Bay, Canada, and now lives in Southern California, where she spends her non-writing time playing at sound baths, taking in live music and stand-up comedy, and cheering on her favorite hockey team during hockey season.

TikTok: @jennfarwell
Instagram: @jennfarwell
Website: jenniferfarwell.com

## *Also by Jennifer Farwell*

One Night Only

Seven Weeks to Forever

Hiding Out in Hollywood (A Hollywood Dating Story, Book 1)

Billion Dollar Boyfriend (A Hollywood Dating Story, Book 2)

All Summer Long *(coming in 2026)*

www.ingramcontent.com/pod-product-compliance
Lightning Source LLC
LaVergne TN
LVHW100513110826
845146LV00002B/624

*9798999401823*